# CHLORINE

# CHLORINE

*a novel*

## JADE SONG

*WM*

WILLIAM MORROW

*An Imprint of* HarperCollins*Publishers*

CHLORINE. Copyright © 2023 by Jade Song. All rights reserved. Printed in the United States of America. No part of this book may be used or reproduced in any manner whatsoever without written permission except in the case of brief quotations embodied in critical articles and reviews. For information, address HarperCollins Publishers, 195 Broadway, New York, NY 10007.

HarperCollins books may be purchased for educational, business, or sales promotional use. For information, please email the Special Markets Department at SPsales@harpercollins.com.

FIRST EDITION

Designed by Leah Carlson-Stanisic

Art by APM Stock and chekart / Shutterstock, inc.

Library of Congress Cataloging-in-Publication Data has been applied for.

ISBN 978-0-06-325760-3

23 24 25 26 27  LBC  5 4 3 2 1

For those who swim to stay afloat

# Author's Note

This is a work of fiction that nevertheless draws from aspects of my own experiences as a competitive swimmer for twelve years. While I am hesitant to say it gets better, because oftentimes, in all honesty, it didn't—and doesn't seem like it will—I do hope, even as *Chlorine* dives into abyss-like waters, that the fierce love, joyous triumph, and humorous absurdity of existence as your true self, whether hidden or free, can be felt throughout this book. Please note these pages contain discussion and instances of racism, misogyny, self-harm, eating disorders, homophobia, depression, and sexual violence.

Thank you for being here—may we all transcend into whichever and whatever states of being we long for.

"But they hurt me so," said the little mermaid.
"Pride must suffer pain," said the old lady.

—HANS CHRISTIAN ANDERSEN

# CHLORINE

# One

You are not here of your own free will. You are here because I desired you first. I lured you to me using my intentional charms: my ethereal beauty, my siren song, my six pack, my tail with scales embroidered in flesh.

Forget what you know about mermaids. For too long you've been inundated by G-rated fairy tales, the blood and dirt in their original drafts scrubbed clean by salarymen in suits. They sold you false love disguised in pastels. Thanks to them, and the cubicle corporations they work for, you think mermaids wear bikini tops made of shells, swim in saltwater, and have flowy red hair. You think mermaids desire either to copulate with two-legged male sailors or lure them to their watery deaths—always or, never and. You think mermaids hate their bodies and their tails, though these are the parts of them that hold their power. You think mermaids have no power.

You are wrong.

Mermaids wear one-piece swimsuits sculpting severe camel toe. Mermaids have neither hair nor scalp, but latex swim caps, squeezing forehead fat out like dollops of leftover toothpaste from near-empty tubes. Mermaids swim in chlorine, thrive in locker rooms, and dive under and over lane ropes. Mermaids sprout thick and luscious body hair, until shaved off for aerodynamics. Mermaids would rather eat four bowls of pasta than a man—though a man does taste good, mermaids prefer not to waste precious stomach volume on such non-nutritious fare, for a man is not sustenance but an occasional dessert.

Mermaids are not born. We are made.

I burst into being when I was seventeen years old. I became a mermaid not as a pearl in a clamshell, but as a girl in a locker room shower stall at the University of Pittsburgh pool during my junior year of high school. I alone saw myself as a rightful mermaid, finally free of my short and pitiful life as a human girl. The others assumed I remained whatever they perceived of me before I ascended. But those were *their* impressions; *their* perceptions.

As a daughter: My parents refused to recognize my metamorphosis, pretending I was not a mermaid but their two-legged, high-achieving offspring.

As a top competitive swimmer: Jim believed me still his athlete, who won meets, races, and points, for him and his team.

As a best friend: Even Cathy presumed me remaining a girl. Her girl.

They are all wrong.

The media will corrupt you into trusting such nonsensical concepts as overnight success, but in reality, the journey from girl to mermaid is long. Mine took thirteen years, beginning when I was four, though I would not touch chlorine for another three—would not desire and then eventually learn to reject its chemical embrace. I look back to these beginning days with some fondness, and much exhaustion.

My mother gifted me a book of mermaid folklore from around the world for my fourth birthday, thinking the illustrations would captivate and distract me while she was too busy working to provide proper attention. Her plan worked, and I carried my book of mermaid lore everywhere, from preschool to the booster seat and back.

"Wow, she must love mermaids. She can't put the book down," Mr. Osborne, my preschool teacher, said to my mother when she came to pick me up. "Can she even read the words?"

"Of course she can," my mother huffed. She stormed off and tugged me away by my wrist. How dare anyone think her daughter illiterate, even at such a young age. Never mind Mr. Osborne was more worried about the content, thinking my underdeveloped brain would be warped by the darkness penetrating each tale: young girls disfigured, men drowned, voices silenced by witches. Never mind my mom did not read the book before she gifted it to me and remained wrongful in her thinking of mermaids as happy, bright, romantic. Never mind the book teaching me that the shadows inside need not be snuffed but treasured—that darkness existed to hide riches from ordinary mortals unable to handle their brilliance, and if I mustered the courage to dive into those veiled depths, these riches could become mine.

I dreamt myths larger than my girl body could hold.

Mr. Osborne, incredulous at my mother-approved precocity, would give me what he called his Five Finger Test: He'd grab the book from my fingers, flip open to a random page, point to a grouping of five words, and challenge me to read it out loud. He'd hold up five fingers as if offering me a high-five, planning to lower a finger with each word I recited wrong, until he'd wield a fist—a fist that never appeared, because I delivered the correct words every time. Yet he continued to steal my book and test me throughout the day, as if he believed I could read only in the morning and forgot how by the afternoon.

I cannot describe Mr. Osborne's face or his classroom. The tiny details comprising insignificant men like him have long since been discarded from my memory. But I can easily recall the shapes of his greasy fingerprints on my book's laminated cover. He gave me my first experience in attempting to prove myself to a man, with no avail.

My favorite folktales in the book were not the most famous. Likely you have heard of Hans Christian Andersen's and Disney's *The Little Mermaid*—I have already told you to forget what you know, but I know you will not, because you are human, and you are eternally trapped in your conventions. But know this then: the Little Mermaid was too desperate, too frivolous. I hated her disregard for her fantastical tail and family, her desire to ruin herself into sea foam for a man open to incest, who loved her like a sister.

It wasn't just the European mermaids I disliked. I also disagreed with the Chinese mermaids featured in the book. Two of them were dependent on men: One stranded on the sand with no legs, needing a ship captain to carry her back into the water; the other covered in tiny rainbow hairs, marrying a man who stole her from the ocean, losing her voice in the process, returning home to the water after her husband's death. While I do admire the latter's rainbow armor, I refuse to follow their male-dependent trajectories.

The third Chinese mermaid in the book was named Nüwa, a deity with a beautiful woman's face and a serpentine body. Nüwa wandered the Earth after it separated from the Heavens. Though the land was beautiful, decorated with rivers, mountains, trees, and flowers, with many living creatures to accompany her travels, she was lonely, craving a companion with whom she could converse and dance. So she used yellow clay, damp from the riverbanks, to mold shapes with faces, arms, and legs. The figures came alive, laughing and twirling around her, ridding her of her isolation. Every human being has descended from Nüwa's clay sculptures. While I empathize with Nüwa's loneliness, and thank her for her contributions to my birth, I disdain her desire for human company—there are many other beings whose camaraderie provides far greater enjoyment than humans'.

The folktale I loved most was the Passamaquoddy tale of two girls changed into water-snakes. Every Sunday, the two girls went to swim and play in their local lake together, naked, wanton. Men in their village spied on the girls and warned of sin, while, as usual of men, disregarding their own lust and hypocrisy. The girls did not listen, so the men came to snatch them away, intending to fix their purity—and discovered the girls had been transformed into water-snakes, their long hair and girl heads connected to wriggly and reptilian snake tails. The story, colored by colonialist Christian values, was meant as a warning against evil behavior on Sundays, but they didn't see the truth of the ending. I was convinced the two girls were free, freer than I could ever be. I envied their ability to slip through those men's grasps. I saw their evolution as a gift, so they could play in the water forever, not beholden to men's needs or a moralist God's schedule.

I reread the pages of the Passamaquoddy tale as my nightly bedtime story, wondering if I'd meet a girl friend someday, and if we'd intertwine into water-snakes. Where was she sleeping each night, without me? And where would we sleep each night, together, after transcendence?

I gave up my daily mermaid recitations when I entered elementary school. There was no use for illustrations or folktales in the American education system, diluted by the dead white male canon. The rigid schedule of school, homework, and the general existence as human wore me down, though not completely: I never forgot my mermaids. Outwardly, I studied. Inwardly, I sought the weightlessness of water, to be as liberated as the aquatic beings in my imagination.

We couldn't afford a pool in our backyard, so I begged my mother to let me join a swim team. She refused for an entire year, thinking piano was the right path for me, until she read a viral article online about the best extracurricular activities to teach kids time management. Armed with the listicle advice, she capitulated to my begging and pulled back on car repair to save money for team dues, in the event I did manage to qualify for the team with no prior experience. It was more important for me to learn control than it was for her to drive safely. And she didn't need prior American athletic experience to understand sports were expensive. Any extracurriculars were extra lines on her monthly budget lists, yet all were mandatory for my future.

She dropped me off at the high school, where there was a pool in the basement for tryouts. I was seven years old with the wrong swimsuit and no swim cap. Until that day, the biggest body of water I had been in was our house's bathtub. Yet when I dove into the pool, I felt like I had arrived home, like my seven years of life until then had been one long cross-country car ride, and the pool was the hot shower to wash off the filth collected from roadside stands and gas station bathrooms. I was liberated, unblemished, and one step closer to becoming the mermaid I always intended to be.

When I decided, years later, to sprout my tail, it was a hearkening back to the book I loved and the mermaids encased within. Though the pages were torn, the illustrations remained vivid with the legends and depictions of the aquatic adventures I longed for. I reread the pages each night when my eyes grew tired from squinting at the needle during the many hours of sewing practice. I marked each page with bloodstains from my fingertips, gashes where I clutched the needle too tightly—

I'm getting ahead of myself.

I do not regret much about my seventeen years as a human girl. Looking back in wistful longing is futile. Though, I will admit, I do perhaps wish I let Cathy kiss me sooner, such as during an inevitable game of Truth or Dare at our end-of-season parties. Girls were always dared to kiss other girls, and I should have taken advantage of the despicable excuse when I had it. Then I would've had the memory of her lips against mine to comfort me while I was alone in the hospital, my mermaid tail perfect, but the threat of unraveling so close by.

But let me be clear, so you cannot misconstrue my motives: while my journey may seem lonesome, I was never alone in my scars. I was the sole chlorine mermaid on my team, but I was not the only girl to self-mutilate. As proud athletes, it was expected our mutilations were a natural course of action to reach peak condition. Some cut. Some bulked. Some purged. It's all the same. Together we girls molded our bodies and selves into what Coach Jim wanted. What we wanted.

We mutilated our hair, cultivating our arm leg pit vagina hair for months like farmers growing wheat, until we cropped it off in one hour, together at the shaving party before the big meet. The razors cut lines down our calves coated in whipped cream, finger pads wrinkled and pruny. We soaped up each other's backs, an adolescent lesson in Sappho. *If you shave my back I'll shave yours.* We emerged from the locker room showers as naked mole rats.

We mutilated our guts with bowls of raw oats mixed with applesauce, stacks of banana walnut pancakes, pots of pasta mingled with marinara and basil, shakes of protein powder blended with egg whites, casseroles of coalesced buffalo chicken dip. We scoffed at nutrition labels based on a 2,000-calorie diet and we scoffed at the skinny girls in the cafeteria who pecked at tiny containers of Light & Fit Strawberry Flavored Greek Yogurt.

We were Fit, but not Light.

We mutilated our beauty, though this sense of beauty was an outdated version defined by narrow wrists and bird bones. We created a new and improved beauty from weightlifting, stair climbing, swim practicing. Our shoulders thickened, our thighs expanded, our muscles bouldered, our hair grew limp, our skin cracked dry into a mockery of fish scales.

We mutilated our language: 8x200's middle 100 red, 12x25's off the blocks sprint, 8x400 IMs descending fast, 6x25's underwater kick, 8x50's IM order, flipturns snorkels kickboards pulleys. A secret code, written on chalkboards and whispered among lanes, a dialect only we spoke.

We mutilated our bloodstream. Mr. Venezia, our chemistry teacher, taught us about osmosis, where molecules flowed back and forth until equalized concentrations lay on each side. After class, at practice, we argued whether chlorine replaced the blood in our veins. We prodded one another's skins, imagining the element drifting through our selectively permeable membranes. *Are we bodies of water? Are we swimming in pools of blood?* We licked our dry arms miles away from the pool and the sharp chemical odor wafted from our pores.

But we did not mutilate our girlhood. We were girls, always, first, even when we were fish, and we never forgot it, even if some of us were so overworked our periods disappeared. Under the steaming showers where we stripped naked after practice, young skin red from lack of oxygen, we stole glances at each other's stomachs, judging whose was flatter, or at each other's breasts, wishing our own were bigger. We huddled together to do our team cheer, arms looped around each other's necks as we pitched our heads back and forth, yodeling: *Hear us scream and see us swim, don't mess don't mess don't mess with the best 'cause the best don't mess.* We slid our hands around each other's waists to assist pulling up the $300 technical racing suit. If it took longer than ten minutes to put on, it was too small, but shorter than five and it was too big.

We were tougher than the football players and the tennis players and the track athletes combined, even tougher than the boys' swim team. Our high school swim team was a small world, but it was ours—we ruled with a dihydrogen monoxide fist.

Do you understand the world I lived in? How my mutilations were a gift?

Most of my teammates developed scabs and scars. They were too afraid to draw blood, so their incisions were shallow. I pity their fear. Sometimes I flit back and forth in my watery haven to watch Cathy, Brad, Ally, Mia, Rob, even Luke with curiosity as they head off to frat parties and underpaid entry-level jobs, and I feel nothing but sadness for them—how useless it is to seek healing through unreturned crumbs of affection and meaningless retirement funds!

Despite their past torments inflicted upon me, I have forgiven them a long time ago. Mermaids do not trouble themselves with the petty troubles of their human past.

As we delve into my tale, I must caution you every mermaid is different. Some tails are made of shimmering scales, and some, like mine, are made of skin and thread and knots. Popular discourse may force you to assume all mermaids have the same experiences, opinions, looks, and emotions, but I assure you, everyone has their unique points of origin contributing to their mythology and the overall canon: The Little Mermaid for a man, the Starbucks mermaid for corporate coffee, Nüwa for friendship. My own reasons were neither for partnership nor for profit—mine were simply a slow uncovering of my true self. While the people I swam with, and their behavior, can be considered catalysts to my transformation, their impact was—in the end—minor. Neither my Coach Jim, nor my best friend Cathy, nor my parents, nor my teammates, nor their viewings of me as an object of intense perverse affection, can be listed as the main reasons. I transformed because I became who I was meant to be all along. A mermaid who thrives in fresh water, chlorine water, seawater, ever adaptable, if I had my tail.

Back then, I was a girl, a body of water, a liminal state of being, a hybrid on the cusp of evolution.

Now, I am Ren Yu.

I am 人鱼.

I am person fish.

I am mermaid.

And so goes my tale of becoming.

Are you ready?

# Two

Like many other stories, mine begins with a wretched man. His name was Jim. He was my swim coach, and I his vessel for his second-hand glory.

The glory he gave me hung off my neck in medals of gleaming gold. The more he gave, the more I wanted, and the more I took. With each swim meet I gained laurels, yet my craving was never satiated. Jim offered me the training to secure these victories, so I bestowed unto him my love in return. I loved Jim because there was no greater intimacy than that found between athletes and their coaches.

The day I first met Jim was the day I first entered a pool. It feels perverse to recall my first time in water, my now home and most vital resource, as a simultaneous memory of the introduction between Jim and me, but alas. Nearly every human memory is corrupted by the fact that it is a memory of being human.

I showed up on the pool deck during tryout week mortified by the pink swimsuit my mother had forced me to wear. The swimsuit had a frilly tutu attached around the waist. It bobbed wildly, reminding me of its hideousness with my every step. The other team hopefuls looked like professional swimmers, having been dressed in second-skin swimsuits with their hair hidden by swim caps, their demanding parents wanting to vicariously relive their grand ol' swimming days through their kids. I had no such equipment. It was obvious neither I nor my mother had any real idea what to expect for competitive swimming, but my desire for water compensated for my lack of knowledge.

I had overheard other kids in homeroom at school talking about their prior swim lessons. They bragged about their progress through the YMCA levels, from eel to guppy to minnow to shark, like we were in biology learning about marine animals, while I had never even touched a YMCA membership card. If our outfits and their experiences were any indication, I would likely soon prove myself to be the worst swimmer at tryouts.

High-pitched laughter echoed around the pool deck. I reverted to awkwardly plucking at the mesh fabric of my tutu as an excuse for not initiating any conversation. My arms and legs were overly exposed, like peeled uncooked shrimp. I wasn't used to being so naked in front of other people who weren't my parents. My thighs chafed with no fabric between to soothe the abrasions.

Despite my uncomfortable state, the warm air on the pool deck lulled me. I was not familiar with pools, but I could sense I would soon love being there, surrounded by the heavy chemical scent, the lane ropes resembling caterpillars, the unnatural aquamarine-colored water. I was buoyant with the heady sense of a love soon to be, a sort of tingling premonition in my fingers.

A splash rang out, the first of the day. The kids parted to form two columns, everyone laughing at the commotion. The lanky sister who had pushed her younger brother into the pool bowed proudly in the center of the divide. I stood on the right side, watching the spluttering boy tread water, and swiveled my head to the left to observe my competition. I scanned a pasty boy, then a girl with frizzy red curls and thick freckles, dressed in a shiny new swimsuit I immediately coveted. I could tell her parents were ex-swimmers—the girl was prepared, looking sleek and competitive in a way I did not. She plucked at her shoulder strap, which was digging into her shoulders, leaving long, red, aching tire tracks on her skin.

"Enough!"

A man emerged from the pool deck office, bringing in a musty cigarette smell. As he stomped, he shoved a handful of mini cookies into his mouth, followed by a swig of Mountain Dew. Parents were not allowed into tryouts, giving this man full rein of adult authority; intimidated, we instantly quieted, leaving only the sounds of the boy's flesh gently slapping against water and the low hum of our nervous breaths.

The instant I laid eyes on the big man, my tutu unraveled, its pink thread leaving my fingers to dangle downward, grazing my thighs. I shivered, confused whether my body's stimulation was from the breezy kisses of the tutu thread or from the sheer presence of such a man. I never forgot the sensation of our first meeting. My body quaked with each tremor of the ground, corresponding with his stomps. I contemplated how he could make me strong. I hoped to impress him, to thrill him.

He stopped at the pool's edge, between our two rows. His fists were clenched, and his jaw was tight as he ground his teeth.

A twitching vein trailed from his neck into the collar of his polo. I stared at him, feeling like I had belly flopped off the diving block into a bottomless pool, and I was sinking down, down, down, with no air in my lungs and no lifeguard on duty. He was scarier than any human male I had ever seen, even scarier than Mr. Sullivan, my third-grade teacher, who showed us National Geographic videos of a ruined Earth during science class. Mr. Sullivan liked to make grand declarations about incoming catastrophic global warming. Because of Mr. Sullivan I couldn't bear dry summer heat—I craved damp, cold, and rainy days. I craved cold water over hot air.

The man pointed to the boy in the water. "You. Get out of the pool. You're out."

He switched his anger onto the sister. "You're out too. Get out. Go home."

We watched the boy clamber out of the pool. His sister gathered him into her arms. Both were silently crying. Their wet footsteps echoed as they left the pool.

The man surveyed us, his eyebrows creased. There were thick paunches of skin under his eyes, and I winced when the bags twitched over me.

"If any of you make it on the team, you'd better learn to keep your hands to yourself," he said.

He chucked the bottle of Mountain Dew toward us. We collectively ducked, and the empty bottle bounced as it hit the tiled floor.

He began pacing back and forth. "I'm your coach. Call me Jim. If you want to make it on the team, you better listen to me." He fingered his whistle, his large meaty hands obscuring it from sight. He blew a loud shrill. I clapped my hands over my ears. The boy next to me snickered.

Jim began to group us into lanes, herding the taller and older to Lane 1 and the shorter and weaker to Lane 6. I was shunted to Lane 5.

"Okay, everyone. Line up behind the lane."

I immediately stepped forward, the other kids shuffling behind me. They had proper gear, but I had confidence. I had *yearning*.

Jim began to pace again. "We'll start with a simple warmup. When I blow my whistle, the first person can dive in. Count to five after them, and then the next can dive in, and so on. Give me four laps of freestyle to start."

He inhaled and lifted the whistle to his mouth, but before he could blow, I dove into the pool. I couldn't wait any longer. I was so close. I wanted to touch water without other children inside it too. Their bodies would have corrupted my experience. And I had already grasped how men liked it when I did things they wanted without them needing to ask first. I wanted to prove to Jim I belonged, despite my unraveling tutu and capless head.

When my body touched chlorine, I grew. The tutu into a tail. My skin into scales. My fingers and toes into webbed appendages. My lungs into voluminous containers. My eyes blinked, and the blindfold I never realized had been tied around my face since birth fell off—I saw clearer when submerged in blue depth. I wiggled through the water neater than how I walked on land. I spun my arms in a messy windmill, scooping water out of my way.

I was alone in the pool the first time I dove in, and I've sought the same sense of isolated grandeur ever since.

When I reached the opposite wall, I lifted my head to turn, ears in the air. Jim blew his whistle.

I stopped and looked back, one arm treading water, the other atop the pool gutter. The tutu flared out of my body and spread onto the surface with my hair, forming a pink-and-black composition amid blue. My head was heavy, my hair soaked. Every kid watched me.

I waved. What else could I have done? I understood even then of humans' thirst for spectacle.

Through my stinging eyes I caught sight of the red curls I had seen earlier, their owner staring at me with her mouth ajar.

Jim strolled along the length of the pool toward me, a patient saunter much slower than his previous pacings. Anxiety flared within me as he neared. Perhaps I had been too brash. Perhaps this man believed I had undermined his authority. Perhaps he would banish me from my newfound shelter, like he had done with that brother and sister.

He stopped in front of where I tread. My eyes were at the same level as his feet. His sneakers were untied, the tongue floppy, the laces soggy with chlorine and old mud.

"Nice initiative!" he announced to the watching children, clapping his hands. "You all should be more like—what's your name?"

He crouched down and put his ear to my mouth. Pleased, I hissed my name, tasting remnants of evaporated chlorine on my lips.

Jim stood up. I heard his knees crack.

"Ren. You all should be more like Ren," he declared. My feet, treading water, spazzed in glee. He stuck his hand out for a high-five. I tapped his palm gently, hoisting myself out of the water like a jumping dolphin to reach his height. His hand was moist and humid. His thumb was long enough to wrap around my palm and crush my bones. When we touched, he smiled, and the pool water lapped at my collarbones.

"Beautiful. Just beautiful. And very talented. We're going to have a great time together," he whispered, winking.

He blew his whistle.

The other kids dove.

We began.

My mother picked me up after tryouts with a Tupperware of halved grapes plucked off their stems. She wrinkled her nose when I climbed into the car. My wet hair perfumed any small space with rotten chlorine. As we drove home, I profusely thanked her for taking me, but she looked nervous that I had fallen in love with a sport. To her, I was not supposed to fall in love. I was supposed to swim well enough to put it on my résumé, to get me into a good school. Love was too powerful a feeling.

"Are you sure you want to keep going?" she asked.

"Yes, Mom," I said. "This feels right. Swimming can be my extracurricular activity on my college applications." I knew how to appeal to her sensibilities. "The coach said I showed raw talent."

"What's the coach's name again?"

"Jim." I popped a few more grapes in my mouth, sucking the juice off the skin. Jim had pulled me aside at the end of the session to tell me he couldn't wait to have me on the team. He had stroked my cheek, and the droplets of chlorine stuck on my skin had trickled off with his fingertips. Absentmindedly, I rubbed my cheek, leaving grape juice glistening where chlorine had been.

"Where did he go to college?" she asked.

"Moooooom, why do you care so much about where people go to college? Stop prying." I rolled my eyes and spat out a grape skin onto the dashboard. "He's a swim coach. It doesn't matter where he went, as long as he can coach well."

I needed to protect Jim from my mother's high standards. Admiration from an athletic leader was new, and I didn't want to lose it so quickly—I was surprised to discover how good it felt to be deemed special for my body. I had always hated gym class, my gym teachers judging me useless. I spent that period walking when we were supposed to run laps, ignoring their whistles in favor of looking for four-leaf clovers. Land sports and recess games were impossible too. I didn't understand why all the kids my age constantly wanted to play outside. I tried my best to fit in. I went along with whatever games the neighborhood kids came up with, learning the rules without prior explanation. But I never dodged quick enough in dodgeball—after every game I'd have circular bruises all over my body. I fell facedown in the dirt during games of tug-of-war. When we played freeze tag, I'd pretend I was frozen even if I hadn't been tagged, so I could stay still. I was never strong enough to break through arms in red rover, and I played every game in petrified fear of getting called over.

The water was different. My home. And Jim was an adult who clearly saw something special in me.

Under Jim's watchful eye, my body would blossom.


I was accepted onto the team, along with the girl with red curls, and some other kids from tryout week I recognized but did not know. I eventually learned their names: Cathy. Mia. Luke Jr. Brad the Third. Ally. Rob. Basic human names. English words given meaning, passed down from their grandparents or uncles, some sort of elevation added, like *Junior* or *the Third*, to emphasize their long American lineage.

My name was simpler than theirs: Ren, 人, meaning person. Yu, 鱼, meaning fish. Ren Yu was neither a traditional Chinese name nor a typical American English name, but my mother thought it symbolic of the way her first and second language deteriorated from immigration, creating a new language with threads from both.

Ren Yu was an easy name to remember too. My mother believed having a simple name with a simple meaning would help me survive unscathed. Keep me inconspicuous, unnoticed. Yet when Jim made us do icebreakers during the first week of practice, my name drew me special attention. My teammates had trouble with its pronunciation, despite its one syllable.

Brad, thighs and eyebrows as thick as the pool lane ropes, picking his nose: "Your name is Ren? Did you cough?"

Luke, blue eyes crinkled in confusion, scratching his blond head, hands proportionally bigger than the rest of him, effective oars that would help him grow into the fastest boy on our team: "Did you mean to say Jen?"

Ally, standing next to Luke, unrelated, but the two together were the ever-classic question of "siblings or dating"—blond, blue-eyed, and perfect: "Can I call you Renny? It makes more sense to me."

Mia, stretching her long legs that would eventually propel her to become one of the state's top backstrokers: "Ren? Never heard of it. Is Ren short for a longer name?"

Rob, the only teammate besides Cathy to ever offer a semblance of kindness: "Hey! We share the same first letter!"

Cathy, with her red curls, who saved me from jumping into the pool during the icebreaker to drown myself from embarrassment: "I love your name."

Jim, who had already noticed me during tryout week, paid me close attention as the weeks went on. He noticed my beauty at the same time he noticed my swimming talent, because Jim had two great skills: swim coaching and predicting who would be hot. The two skills went hand in hand. The pretty ones were always fast. Did skill beget beauty, or did beauty beget skill?

Jim would compliment me, guide my arms and legs into proper forms. He loved to touch me. Never where it would count as illegal, as abuse. None of his touches would compel you to stop reading in disgust. None would make you want to stop understanding my story. Everything was coach appropriate: His hands around my arms, pulling them up in a tighter streamline, his hand against mine in a high-five, his hands pushing my hips forward to show me how to undulate on land before I tried in the water. I didn't mind—I was a beautiful human girl. So beautiful I could understand why he wanted to touch me. Beautiful things demand touch. Hence the taped floor lines at art museums and the roped boundaries between paparazzi and celebrities on red carpets. I was honored to be Jim's favorite acolyte. I was so radiant under his gracious older male gaze. He directed and I listened, even when the instructions were unrelated to swimming.

"Make sure your clothes aren't too slutty."

"Make sure you don't tease anyone too much with your good looks."

"Make sure you always come back after graduation to visit. You'll have to tell me all about the boys you're dating."

Even now, years later, I wake up some nights from haunted slumber, panting, my salty sweat droplets mixing with the salt in the sea, his demands echoing through my brain.

With the touching, the purring, the perversity, came protection too.

Every first day of fall, Jim would go apple picking off the funds from the Parent Swimmer Association and toss barrels of apples into the pool. He'd divide us into two equal teams, with an equal number of boys and girls on each. All's fair in apple bobbing. He'd blow his whistle, and we'd dive into the pool, mouths open wide to bite into the apples we swam past. We'd spit them out onto our team's respective side of the pool deck. Jim would count them afterward, and the team with the most apples collected could skip practice for the rest of the day.

One first day of fall, a year after I first began swimming, Ally mistook Mia's forehead for a Red Delicious and tore off a chunk of her skin, swallowing it whole. Red blood streamed from Mia's forehead and turned the blue pool water purple. Mia had to rush to the emergency room and get ten stitches in the jagged shape of Ally's teeth marks. Ally joked Mia tasted like a sour crabapple. After the incident I was too scared to join in the game—I'd swim along the wall at the deep end, avoiding my teammates' chompers. Jim yelled at everyone else for not moving fast enough, not biting hard enough, but he'd let me wallow and stay out of the way. When all the apples were out of the pool, he'd gather apples kept hidden behind his desk and congratulate me, claiming it was my own unbeatable pile. I went along with his lie, basking in my teammates' envy.

———

Jim encouraged me to specialize, as having one best stroke would give me an advantage when college recruitment eventually came.

Freestyle, backstroke, and breaststroke were such uncomplicated strokes, with legs kept apart and arms with intuitive movements. Why take the easy way out? So I chose butterfly, the hardest stroke of all four, the only stroke with legs together, using the entire body at once, requiring strong abs, powerful arms, great kicks, and flexible hips.

I loved butterfly because of the way my body skimmed atop the water, gentle as Jim's caress. In the water I fluttered my arms like wings, dipping my head forward and back to search for pollen, chlorine as my flower. I wrapped myself in a swim cap and goggles like a chrysalis, bursting from its cocoon to drop time.

I began to win heats. I caught the attention of local coaches and competitors, who before would have never considered a girl who looked like me able to beat them.

As a human girl, I adored winning. To win was euphoria, and euphoria was a blackout—black holes, stars, and galaxies forming at the edge of your goggles, an entire outer space dedicated to the Big Orgasmic Banging of first place. Euphoria was the feeling of ascension, a path I recognized when I later shed my human self for mermaid. Euphoria was reaching the edge of fatigue, near fainting, until adrenaline slapped you awake. Euphoria was muscles on fire. Euphoria was to slap the wall first, fist pumping the water, then to bask in the crowd's uproar, hollering your name. Euphoria was to dip your head in an act of humbleness for the gold medal to be placed around your neck. To shake the hand of your coach as he wipes happy tears from his eyes. To call your parents and tell them you won, again. *Yes, again, Mom. I won again. You heard right. Are you proud of me now?*

As a mermaid, I now recognize how winning places the self within a construct of hierarchy over other bodies—a false construct. There's no victory when someone else loses.

But back then, oh, how I adored winning. The rush of it all! You poor humans. You'll never learn to be better, not when winning is so addictive.

# Three

My father left around the same time I began to win. I came back from each swim meet high off first place, deflating as soon as I stepped into our fatherless house. He wasn't an alien in status, but as we resided in a boring American region of Earth, he was an alien in looks and personality. Though my mother and I tried to convince him that aliens were more captivating than plain human beings, he craved supply and demand in a language he understood. English was the language for colonizers and my father was unable to narrow his mind to learn it well. America would never let him accomplish anything in his accented speech, so he went back to China to build a business. He promised to send the money to us. What is it called when immigrants reverse, when they wake up from the nightmare masked as a dream?

We dropped him off at Pittsburgh's airport, a tiny building with only one security line and two gate sections, clear evidence of the city's trivial stature compared to the rest of the globe. It was four A.M., and we were exhausted, the sky still navy from the night's passing. Though my father's flight was not until eleven A.M., he insisted on arriving early, to offset potential security or visa issues. He had never managed to pick me up from practice or school on time, yet he was seven hours early for his own departure.

The overhang of the drop-off flashed red and blue from the circling police, who occasionally stopped next to cars to ensure nobody overstayed their goodbye. Though my father was leaving for many months, the number of which to be determined, he carried only one small suitcase.

"Don't worry about me. I can get everything I need in China," he said, kissing me on the cheek after I questioned where his clothes were.

"When will you be back?" I asked. My mother tapped the steering wheel, perking up and straightening her posture. She, too, wanted an answer for his return.

"As soon as you go under a minute in the 100 freestyle," he answered. The police siren lights glinted off the lens of his glasses, flickering his black eyes to blue. He pushed them up as his glasses began to slide down—he had promised me he'd get a new pair befitting Asian noses as soon as he landed in Beijing.

I nodded solemnly. I was close—my time was four seconds away to :59.99. I'd practice and practice and practice to get there. Anything to convince my father to return sooner. Anything to appease my mother's sorrow.

He patted me on the head and walked off, the suitcase limping behind him with a rumble against the concrete. Its back wheel was cracked and broken. He was too stubborn and too cheap to replace it because what was the point of spending money when the object's core function was intact? The suitcase might limp, but it could still carry his possessions across oceans. I waved goodbye though he did not look back. I tried to ignore my mother's crying. She had refused to exit the car to offer a proper farewell.

My father's figure shrunk into the yawn of the airport entrance cave. He disappeared, and my heart cracked in recognition at our severance. A human tie of mine, broken.

If the father left home, the mermaid daughter could too.

My mother tried to make up for my father's absence in her own small ways. She brought me meticulously prepared fruit every day she picked me up from practice: sliced peaches, orange wedges, strawberries cut in half into a heart; once, even a persimmon, quartered, rare in the American corner where we resided, and as we drove back home, she told me stories about the many persimmon trees in Beijing, how growing up she would buy frozen pulpy ones from the street vendors and slurp out the sweet juice.

She was a single parent with my father gone. It would've been easier to carpool with other families. But no one wanted to carpool with us. No one talked to us. And we weren't aware we could ask, because my mother and I didn't realize that to carpool was to pool humans inside a car, not a joke about a car driving to the pool.

Despite the cost, time, and energy, she was supportive of my swimming. Every night my father called through WeChat to catch up—morning for him, night for us—and though I sat in a different room, I could hear them arguing through the walls about how to pay for the travel meet hotel room, the competitive swimsuit, the team dues, the future plane tickets for my father to fly back and forth. Everything was expensive. Everything *is* expensive. But my mother never told me no.

I couldn't stay angry at my father for too long. His leaving was for the best. Holding on to such anger, such pain, was counterproductive. Grudges are for humans too small for forgiveness. I understood he needed to reclaim his pride, and I needed to focus on school, on swimming. Besides, there was already a growing pain inside of me, more vicious and visceral than yet another human father gone missing—a cliché tale itself.

The week after my father left, blood clots ejected out of me like burst water balloons. Red mucus came skidding out of me at a rate faster than my best 100 butterfly at an all-out sprint. I was in denial that my so-called period had come, shooting out of me more a bold exclamation point than any gentle tiny dot. A shout rather than a sentence. Why had I not learned more about the horrors of puberty in school?

In health class, menstruation was described in neat and clinical terms. Ms. Reggie, who wore crinkly tracksuits and doubled as the health teacher and the gym teacher, used a projector to indicate how the uterus would shed its lining to confirm the absence of pregnancy. The medical illustrations were clean, organized, easy to follow. But my period was the opposite—gut-wrenching, gross violence, marking the beginning of the end. My mother insisted periods marked the beginning of womanhood and the end of innocence: periods brought about breasts and butts and hips and drooling boys. Jim claimed periods marked the beginning of womanhood and the end of fast swimming times: womanly curves were not conducive to streamlines in water.

I was thirteen years old. I did not understand what was happening. I bled through my underwear, which we bought from Target using the 5 for $20 deal, my mother and I sharing the treasures of our haul—she used two of those five and I used three. I leaked onto our dining room's upholstered oatmeal-colored chairs. I left skid marks evoking roadkill, whose carnage I knew well—Pennsylvania had a deer-overpopulation problem, and anytime I hopped into our car, I prepared myself for the inevitable sight of a deer carcass in the road gutters, no matter how short our drive. Once my mother had hit a deer when we were driving to swim practice; its body flipped and landed on the windshield with a thud before sliding off onto the road. We didn't have the time or money to repair the crack for months. When I took off my pants, the clump of blood there reminded me of the large shovels attached to the municipal Department of Transportation trucks scooping up the gore once composed as a doe.

On the day of my first period, I was more dead doe than human woman. Was womanhood always so violent, raw?

I tried to deny it. I threw away the underwear so my mother wouldn't see. But she had been bleeding for more than twenty-five years. She recognized the stains on the dining chair's beige upholstery when I stood up.

"You got your period, bao bei. You're a woman!" She clapped her hands and squealed like I had gotten straight A's instead of menstrual blood on the furniture.

"No, I didn't," I said. I crossed my arms stubbornly.

She slammed her chopsticks down on the table. "You are a woman now, so act like it," she said. "It's time."

My mother herded me into the bathroom and watched me poke at my vagina, her sympathy transforming into impatience as the night went on. I had a swim meet the next day, and I couldn't swim if I didn't wear a tampon—apparently, it was bad to excrete blood and other bodily functions in the pool, which was news to me, since buckets of urine flowed from our bodies into the water at practice every day. Jim would never let us miss a second of practice to empty our bladders, and I never forgot the way Mia's bloody bitten forehead mixed with the pool chlorine.

"Slide it in and push the ejector up with your thumb, wo de sha bao bei."

"It won't go in!" I sobbed, my hands slippery.

"Stupid child, do you not want to swim tomorrow? Push it up and in. Easy." She frantically mimed the action. "It hurts but it will get easier. Ta ma de."

I began to wail, discarded bloody sticks of cotton on the floor around me, evidence of my failure. My thighs were weak and trembling from holding myself upright in a squat. Whatever rest Jim allowed me pre-meet had been wiped away. I was furious I was forced to push a cardboard-and-cotton tube into my vagina before a dick or a finger—pain before pleasure. I was crying. I was sweating. Chlorine and saltwater and blood poured off my skin—physiological secretions of a stressed young swimmer girl.

She sighed. She stomped over to the drawers underneath the sink and rifled through. She turned and handed me a dusty plastic bottle.

"Rub this on the tampon," she said.

I squinted and read the label: *Organic Natural Moisturizing Personal Lubricant.*

I swallowed my questions and squirted the lubricant onto the rod liberally, my hands sliding across the applicator. I reached down, blood and lube and other fluids following gravity to trickle down my wrist as I jabbed upward.

With the lubricant, the victory was easy, swift. My vagina gobbled the tampon as if starving. My first tampon insertion happened at 2:01 A.M., seven hours after my mother discovered the ruined chair.


3:00 A.M. Four more hours until we'd have to leave for the meet. My insides hurt too much to sleep. I stood in front of the mirror instead, examining my reflection.

Ms. Reggie claimed my body would change upon bleeding, but I didn't see any strident difference. I prodded my sore breasts, the fat reinflating like a sponge, but the only visibly growing part about me were my swimmer shoulders and back muscles. *You literally have the world on your shoulders*, teased non-swimming acquaintances on the bus rides to school. I didn't mind their taunts—I liked being muscled and firm and broad, though many women's shirts did not fit me. I had ripped a few in their back seams after moving my arms in the shape of a hug. My breasts and hips would have to grow rapidly if they wanted to keep up with the rest of me.

I flexed. My biceps hilled in the reflection. I stroked the canyons of muscle indents eroding through my skin. I debated walking to the kitchen, grabbing a knife, and pressing it against myself to carve out each muscle for greater prominence. Jim said the more muscles I had, the faster I would be. Using a knife would be easier than lifting weights. Bloodier, but I was already bleeding anyway.

A cramp rippled through me. I forgot my muscles and doubled over, concentrating on the cruelty inside me. How awful it was to be constrained to the pubertal development of the female body.

My mother dropped me off at the swim meet with a gentle *good luck* and a reminder to *push it up and in*, her arm wildly waving the air in an exaggerated motion. The sweat that had gathered and dried underneath my thighs onto the muggy leather seat squelched as I ejected from the car's protective cocoon. I winced as I motioned her off, hoping nobody had seen her with such a strange arm movement. She had offered to help me put a tampon in again before we left, but as I had slept past my alarm, we were already running late, warmup almost over. It was better to show up as soon as possible, for the more minutes that passed, the more likely Jim would throw a chair at my head. He hated tardiness. He had ingrained in me the lesson that *to be early was to be on time.*

I would have to put the tampon in solo—my mother would be absent. She never came to my swim meets because she cared too much. My disappointment was hers if I swam badly, and my high was hers if I won, and she lacked the ability to handle the comedown, the mood swings. Besides, she hated the other swimmer parents, who somehow became hollering, windmilling-arm animals while their children swam. When she did try to strike up conversations with them, they would answer every question with a *sorry, couldn't catch what you said through your accent.*

I entered the pool deck to drop off my bag and take off my

clothes. I waved to Jim, who was standing on the other side of the deck. He jabbed his thumb toward the pool, indicating I had to hurry and begin warming up, and I nodded, gesturing toward the locker room, to tell him I would start as soon as I was ready. I shoved the pastel tampon wrapper deep into my fist and headed toward the locker room, passing bleachers filled with our competitors, decked in varying levels of swimsuit technicality and team colors. I held my breath when I wove through the mass of coaches wearing baseball caps, holding clipboards and stopwatches. They stank of man sweat, cigarette butts, and faded glory.

The locker room was empty, most girls still warming up. The bathroom section was dark, stale, and musty, like all the other pool locker rooms I had grown up in, the sole sources of light from the overhead fluorescent bulbs. Dried chlorine, sweat, and Gatorade made the floor sticky, and I shivered at the invisible microscopic germs and bugs crawling over my bare feet. I wished I had remembered to put on my flip-flops.

I entered a stall and clicked the lock shut, rattling the door, testing its strength, fidgeting from one foot to the other, hoping my shifting would scare the floor toxins away. Through the walls, I could hear the announcer indicating the beginning of the meet. I shoved my swimsuit down to my ankles, shivering in the clammy air, and unwrapped the tampon. I stabbed myself, blindly, skin still sore from last night's pounding.

My vagina clenched. My aim was off. The tampon did not go in.

I sat down heavily onto the toilet seat, giving my arm and vagina a break. I heard a shuffle through the locker room, then the sink running. I wondered if help had arrived. I stood, unlocked the door, and peeked out.

Red curls untamed by water, frayed out from a head atop a pale body. In the mirror, freckles, dotted like dirt.

Cathy.

She looked up in the mirror and saw me and my bloody hand peeking out of the door. She shrieked and turned around, clutching her chest.

"Ren! What are you doing? What's on your hand—blood?" She gasped and turned even paler under the fluorescence.

"Cathy—I need your help. Please."

"What's wrong? Why is there blood?" Cathy squinted at me. "You look tired. Are you okay?"

Though we were young, we had duplicate facial characteristics indicating how we relinquished rest for swim practice. That day, I looked the worst out of all our teammates, the little rest I had last night written clearly on my skin in the form of dark eye circles, swollen lids, and haggard wrinkles.

The announcer's muffled *take your mark*, BEEP, filtered through the room, echoing off the tiled walls, indicating another heat gone by.

"Can you come inside the stall?" I asked. "Please."

"Uh—"

I didn't let Cathy refuse. I reached out and gripped her wrist with my clean hand, pulling her forward, her body following. I was near naked, my suit at my ankles, and her body pressed against mine as it crossed the threshold of the stall door. Despite the narrow space, our bodies had enough room to remain separate, but I felt like if I inhaled, I'd swallow her.

She stared at me, mouth agape, reminding me of tryouts, when I saw her across the pool.

"Have you ever put in a tampon?" I asked. I drummed my fingers on the tin receptacle, impatient.

"No. I don't use them. I'm on birth control."

"Fuck."

Cathy perked up. "My mother showed me once how to put it in though," she offered.

The announcer's voice declared the start of the boys' 50-yard freestyle, heat one. My event was next. I was in heat three. I had to hurry. I raised and rested my left foot on the toilet rim, and gestured wildly to my vagina with my bloody hand clutching the cardboard tube, soggy and red.

"How do I get this stupid thing inside me?" I asked.

Cathy determinedly studied the wall above her head. Anywhere but my vagina.

"I think it has to be at a forty-five-degree angle," she replied.

"Like, toward my stomach or toward my back?" I asked.

"I think stomach," she said.

I bumped my elbow against the stall. "FUCK!"

Cathy giggled.

"Stop laughing! You're lucky. My mom would never let me go on birth control." I glared at her. A trail of blood ran down my wrist. Beads of sweat dotted my face. There were spots of dried blood on my thighs, leading up to my naked vagina. No pubic hair. I was sure Cathy's looked the same. We were all shaved clean. Less hair—even covered by the suit—meant faster swimming times. No drag.

I couldn't decide what was more beaten up. Me or the tampon. Or both. A mild cramp tore through me. I winced. Cathy noticed, frowning.

"How do you want me to help you? It's not like I can shove it up for you."

"Why not?" I asked.

"*What?*"

"Pretend my vagina is a close friend and you're lending her a helping hand. C'mon, I can't go out there without it inside," I said.

"I can't do that!"

Inspiration tore through me. "Call her Penelope, or something, if it makes it easier. Penelope, because she pees."

"You're naming your vagina Penelope?" she asked.

"Yes. Penelope goes pee-pee," I teased.

"Oh my god. Shut up," she said.

"Penelope needs your help, Cathy. Please?" I begged, I pouted, I fluttered my eyelashes.

She grabbed the tampon from my hand. We were close. The locker room's musty odor of rotten chlorine and sweat intensified.

"You need to squat," she said.

"How?"

"Like this." She slapped my thighs to force them horizontal. My skin buzzed where she hit me. When I moved into position, she thrust the tampon repeatedly into the empty space between my legs and below my vagina, toward the back of my stomach. Cathy placed a hand next to my head to balance herself. I was pinned. She leaned between my knees. Her breath flirted over the side of my neck. I watched a trail of chlorine drip from her hair to her shoulder.

When I didn't respond, she kept jabbing to emphasize the proper movement.

"Yeah, just like that," I half moaned, half giggled.

"What did you say?" Aggravated, unnerved, Cathy straightened and frowned at me.

I began laughing so hard even my hard muscles were jiggling. "You kinda look like you're jacking me off," I howled.

"What does jacking off even mean?" she demanded.

"Never mind. Here, give it to me," I said, wiggling my fingers.

I snatched the tampon, so soggy I wasn't sure it could stand up by itself. I squatted and jammed it up my legs at the angle she had shown me. It slid in easily, as if mocking why I had ever been worried.

"Okay! It's in. I think." I straightened, my arms horizontal like a cross, bracing myself upright using the sides of the bathroom stall. I thrust my hips around, wiggling to see if I could feel the tube inside me.

"Your blood is all over my hands," she said. She poked my upper arm and left a red watery dot.

I exploded in laughter, and she followed. Her laugh was deep, belly-bursting. My hands left the walls to clutch at my sides, drawing a trail of bloody handprints across the stall partition, a crime scene of hormonal evidence, which made us both laugh harder.

"Caught red-handed," I choked out.

"Shut up. What matters is Penelope. Is she happy?"

"She says yes!" I said as I coughed, gagging on my own saliva, too busy laughing to remember how to breathe.

The announcer's voice echoed through the locker rooms again, announcing the beginning of the girls' 200-yard freestyle. I cleared my throat, the giggles dissipated with the impending race. I patted Penelope. I wiped my mouth with the back of my hand. I tasted blood.

"Okay. Let's go. Can you help me pull my suit up?" I asked.

Cathy nodded, hand clapped over her mouth in an attempt to stop chuckling. I pulled my suit up past my boobs, and raised my eyebrows at her, waiting. She came close to me, again, and pulled up the left strap, then the right, around my arms and onto my shoulders, readjusting where they fell on my deltoids. My skin burst white around the thin spandex. The suit was tight. Perfect.

I walked over to the sink and rinsed my arms up to my elbows with soap. Red whirled down the drain, coloring the porcelain.

"You should wash your hands." I eyed her from the reflection in the mirror, where she stood behind my shoulder, looking at her open hands. She ignored me, entranced by the stains on her fingers and palms.

"Thanks for helping," I said under my breath, so quietly I wasn't sure if Cathy could hear my thanks above the muffled clamor of the swim meet: the murmurs of the crowd, the babble of the swimmers, the chirrups of coaches' whistles. Sound had suddenly filtered back into the locker room after our laughter, as if the previous moments between us had been too solemn, too weighted, for petty clangs of the outside.

"Let's go." I marched away, tucking my stray hairs under my swim cap, rolling my muscles as I walked, my arms in a streamline above my head, legs alternating kicking against my butt to stretch my quads. I'd had enough warmup in the stall. I was back in competition mode.

The heat before mine was already on their last lap. Any later, and I would have missed my race. We reached my lane, and as I stepped away, she held up a hand for a high-five.

"Good luck," she said.

Her palm was crimson. She hadn't washed her hands. My blood was stuck on her skin.

The audacity of my biological clock had me curled up around a hot water bottle instead of around a swim towel. I tried not to miss practice when my period came, but sometimes the pain was too great, even for me. When I finally admitted to Jim how occasionally, my periods would force me to bed instead of to the pool, he embraced me, and said I was growing up. His meaty hands squeezed my hips, checking to see if the weight there had already crept on. Jim joked how as a coach, he was angry that breasts and hips would slow me down in the water, but as a man, he was eager for breasts and hips to bring divine things for his viewing pleasure. He winked and reminded me he had been a star breaststroker at Penn State. He was proud of me for bleeding.

My period continued, an inevitable cycle, yet every month I was somehow surprised by the violent pain. It was as if I refused to believe my body, something I'd trusted for years, would repeatedly betray me. My stomach ate itself from the inside, a revelry I had been dragged to, a feast I was forced to join though I was not hungry. The meal lasted four to six days, gorging on cramps, the spilled crumbs falling out of me stained with raspberry jam. My stomach was never a clean eater, gnawing on my uterus and fallopian tubes, leaving bite marks. I counted each rotation of the sun with heightening anxiety until it passed and I reset the clock. The knife carved my insides into pot roasts; the fork jabbed my sides into holey cheese. I could distinguish each fork prong—the pain was profound. My guts twisted around the spoon like spaghetti, tangled noodles slathered in scarlet marinara. Menstruation was more smashed acidic tomatoes than sweet fruit compote. I wiped my fingers on white jeans made of napkins and left streaks dried to rust. The stains came out with bleach and detergent. I died and regenerated every month. How else could I define the experience? The reasonable explanation was death. I decided when my body was wheeled into the morgue, the coroner would declare I died of being a woman. Which was far better than dying of being a man.

Every day I contemplated how mermaids do not menstruate. There was no mention of cramps in my mermaid book. I was jealous of them. I wished to be freed of my uterus's commands.

I did not swim well at that swim meet, the weekend of my first period. I was too tired. Too unused to the sensation of blood pouring out of me. Jim's punishment set for my slow results had my muscles sore and swollen for days. But the swim meet did bring me something beautiful.

I finally had a friend.

Cathy and I were acquaintances until she jerked me off with a soggy tampon. I pulled her inside the bathroom stall because she had been there at the right time, but also because she seemed the friendliest out of all my teammates, and though we had not been teammates for long, I could already tell she wasn't the type brave enough to say no.

I may have initiated with her out of desperation, but we became close friends after the meet because it was impossible to stick a hand up a bloody vagina and not fall in love with its owner.

# Four

Humans are the downfall to myths. Whether the human razed the home, broke the heart, or betrayed the trust, the mythical is always in a worse state after the introduction. I read countless stories of mermaids dragged forcibly from their oceans, mermaids condemned to marriages with men, mermaids stricken with voiceless throats. My ancestors' lessons forewarned me to close my heart to human advances.

But I was so lonely.

Looking back, I think Cathy was lonely too. She tried so hard after the bloody tampon to befriend me. We both did not fit in with our teammates. She was too chubby and too slow of a swimmer. Though I have always found her beautiful, human teenage popularity standards were unyielding, especially for athletes. Cathy couldn't rise to their expectations.

Cathy was the kind of blue-eyed white girl reminding me of the Blue Eyes White Dragon YuGiOh card I coveted when I was younger. And like blue eyes and whiteness, eventually I learned the Blue Eyes White Dragon was simply a construct too. A piece of flimsy card stock, its value ascribed by a mysterious higher power. I could go online and buy a million Blue Eyes White Dragon cards, and similarly, I could walk down the street of our suburb and see blue-eyed white girls everywhere, available a dime a dozen.

Ten cents can't buy much these days. Blame inflation.

I did admire Cathy's attitude. She was free from expectation. She spent her days swimming, eating, and going home, picking up a piece of assigned homework if it suited her sensibilities in the evening. She never cared about anything past the initial pleasure. Her life was so easy. She had normal parents who shared a bed. She had a grandma who lived in America, who celebrated Thanksgiving and baked her warm chocolate-chip cookies. I judged her days as remarkable for their mediocrity.

Because I enjoyed watching the parade of her All-American life, and because I was lonely, I let her be my friend.

"Which Faye Wong song should I choose?" I was scrolling through my iPod. Cathy and I sat on the pool deck bleachers, wrapped in towels. The last event of the morning session was under way. I was seeded first at finals in the 100 butterfly later that evening. I had to tell the official which song to play before prelims ended. The first seed was responsible for choosing the thirty seconds of music for their finals heat to walk out to. A privilege of the fastest.

"Who?"

"Faye Wong."

"I heard you the first time. Who is she?"

I looked up from my iPod in shock. "You've never heard of Faye Wong?"

Cathy shook her head.

"王菲?" I asked, using her Chinese name while inwardly cringing—if Cathy didn't even know the Anglicized version of her name, she wouldn't know Faye's real Chinese name either, the name my mother reminded me to use every time we watched *Chungking Express* together.

Cathy shook her head again. "Is her music any good?"

"Yes! My mom and I love her. I'm thinking about playing '胡思乱想' for the walk-out."

"What did you say? Who sah loon? Did you sneeze? Bless you."

Hurt, I shook my head and flashed the iPod screen toward her. "No. It's a song. In Chinese. One of my favorites by her."

Cathy took the iPod from me and stared at the album cover with a skeptical expression on her face. "I don't think anyone here has ever heard of any Chinese song, let alone this one."

"Well, I have," I huffed. "And if my mom was here, she would know the song too."

"Okay, so? Your mom's not here, and just because you're fast doesn't mean you can choose weird music." She pulled out her own iPod from her duffel bag behind her. "I can give you some other options," she said, waving me over.

I slid closer to her, the towel around my body smooth on the bleacher metal. Our thighs touched.

"Okay. Here's an option for you." She placed a neon-pink Skull-candy earbud into my left ear and the other bud into her right ear. She bobbed her head as she pressed Play.

A piano banged, high then low chords.

*Just a small-town girl, livin' in a lonely world*

I ripped the earbud out. The water stuck in my eardrum squelched with the release. "Are those lyrics supposed to be inspiring?" I asked.

"Yes! It's a classic. 'Don't Stop Believin',' " she said.

"Don't stop believing in what, exactly? I guess I'm a small-town girl, but I don't want to be livin' in a lonely world or whatever—how are those words supposed to hype me up before I swim?"

"No, silly, it's the whole piano anticipation thing, like, it's supporting the buildup to your race," she said.

"I don't think it'll work."

"The beginning, those chords—doesn't it make you excited?"

I tapped my chin. It wasn't as catchy as any of my Faye songs. "Any other recommendations?"

Cathy scrolled through to the bottom of her playlist. "Here."

I jammed the earbud back in.

Ominous synths, a low electric guitar, cymbals.

*Ooo wah ooo wah ooo wah ooo wah…*

I took out the earbud again. "Is the voice supposed to be singing?" I asked. "Ooo wah ooo wah ooo wah?"

Cathy paused the music and tucked her iPod back in the duffel pocket. She sniffed. " 'Livin' on a Prayer.' By Bon Jovi? It's a classic." She wiped her nose on her towel. "Trust me. You should choose one of those two options. If you play the weird song you mentioned, people are going to make fun of you."

She had a point. I cradled my head in the crook of my arms, resting atop my knees.

"It's not my fault I've never heard of either of those songs," I argued, my voice muffled and petulant. How could I have heard of them when my parents preferred Chinese over English? My dad loved Teresa Teng, stacks and stacks of her pastel-pink CDs overflowing the shelf above our television. Her warbles would float out from the basement where he worked on his software business before he left to rebuild it in China. I memorized the sounds she made and learned Chinese from her songs. I memorized the phrase for *the moon represents my heart* before I learned *hello, thank you*.

I enjoyed Teresa's music, but like my mother, my heart lay with Faye Wong. My mother and I considered Faye the most beautiful woman in the world. Neither of us had ever seen anyone else carry such an ethereal face, either in China or in America. Faye was the epitome of cool. I didn't care about Abercrombie logo T-shirts or milkshakes or Tamagotchis. When I wasn't thinking about mermaids or swimming, I was thinking about Faye. My mother played her CDs to and from practice, Faye's crooning accompanying our journey. When I recall the lactic acid cooldown of post-practice drives, I hear Faye's slow yearning beats of nostalgia.

Faye was our favorite movie star too. My mother and I watched *Chungking Express* every Friday night after swim practice. As the movie played, my mother would sew tablecloths, pencil pouches, pillowcases—anything fabric and thread and her sewing abilities could construct—so we could save money, while I would halfheartedly finish some homework, shaking my head every so often to air dry my hair. She would cover my eyes when Brigitte Lin, in her sexy trench coat and blond wig, shot her gun at the disgusting white man's head (how dare any white man show their face in such a gorgeous work of Asian cinema?) or when Tony Leung shoved Valerie Chow against the closet and flew a toy airplane down the curve of her back. Though she tried to shield me, I understood the violence and sex on-screen the way a young child can interpret a parent's vocal inflections. I watched the movie obsessively, bobbing my head to "梦中人," watching not for the classically handsome Tony Leung or the smoldering, pathetically sexy Takeshi Kaneshiro, but for Faye. Faye, with her hot boy haircut and tiny round sunglasses and yellow polo, heaving a bucket of carrots and onions through a dusty outdoor market. Faye, leaning against the takeout counter, chin in hand, dreaming of escape. I learned the absurdity of human sorrow from *Chungking Express*, and I learned that to love for ten thousand years, as Takeshi murmurs into the phone as the password for his nonexistent voicemails, was a very long and lonely time indeed.

And Cathy wanted me to play such meaningless sounds instead?

"Well, you've heard the two song options. You better like at least one of them." Cathy nudged me. "Go on. Tell the official. The name of the song is enough, no need for the artists' names, they're super popular."

"Fine. I'll choose the first song. What's it called? 'Don't Stop Believin'?" I stumbled up off the bleachers, wrapping the towel tighter around my body. I shivered.

"Yep, you got it," Cathy said.

I was the sixth "Don't Stop Believin'" to play at finals. Every event before mine, and every event after, had the beginning thirty seconds of either the small-town girl, or the stupid bouncy ooo wah ooo wah ooo wah.

After the meet, I never listened to Faye in public. I kept my love for her private, through my headphones at home or through the CD player in the car. I learned the idea of fitting in was not to be exceptional, but to be the same as everybody else, regardless of taste. For both Cathy's sake and mine, I memorized the few acceptable songs in the American athletic musical canon, all in English. Journey, Bon Jovi, Eminem. M&M. Is there anything more American than a musical artist named after candy? Anything more American than living on a prayer and nothing else?

These days, sometimes my marine neighbors in the next coral over blast Bon Jovi and Journey during parties. Playing human music for enjoyment gives them a sense of control over the hierarchical animal kingdom. I leave my dwelling when they celebrate because I cannot stand their music. Besides, I prefer the quiet. I head upward to bask on a rock in the sun with my tail fluttering behind me, reflecting on how happy I am. How free I am.

My sole complaint about my life now is I haven't been able to find a waterproof way to watch *Chungking Express*.

# Five

## CATHY

Dear Ren,

How are you? I hope you're doing well. You seemed happy when you left. I hope the happiness has stayed. I'm writing my letter by hand because I think you'll appreciate the personal touch. I apologize if the handwriting gets messier as the letter goes on. I'm worried my hand will cramp up as I write, since I'm trying to keep the size of my writing small. I went to the thrift shop where you used to get your clothes and bought some old glass bottles with stoppers, but they all have rather skinny necks. I can't use too many pages of paper, or else the letter will be too thick to fit in the bottle. I'll try to keep my message as short as I can.

Were you aware when I realized I was in love with you? I keep thinking back to the dawn of my awareness. I try to grasp its rays so I can stay warm, but they fly out of my hands. I have trouble holding on because you're not around to remind me how.

I guess hearts are slippery because they're covered in blood. I wish I could bleed mine dry. Then I'd miss you less.

I realized my love for you during a streamline perimeter walk at practice during freshman year. Remember those horrible walks Jim made us do, because he insisted we wouldn't learn unless we did it for hours? I know loose streamlines meant water could rush through the gap between our ears and upper arms, but did he really have to be so cruel? We'd trudge around the pool with our bodies ramrod straight, our arms pointed upward, our biceps pressed firmly against our heads, our hands stacked, dominant thumb wrapped around the other palm—we resembled sharpened pencils rolling around a box as we circled the pool. You'd probably argue that Olympic races had been lost due to loose streamlines, but I still don't think Jim really needed to circle us in reverse, slapping at our arms with a ruler. Even now I can't look at a ruler in the office supply store without hearing echoes of ruler thwacks against flesh.

We were so used to pain. Jim forced us to do horrible things. Remember those wall sits, where we balanced our backs against the wall with our legs at ninety-degree angles, our quads burning in infernos far greater than the guy we read about in English class? Dante. Divine Comedy. You loved to ridicule the idea Dante was in hell, because we already knew hell. Jim didn't let us stand straight from those wall sits until one of us collapsed on the ground. Remember once Luke passed out and there was a nasty purple bruise on his tailbone for weeks? He kept flashing us the bruise at practice, pulling his Speedo down. His ass was so pale.

*Remember those stair runs? Us running up and down stairs like an army of ants, Jim our queen at the top, blowing his whistle in warning whenever one of us reached a hand out to the railing for support.*

*Remember those underwater dolphin kicks, those laps of undulating kicks underwater, back and forth until one of us passed out from lack of oxygen? Brad passed out the most often, his lips bright blue. Jim said it was because he was a weakling with small lungs.*

*Remember, remember, remember? Feels like all I do is remember the times I had with you.*

*I still think streamline perimeter walks were the worst of all of Jim's creative tortures. Wall sits, stair runs, underwater dolphin kicks—those were all doable because our bodies could form the positions naturally. From childhood we can sit, run, and kick. But there was nothing natural about streamlines. It was us against gravity and we were destined to lose.*

*Anyway, let me get back to my yearning:*

*We were on our second streamline perimeter lap around the pool. My body had long since entered a state of burning numbness. I had no sensations left. To survive I stared ahead.*

*You were in front of me. We were best friends. It was freshman year already. By now, you could rap every word to "Lose Yourself" by Eminem, even though we both agreed your pronunciation was in poor form.*

*On your head was your usual swim cap and goggles: tight purple straps, smooth latex. On your body was your new swimsuit. Do you remember which one I'm talking about? You had told me as we changed in the locker room before practice that your mother agreed to buy the suit if you finished five SAT prep practice tests with perfect scores, and of course you succeeded, in part because of your own brilliance, but mostly* because the answers were available online. Your new suit was the year's latest edition of the Nike swimsuit, rather controversial, as the suits had an open back, deep thigh cuts, and a swatch of fabric hanging low, swooping right above the butt crack. The suit bared more skin than we were used to. Of course, the exposed back and higher thigh cuts meant water rushed in during any flipturn, a glaring flaw, but it was sexier to show more. Among our teammates, only you and Ally wore these suits so far, though we all wanted to.

Your suit was a deep scarlet, matching your swim cap, with white and orange spots splattered across your butt, and those spots swayed in conjunction with the rhythm of our marching, hypnotic, like a swaying pendant. I gawked at the suit, following the spots, straining to enter nothing, a dreamless sleep. My eyes trailed upward, over the smooth expanse of your back. Fluid. I watched your muscles ripple as you straightened your streamline.

THWACK

I heard the stomping too late. Jim's ruler hit my left arm. Pain shot down my limb to my left butt cheek. The flames leapt higher. I gritted my teeth and tightened my arms.

Jim sternly reminded me to pay attention. He walked on in the opposite direction. I peeked up at my arm. The skin was bright red, a cherry rectangle on my forearm where the ruler made its mark. I'd press the spot later at night in my bed before sleep, to watch the blood rush out, then in.

I strengthened my streamline. I pressed my thumb harder into the opposite palm. I hardened my back.

We kept walking. Needles pricked my skin. My body heat climbed to feverish levels. Instead of tracing your body, I stared forward, immobile, straight at your head. I couldn't be distracted by scanning any lower;

there was too much at stake during streamline perimeter walks to interrogate the curious hypnosis while examining your exposed back, your butt, the spots on your skimpy Nike swimsuit. Your head was as entertaining as your body, encased within your red swim cap, bobbing like the apples we threw in the pool every first day of autumn. The red was framed by your arms, no gap visible, of course, as you were Jim's star swimmer, always perfect. Perfect streamline form, perfect swimmer body, perfect race. I kept walking. Your red sphere was interrupted by a purple line, your goggle strap. I traced the strap and wished I could tear it with my teeth; lift the strap up and slap it down. My eyes burned. My shoulders burned. My back burned. My skin, ever chlorine-chapped, burned. Everything burned. I lost track of where my streamline began and where the pool floor ended. Perhaps my body was cursed. Perhaps the myth my mother had recited to me whenever I was caught sticking my tongue out was coming true: if I made a certain face for too long the expression would permanently freeze. Perhaps I would be trapped in streamline forever. There were worse fates—

I reversed. I smacked into you. My nose bounced off the red silicone of your head. I wasn't paying attention. My streamline broke, my foot slipped, and I flailed, trying to regain my balance. You turned, arms down by your sides, and yelled at me to watch where I was going. You swore at me—I remember clearly how you said, What the fuck are you doing—I can replay these five words in your voice because though you liked to swear often, it was the first time a swear word from your mouth was directed at me with venom.

I lost my balance, tipping over and toppling belly first into the pool, clumsy, like I wasn't a swimmer but a child at their first pool party. Gasping, I came up for air, my arms relieved, my body doused from flames.

*I locked eyes with you. I spat out water. I apologized.*

*I treaded and debated whether to drown myself or deal with Jim's inevitable punishment. Drowning would be less painful.*

*Too late. Jim's shrill whistle blew. I heard his stomps before I saw his stomach. I saw his hands push aside Rob and Mia. Jim's knees cracked as he crouched and motioned me over.*

*My hopes rose. He hadn't thrown a chair, hadn't raised his voice yet. Jim would take pity on me. A kind gesture from an unkind man, which made it more meaningful. I doggy paddled to the gutter.*

*When I drew closer, he took out the kickboard tucked hidden behind his back and whacked me over the head. I had lowered my guard down and had no time to dodge. The foam was soft and his precarious position at the edge of the pool meant the hits were more symbolic than actual punishment, but my insides writhed with embarrassment. I didn't chance glancing at you. I didn't want to see pity on your face.*

*After seven whacks, he stopped hitting me, panting. I kept my head lowered, like his smacks had bent my neck into a permanent angle. Better to let him think he hurt me.*

*Jim clambered up to his full height. He dismissed the team, including you, then gave me a punishment set: 8x100 breaststroke, four of them within five seconds of my best time. When he said the word* breast *in breaststroke, it made me think of both of yours, nestled within your Nike swimsuit.*

*I lowered my goggles to my eyes and swam freestyle to the far wall. As I shifted my head to the left for air, I saw the girls walking toward the locker room in groups. But you, in your distinct red swim cap and new red gear, walked alone. I could tell, even in my blurred waterlogged vision, you were watching me as I swam, your head turning with each inch I moved.*

What were you thinking? Were you feeling sorry for me? Were you thinking the same burning thoughts?

The whistle blew again. I was fucking sick of Jim's whistle.

Jim towered above me, raising his eyebrows.

I rested my hand atop the gutter. I brought my feet to the wall.

The whistle.

I pushed off, underwater, in a streamline once again.

As I broke through the water, my mind wandered—separation of mind and body was the sole way to get through Jim's punishments. After so many years the body moves automatically, like a waterproof robot. As I swam, I wished I could praise how your body looked in red, and I wished I could say hello to Penelope. I wished I could leave the pool and join you in the locker room, where we'd strip ourselves bare.

Anyway, I'm writing all of this now because I couldn't say it then. Jim was in the way and my own fears were too.

As I write, I feel the same fire from that streamline perimeter walk, relighting itself inside me, licking, inside my core, a slow smolder, a wholly different sensation from the numbing conflagration brought by streamline and the irritation of chlorine on skin—the feeling you give me is more like embers. Glowing.

Okay, enough from me. After the ink dries, I'll stuff my message into a bottle, then head to the creek. I've been going there alone. Sometimes I pack egg rolls and dumplings and leave them by the shore. For you, for the fish, for whoever wants these trivial offerings. I stroke the sand where we sat.

I cry when I'm there.

Sob, really.

I search for you in the creek. Sometimes when the sun shines on the *water, and it glitters, like diamonds, I see your face in the glimmer—but then I blink, and you disappear.*

*God, I miss you. Do you miss me?*

*Anyway, I'll throw my message-in-a-bottle into the creek, and I'll squeeze some jeweled touch-me-nots for you too. I hope my letter finds you, wherever you are. And I hope you're thinking of me as much as I'm thinking of you.*

*Love,*
*Cathy*

# Six

Humans break so easily. They break their bones, their bodies, their hearts. I, too, as a girl, once broke. My head. And when this happened, I, like many other humans, did not allow myself the time and resources to fully rest, heal, recover. Of course, there are excuses: No health insurance. Boss wants me back in the office tomorrow. You must pay for the ambulance. I'm out of sick days. No paid maternity leave. Need to get back to swim practice.

These are, essentially, human excuses, but more specifically, American excuses. I'm confined to a comprehension of human difficulties through an American lens, no matter how hard I try to break out of the star-spangled brainwashing I was subject to from a young girl's age. In a way, the recognition that these issues are uniquely American makes it worse, because they are entirely avoidable.

Luckily, I have no need to worry about American human problems anymore. Here, in my marine dwelling, we reject the human dependence on such ridiculous things like employee-offered health insurance and paid time off. Mermaids aren't beholden to human economic constructs. Under the water, we aid, love, give, heal. Freely. After I hit my head, I barely held on. I had little consideration for anything other than myself. How selfish I was. But I was meant to be selfish—my self, meeting the fish. In a way, my breaking compounded my ascendancy, though it was never I who did the actual breaking. It was my head, the people, and the systems around me.

As a human, I was weak. I allowed myself to crack.

Today, as a mermaid, I am strong. Unbreakable.

You cannot touch me.


My head broke during sophomore year of high school, during the winter. Pittsburgh was a dull, gray, human city full of bridges, prone to hiding the sun behind stormy clouds and bisecting family neighborhoods with four-lane highways, and as a human girl I was both annoyed and enamored with the city. The home was a hard place to love, perhaps because it was the home, and you therefore expected so much more from it, and felt its failures more acutely. Twelve inches of snow couldn't faze even the feeblest of Pittsburgh residents, and so life went on in the winter without reasonable inconveniences like event cancellations or road blockages. The city's salt trucks, outfitted with the hardiest equipment, were on standby at the mere hint of flurry, beginning November, their sentry lasting until May. Jim didn't care about the dangers of driving in wintry conditions; once Brad was going down Eichner Road for morning practice, too early for even the sun to come out yet, never mind the salt and deicing trucks. He lost control of his SUV, spun off the road and hit the guardrail. He never made it to morning practice and Jim threw a chair at him when he showed up in the afternoon. Car crashes were no excuse to skip. Using Jim's logic, why hadn't Brad ditched his wrecked SUV and walked the rest of the way?

Cathy and I were leaving Mia's house, a shingled construction in one of the nicer neighborhoods on the opposite side of the school district. We called her side the money side. Ally and Luke lived nearby too. Mia's house was the host because her mother was bored—she spent her days cooking thick sauces and lumpy dips and wilted salad dressing. Cathy and I were both stuffed from her creations.

We had been there after afternoon practice for the annual kickoff Parent Swimmer Association meeting, where Jim had lectured on his hopes and dreams for the season. My mother was the only mother to not show up. She was working. I didn't care. Why would she waste her time with such trivial matters? I always swam well, so she had no need to harangue Jim with endless questions about my results.

The kids were kicked out of the meeting after two hours, because the parents had more important things to discuss with Jim: the team budget, the team dues, which college recruiters had contacted him so far, the meet chaperone schedule. But Cathy and I were alone in leaving—our teammates had stayed at Mia's home, piling up in her bedroom to gossip and cuddle and giggle—Cathy and I had excused ourselves, citing homework, although our teammates hadn't extended an invitation to us in the first place.

We strode across the driveway to our cars. We were sixteen years old, finally achieving suburban vehicular freedom, and whenever we had to go somewhere after practice, whether for a team dinner or meeting, Cathy and I would drive together but separately: me first, leading the way in my beat-up hand-me-down old car with thousands of miles clocked on the odometer, bestowed from my mother, who, after careful calculations, realized she would, over time, save money and office reputation by giving me the family car and buying another used car for herself so she could stay longer at work instead of leaving early to drive me; Cathy following in her own sparkling new sixteenth-birthday-present car because her mom didn't think twice about it.

It was nighttime already by the time we left Mia's house. In Pittsburgh, winter darkness settled in early. The sky and stars faintly winked at us. A tentative flutter was all outer space could muster, even in the relative light-pollution purity of our suburbia. It was freezing. I shivered. Cathy was talking about her mother again, about how maternal affection in her household came in the form of body admonishments, and I was half listening because I was sick and tired of hearing about her hatred for her weight—I loved her body, its thickness, its absolute denial of nonexistence. It hurt me to hear her hate herself. So I tuned her out, interjecting with occasional monosyllabic sounds of agreement to indicate my attention as we neared the getaway vehicles, and I was concentrating instead on reviewing the latest chemistry equations in my head when the ground went out from under me and the stars disappeared.

Silence.

Darkness, never-ending.

Was I dead?

I blinked, and my vision rushed back. I blinked again, and small bursts of stars fought their way through neighborhood streetlights and car headlights on the highways—I blinked—the stars moved to form numbers, and I recognized what they composed—my swimming times to the millisecond: 1:02.09, 4:59.08, 1:12.47, 1:58.36. Were the heavens communicating their significance? I blinked. The stars rearranged, again—a tail. There was the fin, double-pronged, and connected to two longer curved lines. The stars were communicating something about a fish. A mermaid tail?

I blinked.

I refocused.

A hammer pounded against my skull. My eyes were the nail heads. I was on the ground, my gaze directed up at the night sky, where the stars pulsed. My butt was frosty. The frigid driveway seeped through my jeans. My tailbone throbbed.

"REN!" Cathy's harried and desperate voice flew into my consciousness. My name was more a gasp than a word. What had happened to make her sound so wretched?

I heard a shuffle of quick footsteps, a thud of knees near my ear. The stars were replaced by freckles surrounding a nose, then red curls, then two blue eyes wide as the dinner plates we'd used at Mia's. Cathy leaned over me.

"Are you okay? You fell on the ice and hit your head. You wouldn't move. I wasn't sure whether to run inside and bother the parents or not. I can go get your mom?"

"Oh." I wiggled my nose, then my fingers. I could move. I had expert control of my muscle function. I was fine, though my head throbbed. I smiled up at Cathy. Perhaps I was dreaming about her. Was she rescuing me? Her curls were fiery, her eyes like deep springs of water, as she hovered, surrounded by winter skies. Worrying about me looked so good on her.

"No, I'm all right," I said dreamily.

"Are you sure?" Cathy asked. Her forehead wrinkled deeper in worry.

"Yes. Don't wanna bother them. My mom isn't here anyway. Can you help me up?" I asked. I held my arms out in front of me like a zombie rising from the grave. Cathy wrapped her hands around my forearms and gingerly pulled me to a sitting position. The shift in movement made my vision go blue. My butt was numb and soaking wet, and my head was throbbing with gaining intensity each passing second. I gripped Cathy's shoulder, then together we heaved upward, my weight on her.

"I don't think you should be driving right now," Cathy said anxiously. "Let me drive. Leave your car, it'll be safe here. We'll pick it up later."

I grunted, in too much pain to disagree.

She led me to her car, an awkward shuffling couple, a mismatched double.

When we arrived, I shook Cathy off and clambered inside, wincing with each movement of my body. Cathy rushed over to the other side, starting the car as she looked over at me. It was so cold inside the car that both our breaths came out in gray clouds—I smirked, because they reminded me of Pittsburgh's skies—how funny, I mused, that we breathe the heavens—then I saw black, again, and my forehead tipped to the side, thudding against the frosty window glass.

I sat in the hospital, my body slouched against the weak cushions. Cathy was next to me, one hand rubbing my upper arm, the other scribbling on the medical forms. She had already memorized my birthday, my allergies, my first and last name, but there were a few answers she needed I couldn't recall: social security number, family history, health insurance card. I motioned toward my butt cheek to where my cell phone rested in my back packet, so she could call my mother, the most reliable source of my personal information, but she shook her head and drew my phone out from her backpack—the screen had cracked when I hit the ground. It wouldn't turn back on. We could have tried using her phone, but Cathy didn't have my mother's number saved, and with my head pounding, I couldn't recite the correct digits. Neither of us wanted to call Jim.

I let Cathy fill out the forms while my gaze wandered around. We were sitting in a typical waiting room with white lights and gentle classical music playing from the speakers. Both the lights and the music were overwhelming—there was a sharp whine emanating with the light's wavelength near the bridge of my nose, between my eyes, and the string instruments carried the clashing of a hard metal concert, my head banging with each beat. My limbs were both weightless and weighted, like I was floating in water while clothed in loose, dragging fabric. I looked down at my shaking hands and counted three fingers and two fingernails.

There were many beings in the room, waiting their turn with the doctor, their bodies crinkled like balls of paper in their chairs. I saw humans with neon pink skin impatiently tapping their feet on the ground, boys with three eyes begging for treats from the vending machine, girls with golden snakes wound around their limbs. I saw mothers with spiky black hair like sea urchins and I saw fathers with fins for hands. There was a woman sitting in a chair with crab claws at the ends of her arms, cutting the hair of a girl who sat on the floor cross-legged between the crab woman's calves. The hair strands drifted delicately around them like air bubbles. There was an octopus with its eight slimy limbs spread onto the linoleum tiles, a mask over its flabby face, and next to the octopus, licking one of its tentacles like it was a popsicle, was a young girl, wearing a denim shirt and a long maxi skirt. Under her hem I spotted iridescence. Scales covering her swollen feet.

A mermaid?

I rubbed my eyes.

The scales didn't disappear.

Cathy elbowed me gently.

"Ren, are you okay?" she asked.

"Yes," I said. Squinting at the mermaid scales, I grabbed a children's book on the side table next to our chairs without looking to see which book I chose. Anything to distract myself, to hide my gaze from the aquatic sight before me. Looking down at the pages, I saw I had chosen *The Rainbow Fish*, the glimmering scales of the illustrations similar to the mermaid tail I had just seen. The Rainbow Fish's tail leapt out of the waters of the book pages and slapped me in the face. Frantic, I dropped the book back onto the table and returned to searching the room, confused, panicking, believing in the reality before me. There was a man with orange and white stripes on his face like a clownfish, holding the hand of a smaller boy, his son, who had a shrunken fin instead of a right arm. I saw a bearded man with a golden trident stabbed into his chest, on the left side where his heart would be, and a woman next to him with a turquoise fin jutting from the top of her head, waving her arms in panic as blood spurted from the trident prongs. The nurses seemed unbothered with the spill of ruby over the floors, as if they did not notice, or as if it were not really there. I took their cue and ignored the spreading puddle.

I closed my eyes and sank farther down into my chair. The cushion deflated further with my weight. I let Cathy take the lead.

It was a concussion, probably a major one, the doctor said, when we were finally invited inside. Though the doctor excused his uncertainty by claiming how brain science had not yet progressed enough to provide an accurate diagnostic, he was sure the impact, the blackout, and the subsequent memory loss and pain coinciding with aversion to the waiting room's bright light and music were indicative of Jim's greatest fear: medically induced time off from practice.

The doctor clarified nothing was certain. He said diagnostic tests were helpful but ultimately inconclusive. Concussions were uncharted territory and doctors were explorers fighting through the poisonous forest. He said we had to trust my feelings: if I had a headache come on whenever I moved my head or whenever the lights flickered, I was still a concussed invalid.

"So it's up to me?" I asked.

"Yes," he said. "Be honest with yourself. Concussions are serious. It's your head. Your brain. The most important organ in your body. If your head twinges at all, especially under bright lights, you're not healed. And you can't get back in the water until you've fully recovered."

"But what if my head always hurts?" I asked.

"What do you mean?"

"Like, everything hurts. All the time. Everywhere." So was the extent of my articulation.

The doctor pursed his lips. "You hurt because you've suffered a fall and a head injury. You'll be fine as long as you take care of yourself."

He misunderstood.

How was I supposed to differentiate between the pain due to the concussion and the pain due to the agony of everyday human life?

Instead of going to swim practice every day, I went to the doctor's office, my mother waving away my repeated questions about how we'd pay. My father reminded me, through the crackling weak Wi-Fi connection of my mother's WeChat app, to obey the doctor too.

The doctor forced me to take endless tests on the computer. They were the same questions and activities every time, but my head hurt too much to memorize the answers. I had to alternate pressing between two keys on the keyboard, the letter K if the right image flashed, and the letter S if the left image flashed. Such a stupid test would make anybody's head hurt, concussion or not.

Though the doctor prescribed rest and relaxation after these tests, I still had to study and keep up with my schoolwork. Of course, my head kept aching—if you've ever had to exist in a body form not yours, if you've ever had to read a chemistry chapter on thermodynamics, or an act of *Hamlet*, or a long and winding family history of the Hapsburgs and their weak chins, then your head would pound too.

Without swimming, I became limbless. Oxygen was less nourishing than chlorine and I was starving. Jim texted me every morning when I woke up and every night before I fell asleep with a winky face and a question mark, as if trying to convince me to skip recovery without using the actual words to indict himself. When I called him, three days into my chlorine quarantine, begging him to let me back into the pool so I could achieve the perfection we both craved, he said I had to come back with a doctor's note or else he'd be in trouble with the Parent Swimmer Association. *But*, he whispered, co-conspiratorially, *if you really want, I'll look the other way.*

I still went to school. My mother refused to let me skip. Though I saw Cathy at school, our friendship had changed. Most of our conversations had consisted of swimming discussion and swimmer gossip; now, with me out, our chats petered out after the initial greetings.

She tried her best. She'd ask me how I was doing, how I was feeling. She cared.

In response to her concern, I'd tell her to shut up and leave me alone.

Instead of walking to the pool after class with Cathy, I'd trudge to my car—the doctor had recommended I refrain from driving, but with Cathy at practice and my mother at work, what other option did I have? I'd head straight home, careful to not swerve on the road, then grab a chocolate bar from the kitchen cabinets and head up to my bedroom. I'd take all my clothes off and get into bed, naked, the lights shut off. I'd lie there, under the covers, and will myself inert. I'd pretend I was a piece of coral, stuck in sand, breathing in and out as the fish flitted around me. Sometimes my head would pound randomly, like there was somebody inside my head hammering the walls of my skull. I'd squeeze my eyes shut and splashing mermaid tails made of stars would dance behind the pressure of my lids.

My mother assumed I was studying when I holed myself up in my room. She was relieved I could take some time away from the pool. She hoped I could see how life was still worth living even without swimming. While she appreciated how fast I could swim, she did not like how stuck fast I was on the sport. She worried about my thick muscular body devoid of femininity, she worried about my grades, and she worried about my mental state.

She was right to be worried. I was addicted.

Addicted to the lactic acid running through my veins, to the brittle feeling of my hair, to the damp towels on the bottom of my backpack, to the scent of chlorine ever-present on my body. For some time, in the weeks after my father left, I had a compulsive habit where I licked my skin and chewed my hair—my pores and follicles absorbed so much chlorine that one bite or lick would resurface the chemical's exquisite taste into my mouth. I woke up every night choking on the hair collecting in my throat, coughing up hairballs like a cat onto my duvet. Fed up with the clogged shower drain, my mother sat me down and presented to me in no uncertain terms an ultimatum: if I kept chewing my hair, licking my skin, growing muscles, and letting my grades suffer, I would have to quit swimming.

I couldn't do anything about my unfeminine body. Who declares what is feminine and what is not? Wasn't strength a form of femininity? I loved my muscles. If anything, I wanted my limbs to become even more muscular. But I did promise her I'd stop chewing and licking myself. And I promised I'd keep my grades up if she indulged my chlorine-fueled fantasy.

She acquiesced. So I ate food instead of my hair. And I studied hard, though I didn't actually care—grades were merely the vehicle to get me where I wanted to go: the pool.

And now I was barred from it by my usually reliable head, now turned villain.

Chlorine. How I loved thee! In chemistry class I'd peer at the periodic table and narrow in on the Cl block; I was acquainted with Cl better than I was with Au or Fe. And I preferred chlorine over fresh $H_2O$—drinking and showering second and third to swimming first.

My body shook with cold-turkey shakes, the chlorine withdrawal terrible and profound. I read in health class during the Tobacco Prevention component of the syllabus that experts would often recommend the cold turkey method to quit certain addictions. Even as a mere young high schooler, with chlorine as my unstudied and uncharted addiction, I had perceived this phrasing ridiculous. As if the way you quit could be a choice. Not a necessity. Not an action imposed onto you.

With my concussion, I floated even further away from humanity, unconnected to what had kept me grounded. Who was I? What was I? What was my life worth if I couldn't stay in the pool?

Monkhood was boring. After a week, disgusted with my dormant self, I told the doctor I was no longer having headaches. There was no need to lie in a dark room on the bed without stimulation. My brain pummeled my skull with each uttered falsehood. The doctor reminded me I'd regret it if I didn't let my head heal. I'd feel the consequences for the rest of my life.

Whatever. The doctor might have a fancy medical degree, but he did not understand how a life of head pain was nothing compared to a life without water.

"Welcome back. We missed you." Jim crumpled the doctor's note and jump shot it into the trash can. He leaned down and wrapped his arms around me, squeezing me in a tight hug. My swimsuit straps rubbed against my skin. I held my breath through the cloud of cigarette smoke accompanying him the way chlorine accompanied me.

"I missed you too."

Jim ruffled my hair. I willed myself not to wince as he touched the top of my head.

"You're totally healed now, right?" he whispered in my ear, his chin whiskers scratching my lobe.

I shivered. I imagined his tongue licking my ear, from lobe to helix.

"Yes. One hundred percent," I said. I did not tell him I had swallowed three pills of ibuprofen before practice in the locker room. I did not admit I had considered smashing the pain reliever pills to snort lines on the locker room benches—a quicker hit.

Jim grinned. He patted the side of my neck, then scratched his belly under his shirt. He motioned toward the glass windows of his office, to where the team sat on the pool deck, stretching, pre-practice.

I exited and walked over to Cathy. She had seen me walk in.

I brushed my hand over her head in welcome. She blushed at my touch, a red spreading across her cheeks to the back of her neck to her scalp, peeking through the strands of her even redder hair. She focused on her toes, like she couldn't bear the heat of my touch or gaze. She reached out and grabbed her feet, stretching her hamstrings.

I sat next to her. The bruises on my butt from my fall on ice had faded. It was painless to sit on a hard tiled pool deck. I hoisted my limbs into a sumo squat. My inner thighs and hips whined. I closed my eyes. I took a deep inhale of the sharp chlorine scent lingering in the pool air. The pain in my head dissolved as chlorine rushed in.

# Seven

Perhaps it was the concussion opening the floodgates for my hunger, the sharp crack of my head against concrete jolting free whatever restraints had been holding me back. Perhaps I had been hungry all along, too distracted by school and swim practice to pay attention to my body's demands until I was forced to stop and rest for a short while.

Hunger became my longest state of liminality between mermaid and girl. I still followed human cues, ordained by the human body I was stuck in, but I learned to unmoor by way of pleasure. My headaches still bothered me, but they were appeased by newfound ecstasy, whether given by my hand or another's.

When I was a girl, I learned many methods to reach rapture. My favorite was simple. I'd lie on my back in bed, use my fingers, and think not of men but of mermaids. How they braided their tails together on rocks jutting out on the shoreline, how the sun basked their writhing skin boiling. Or I'd think of Cathy, her red hair running its way down my stomach, her hand moving between my legs, her other wrapping tight like a hug around my neck. These fever-dreams of Cathy and mermaids flashed by in my head, where there was all pleasure, no pain. What better way to let loose my overworked, tense muscles? I'd see bursts and bolts of tender, bright light and navy blues, reminiscent of the pool's deep end. I'd see Cathy dropping delicate kisses on my collarbone. Cathy's fingers curling around my hips the way a comma promises a sentence it can continue. Cathy's breaths coming in short gasps like a breathy trombone, the instrumentals of melodramas, my fingers rubbing, Cathy, I'm close. Cathy. I'm close—

Cathy and I never had such an interaction in real life. Our pleasure existed in my imagination. I'm sure if I'd tried, she would've let me. But I admit I was too scared. It's embarrassing to look back on my silly human girl fears and recall the many opportunities I let pass by. I am not alone in contemplating the foolish mistakes of my human past, but alas, only time and distance from that previous state of being allows such clarity.

Eventually not even my fingers could appease my immense appetite. I grew ravenous. I'd built up a tolerance and the hit needed to be greater. So I sought easy prey.

The boys, of course.

When I reflect upon my past male conquests, I realize everything about the male is so easy to win, the steps taken to seduce them so clearly outlined: laugh at their jokes, shake the butt, ask about their parents, let them talk about their emotions. In the end, the outcome is less victory, more concession.

It is the women, the genderqueers, the mermaids, who are hard. Worth the battle. After long romps and long conversations and long nights with them, I emerge sweaty, victorious, exhausted from the lock of our mental and physical wills, the connection between our grappling bodies and hardy memories.

Sometimes I think about Cathy when I'm surrounded by naked, writhing mermaids. I suppose it's rude to think of another person while someone else is trying to give you pleasure. But we mermaids do not mind a wandering heart. Free love reigns in the ocean, with no rules or human emotions to ruin the experience. We listen to our wants and to our bodies. We respect one another's choices and spaces.

Becoming a mermaid hasn't stopped my hunger. Luckily, down here, in the water, there are many lovely creatures with whom to share sustenance; if need be, many humans we trick into providing for our devouring.

I returned to practice hiding the symptoms of my ongoing concussion. My head hurt often, but I convinced myself the ache was not from injury but from the overpowering stack of homework and tightness of my goggles. Jim never asked how my head was feeling, and I did not inform him, choosing to chug ibuprofen instead. Neither of us wanted to admit I had come back too soon.

The day I began my hunt, Jim was feeling lazy. We could tell by the way he sat on his ass in his chair rather than pace around the pool deck stalking us as we swam. When Jim felt lazy, and if we had done well at the previous weekend's meet, he'd allow us to play Sharks and Minnows for the last hour of practice.

The game was not for relaxation. It was coach-sanctioned violence. We played aggressive, mean, and belligerent, the way you'd imagine hormonal teenagers with athletic bodies would play games involving grabbing a half-naked body in tight spandex. *Fishy fishy, come out and play*, the sharks said before their attack. There were at least three bloody noses and four foot-shaped bruises on shins and shoulders after each game. Unlike apple bobbing, where I swam around trying to avoid teeth, I heartily enjoyed Sharks and Minnows, especially when I was a shark—I was so fast at swimming that my caught prey piled up in minutes.

For the fateful game, I was chosen as a shark, as usual, because Jim always gave me what I wanted. I smothered the fear I would be kicked in the head, and bared my teeth, ready for the fight. Cathy was my partner shark. She was terrible at the game and it would be up to me to capture our minnows.

I seized Mia, then Rob, then Ally. I took a deep breath and dove back down, catching sight of a foot, which I thrust forward to tag, too late. Unfettered, I followed the owner down to the other side of the pool, pinning the body into the corner of the deep end. I resurfaced to see who I had followed.

Brad.

Brad was a fine swimmer. Just fine. He was decent enough to earn Luke and Rob's hard-won friendship, but not fast enough for me to pay him any attention during practice. His eyebrows were thick and hairy—the teammates liked to call him Groucho Marx, who I had to google one night when the taunts crescendoed at a pasta party. Cathy said it was weird I was unfamiliar with the classic character of Groucho Marx, while I was rather surprised at her reaction, considering how much of the gaps in my American pop culture education Cathy had already smoothed over. Brad was better-looking than Groucho though, if by virtue of his thickset body and younger, unlined face.

Brad began to wiggle his eyebrows above his goggles, like hairy caterpillars trying to wiggle across a latex branch. He held his hands up in surrender. "Okay, okay, you caught me. Hurry up. Tag me."

"Where's the fun in an easy capture?" I liked to torture my minnows with a slow death.

"C'mon. Get it over with." He thrust his arm forward and I twisted, avoiding touching him.

"Stop it! I'm supposed to be hunting you, Brad. Don't be stupid."

"I hate this game. Tag me!"

"Aren't you going to fight?"

He opened his mouth and let water fill up to his top row of teeth. He spit it out like a dolphin blowhole, aiming directly at my face. I spluttered. In retaliation, I dove down into the water, gripped his ankle, and pulled him deep. He was unprepared—I heard him choking, then we descended like rocks, intertwined. He kicked, trying to land a foot on my head. My grip around his ankle loosened, but I did not let go. My hand began to crawl up his knee, up his thigh, around his waist, while his arms curled around me. One of his legs wrapped around my thigh, and his fingers squeezed somewhere between my waist and armpit. We struggled. I didn't understand what was happening—somehow, I had become the minnow and he the shark—black spots appeared around my eyes, I was drowning—Brad pinched my side. He let me go. I floated back to the top, coughing out water, furious. I opened my eyes. My vision resumed. Brad had already swum away.

Brad's grip left a purple bruise on my thigh. I'd tap it and enjoy the rush of the light pain that followed, fantasizing about the other ways his hands could leave marks on my body. I stared at him across the lane ropes during every practice, daring him to notice me. He tried to ignore my stares but ended up choking on the pool water or tripping over kickboards on the pool deck instead, his failed attempts at nonchalance delighting me to no end.

We had another away meet the weekend after the fateful Sharks and Minnows game. We rode the dusty coach bus to the middle of Pennsylvania, hunched over in the bus seats covered with vintage carpet swirls matted with years of dust and Cheeto crumbs. I was lying down and taking up the entire back row, the sole row with three seats, next to the bathroom, listening to Faye Wong in my headphones, thinking about my upcoming races and how I'd swim them. Cathy was in the row across from me napping, her face pressed against the window, mouth open, fogged glass where her snores hit.

Brad clambered up the center of the aisle, using his arms to balance against the seat headrests as the bus swayed and bumped over potholes. I winked at him when he passed, and he blushed, scratching his neck. He entered the bathroom without comment. I sighed. It was disgusting when people had the shameless initiative to use the bathroom—it made the entire bus's air, especially the air where I was sitting, stink like urine and shit.

I heard the toilet's flush through Faye's singing. The bathroom door swung open, releasing the odor of excrement. My legs were plucked upward, then back down, over two warm bumps.

I scrambled up, resting back on my forearms.

"Brad, what the fuck?"

He had lifted my thighs to sit in the seat next to me, placing my legs back onto his own. I tried to remove my legs from his lap, but his arms, resting against my kneecaps, pinned them down. I took out my earphones, the snores of our teammates and the bus engine overtaking Faye's receding croons.

"Hey, Ren," he said.

"What are you doing?" I asked.

"Listen. I wanted to ask. Are you—uh—I mean, are you trying?"

"Am I trying what?" I wrinkled my nose. "By the way, it smells like shit. Did you have to poop when I'm sitting right here?"

He cocked his left eyebrow. "Can you smell what I ate? Guess my last meal," he teased.

"You're gross. No thanks." I broke my legs out of his loosened grip and settled into a normal sitting position. Outside, the flat Pennsylvania scenery whizzed by; the landscape was painted in gray, from the cloudy winter sky to the crowded asphalt highway road to the branches of the empty trees. In Pennsylvania winters, every leaf died, but bark survived.

"It was a cheese and broccoli frittata. My mom made it," he said.

"Cool?" I turned back to him and tapped my chin. "Anyway, am I trying what? You never finished your sentence."

"Are you—are you, um, trying to—I mean, do you want to—"

I laughed. I snaked an arm over his shoulders and pulled him toward me. I followed what I had imagined in my head and had seen on my mother's blocked websites I could bypass using a private browser. Brad wasn't Cathy or a mermaid, but he would pass for now. I held my breath so I wouldn't have to smell the odor of his shit or the odor of his unbrushed mouth. His fingers stroked my shoulder. They were brutish fingers mimicking his body—thick, coarse. The calluses from the weight room on his palm rubbed my skin through my T-shirt. Our hands were interchangeable; I had matching calluses in similar places, in the boundary between finger and palm, purchases from the barbell. All athletes paid the price of soft hands in exchange for bulky muscles.

Cathy was still napping. Brad's poop odor had disappeared, leaving behind stale, disinfectant-laced coach bus air; either our noses were used to the shit molecules, or they had dispersed.

I rested my head against Brad's shoulder. His nose snuggled against the top of my head.

"Do you like me?" he asked.

I shrugged. "Does it matter?"

His calluses touched my cheek and I obeyed, tilting my head upward; he kissed me. His calluses began to fondle the skin under my ear. It was a dry kiss, no saliva exchange.

We were two frozen plastic dolls smashed together. Neither of us moved our heads like they did in the movies. There was no passion, no fireworks, no burning gut. Then the bus jolted, rolling over a pothole, and my body fell into his, the failure of our state infrastructure the most effective wingman.

I wasn't attracted to Brad. It was more the attraction I'd have toward a cup of raw broccoli if I was starving. When you haven't eaten in days, even flavorless vegetables were delectable. Brad didn't need spices or an oven. He was quick sustenance. Easy preparation. Weeknight meal in three steps. No nutritional value.

The kisses got wetter, perhaps even better, and we slid into sin quickly. Everything Brad and I did together was tinged with cramped secrecy—the back of his minivan with the seats pulled down, his parents' king bed whenever they were out of the house, the secret room behind the pool where broken lane ropes were stored. We never told our other teammates we were hooking up. It was a secret, it had to be. Neither of us would be able to stand our teammates' or Jim's scrutiny. I only spilled the secret to Cathy. I trusted her. I even solicited her help in techniques of sexting seduction. She would never tell anyone. Who could she tell? I was her only friend.

We settled for furtive get-togethers after practice, sweat droplets made more of chlorine than salt in his car as he thrusted, the air smelling like moldy flippers. I learned important techniques like how to suck on his neck so he moaned a low, breathy hum in my ear, how to gyrate my hips. The shape of Brad's dick reminded me of the Chinese eggplants my mother used in cooking—long, thin, curved, thicker at the base. She'd cut up these eggplants into chunks and boil them with green onion and spoonfuls of zhimajiang. I wondered if I could do the same to his dick. My mother's cooking tasted better than he did.

We didn't use condoms. We used the pull-out method. It was sexier to go without protection because I liked him shoving inside me without preamble. The more desperate he was, the more desired I felt. We did try to use them in the beginning, citing responsibility, but I hated the way the plastic wrinkled when I ripped open the wrapper, drying out what was already threatening to be a desert.

When Brad and I had sex, my head stopped hurting, and I was delirious off the clarity.

When Brad and I were fucking, I wasn't thinking about anything else, which was what I liked most—it was the first activity fully taking my mind off swimming.

Somehow, the few months of bliss tricked me into believing that remaining human would be okay if the bliss lasted forever. How ridiculous I was. For humans, pleasure is always fleeting.

# Eight

## CATHY

Dear Ren,

Did you get my previous letter? I threw the bottle as hard as I could into the creek, but like most current and former swimmers, I'm not very coordinated on land. The bottle didn't go far, but the current carried it away. I hope it reached you.

Feel free to keep the bottle. If you put it under the sunlight, the glass sparkles and gleams, creating these beautiful rainbow refractions, like the scales of the mermaid tails in the book you loved. By the way, I don't think I ever told you I saw those pages. I'm sorry if I overstepped your boundaries.

That's the reason why I'm writing today—I wanted to apologize for yet another thing I did, back when you were still human.

*You didn't invite me to your room. I snuck up there without telling you. But how else was I supposed to connect with you when you kept ditching me to hang out with stupid Brad? When was Brad ever there for you the way I was? What did Brad ever give you that I couldn't? You never asked if I was okay with you hooking up with Brad. You never asked why I was hooking up with Rob either.*

*Guess what—Rob and I were pretending. We dated each other for protection, for something to do. Rob was terrified of his military father, and so dating me would be his cover. I agreed to date him because I didn't want you to think I was jealous of Brad, and that I was dead lonely without you.*

*Please understand what I did was out of aching loneliness—the only reason people ever do anything.*

*I snuck in during one of our pasta parties, during the sophomore year season. You were hosting—well, your mother was hosting. Wasn't it ridiculous how we expected our mothers to cook for and host the girls' team, every week? I guess Jim thought it would be more equitable to make each mother host once per season, with all mothers responsible for bringing food. Spreading the burden, he claimed. How kind of him. I thought it hilarious how your mother never cooked homemade food— she always brought microwavable egg rolls from Costco's freezer section. The other mothers spent hours prepping layers of cheesy creamy dip, while your mother simply hopped in the car for ten minutes to the store, with two extra minutes for the microwave at home. It could've been so brilliantly simple for everybody, but yours was the only mother brave enough to try. The best part was your mother's Costco egg rolls were delicious. As good as, and frankly even better than, the homemade food.*

*I actually really miss pasta parties. They're pretty much the one thing I miss about swimming, other than you, of course. Ever since I quit the* swimmer diet for "reasonable" daily calorie intake, I fantasize about those endless banquets of four-cheese ravioli, spaghetti Bolognese, potatoes of all forms, soupy dips rimmed with tortilla chips, spinach strawberry walnut salads, buffalo chicken pizza—and the desserts! These days, I'm forced to limit myself to one square of dark chocolate a day for "health," a habit my mother insists will help me wean off my supposed sweet tooth, but I still crave those cookie platters, so many strains of sugary circles: snickerdoodles, oatmeal raisin, chocolate chip, sugar, ginger molasses, raspberry thumbprint, snowball, pinwheel. And I loved how we could make merry before a stressful swim meet, for we were so lucky to have these celebrations of gorging ourselves, because we didn't have to stay skinny like cross-country runners and gymnasts, and we didn't have to make a weight class and cut calories like wrestlers before competitions. There was no one to shame us, as our pasta parties were split up—the girls to one house, the boys to another. No stupid boy to compete with for the food. We could eat to our content, eat everything in sight, despite Jim's nagging we should watch our diet, because lighter bodies float better. We'd shovel the food into our mouths, chomping our teeth, breaking penne and chicken and pancakes in half, then quarters, then eighths, sending the crumbs straight into our guts, where we left their fates up to the gods of carbohydrates and simple sugars. Remember how we would joke-pray to these gods, begging for their kindness to break down our meals into energy, to propel us across the pool the next day? We'd take seconds and thirds and fourths without asking because we deserved it—frankly, I still think I deserve it.

By the way, I never told you Jim often called me into his office to give his infamous Fat Talks. I was too embarrassed to tell you, especially since you kept reminding me it didn't matter how much I weighed. I couldn't agree with you then, not when both Jim and my mother kept advising me to lose twenty pounds, so I'd make it to states. He'd always tell me to control what I ate, except not to take it too far, or else I'd get an eating disorder. But then he'd wink, like he wanted me to get one, so then I could swim the best times of my life.

I'm proud of the fact I never cried during his Fat Talks. Of course, you never got a Fat Talk. You were flawless for an athlete, exemplary— all muscles.

Do you ever think about your childhood home? I'm not sure if mermaids ever feel homesick. I remember how, when I parked by your driveway, my eyes kept sliding to the grander house next door—your house was nondescript and compact, a cube with maroon shutters and a tan tiled roof, much smaller than the neighboring houses, and the beige shingles gave your house an air of camouflage.

Your front door was unlocked. As I entered, I tripped over the many empty sneakers and snow boots piled up at the muddy entrance mat. I added my puffer coat to the stacked pile on the carpeted staircase to the left and began to follow the babble of voices and clattering silverware, when it struck me how I was in your house for the first time.

So I decided to trample over your boundaries. My hunger for food forgot itself in the hunger to know.

I leapt over the pile of coats, using the railing as propellant. I crept up the stairs, the carpet muffling my footsteps, the commotion of the pasta party disappearing as I rose higher into your home.

I reached the second, and highest, floor. I looked left and right. No one was around, everyone was downstairs. There were three closed doors. I took a chance. I opened the one closest to the staircase.

You waved at me—I gasped. You caught me. I racked my brain for a reasonable excuse.

Then I realized it wasn't really you—just you caught frozen mid-wave, toward an invisible photographer, on top of a wood, unpainted dresser. You and your parents and other wrinkled relatives I didn't recognize posed inside bronze and silver picture frames. I remember this first room was big, containing a king-size bed with enough space for two bedside tables, a desk, and a stack of plastic laundry baskets with broken handles resting in the corner. One side of the bed was more mussed than the other, its ruby comforter wrinkled, pillow dented. I assumed the messy side was where your mother slept, while the pristine half was your absent father's.

I closed the door, crept through the hallway to the next room, tiptoeing despite the carpet.

It was a bathroom, simple, white tiled with a fluffy bathmat under the sink. I entered and locked the door behind me. The mirror and sink were flecked with dried toothpaste. On the counter lay two bottles of ibuprofen on their sides, one empty, the other capped, next to a flat tube of Colgate and a toothbrush. The toothpaste tube was congealed at the top, hardened spheres of mint green clumped around the cap. I ran my thumb over the toothbrush's frayed bristles—I recognized your toothbrush because you always forgot to replace it, until the bristles resembled an explosion of weeds rather than neatly mowed lawns. You were always so forgetful about trivial matters like dental care, with your headaches and your sharp focus on swimming and mermaids and school.

Do you recall how we would brush our teeth next to each other before bed, when we shared a hotel room during away meets? I thought it homey and couple-like to brush at the same time. You'd always brush in a sort of lackadaisical way, with a limp wrist in uneven circles, and I'd observe you in trepidation, because I didn't want to partner with someone inevitably toothless—I'd always demand you brush longer, harder, and in circles, and to replace your toothbrush every few weeks, but you never listened to me, insisting your shitty teeth were genetic, because back then in China, dentists would opt to yank out teeth instead of filling in cavities, and your mother had four fake teeth and she could still chew fine.

When I turned to the shower curtain, I saw pink and purple plastic bottles resting atop the white porcelain shelf. I picked up the shampoo and squeezed the bottle, a wisp of coconut and vanilla with light floral notes puffing out and into my nostrils. If I had a perfume laboratory, I could re-create the scent without pause, even now, without you around as reference. I memorized your smell when we were girls. I craved the smell of your hair, inching down your neck. The smell of you when you weren't corrupted by the chlorine, a smell lingering around your locker.

I used to sneak squirts of your shampoo at travel meets instead of my own. When I emerged from the shower, it was like a cloud of you around my head.

There were black hairballs around the tub, and on the floor surrounding it. Your shedding. I had seen these strands before on the locker room floor, in the shower drain, in your hairbrush. I picked up a few and ran them between my fingers, pretending they were still attached to your head, you purring in pleasure as I stroked your hair. I loosened my fingers and the strands danced down onto the floor, dainty as a feather. Then I looked up and saw—mermaid tails.

I'll never forget what I saw there on your shower wall.

Most of your hair strands had dried, some falling away, their stickiness to the wall faded, but I could still decipher the serpent-like shapes you had outlined. Did you stand in the shower, pull out your hair, and draw tails on the shower wall? Did you drag the strands around with your fingers until they showed fins and scales?

*I didn't dare touch your hair drawings, for fear you'd find out I was there.*

*They scared me, Ren.*

*I couldn't ask you about them. If I brought up those shower mermaid tails outlined with your hair, you'd laugh at me, and then go hang out with Brad instead.*

*So I didn't mention them.*

*I'm sorry.*

*I exited the bathroom, and debated going downstairs, to the pasta party, to banish the tails from my head, but I couldn't leave, not without seeing your bedroom. My heart palpitated like I had just swum a long race. I crept toward the last door, my hand reaching out in a ready grip for the doorknob, leading to where you slept, where you woke. My heart screamed in capital letters. I planned to linger over the Faye Wong posters I figured you had taped up. I planned to land like a cross onto your bed where your body indent rested—back then, hell, even now, I would have been willing to die by crucifixion if you controlled the nail and hammer. I wanted to bury my nose in your pillow and breathe in the coconut remnants of your hair the way I did at travel meets. I wanted to do what lovers do in bedrooms. I wanted to open your closet and trace the clothes you'd have hung there, imagining you had given me permission to take your favorite T-shirt for me to sleep in. I loved your style, and I loved watching you get dressed in the locker room. You'd always ask me why I was blushing, and I'd blame it on the tough workouts, but really, it was because you had the most elaborate outfits, color coordinated with unique pieces I didn't realize existed or were even allowed in our high school, where teachers prowled with yardsticks to measure the length of girls' skirts and tank-top straps. You would start naked, then immerse your body into your chosen clothing, like you* were the queen's personal knight suiting up for battle: brown thigh highs matched with a flowery peasant dress tucked into heeled oxfords, or a black oversized blazer over a graphic T-shirt with high waisted skinny jeans, or a leather skirt over fishnets and platform combat boots. In the locker room you were so strong, muscles so visible, and sometimes, when I caught you curling a weight or lifting your duffel, I'd become distracted, shoving both of my feet into the same pant leg, too busy dwelling on how my head would feel crushed between your biceps, my face smothered against your chest. I can conjure up all your outfits and how they clung to your body, because I wanted to clutch at the fabric and rip them off you, my heart beating your name Ren Ren Ren Ren Ren—

Sorry. I get easily carried away, remembering you.

When the door swung open, I was shocked by how barren everything was. The furniture was plain, purely functional. One small twin bed tucked into the corner, a small white dresser with a cerulean blue vase on top. The vase was shaped like a fish, with the tail as the base, and the open mouth as the opening, with two fins on each side to give it a shapely curve. The scales were indented onto the surface, and there were two dried wheat stalks sticking out of the mouth. I drew close, to touch the wheat, but then spied the other decorations you had cared enough to hang in your room, against the far wall. I tripped over my feet in a haste to arrive.

You had hung up so many strange and fantastical mermaid illustrations. There were girl heads attached to snake bodies, mermaids eating the throats of men, mermaids with rainbow fur, mermaids with tentacle hair, and mermaids clutching their throats, eyes wide open in terror, their voices gone. There were mermaids seducing men, tying chains of seaweed around their wrists. There were mermaids rubbing sand and fish guts all over their stomachs. Some drawings were in black and white, clearly older, some sort of myth or legend from medieval times, but many were in color, garish, bright. Every page you hung up had a frayed edge, like you had ripped them out of a book frantically, but the pages themselves were unwrinkled, as if you had taken care to make sure the illustrations remained spotless.

From where you slept, the shrine would've been the first thing you saw when you woke up, and the last thing you saw before you fell asleep.

Ren, should I have ripped the mermaid shrine down? Should I have run downstairs and asked you why you made it?

Was Brad aware of the mermaid shrine? Did he help you hang all those illustrations, or was it your secret, yours alone?

You could've shared the shrine with me.

For some time, after you left, I was bitter you didn't.

Why? I thought you trusted me.

I'm trying to understand. Won't you help me understand?

I'm sorry I didn't say anything. To you, to Jim, to your mother. I bottled up my sorrys; now, they're in this bottle, and I can only hope they reach you.

I bet your mother tore down the bedroom shrine and the shower stall hair after you left. I wonder if she's remorseful over not confronting you about it, like I am. Maybe we could've staged some sort of intervention, had we known.

I'm so sorry. How many sorrys can I say before you come back to me?

In the end, I guess everything turned out okay. You're a mermaid now, and likely much happier.

Have you met any other mermaids? Have you fallen in love with any of them? Or maybe even with other sea creatures? Do you have a pet fish, a friend fish, who resembles that blue vase? I'm not sure how it works, down there. Do the mermaids you're friends with now look like the ones in those illustrations? They're a bit scary, but I'm sure if you love them, then they're all right. I trust you.

You can write back to me. You can leave the letter on the shore of the creek. You don't even have to show your face. I go there often; I'll see your letter before it gets swept away by the wind or current.

Tell me you're okay. Tell me what's been going on, and who you've met since you've left home. I promise you I won't be jealous, not anymore, not like how I acted when you were with Brad.

I just want you to be happy.

I'll write again soon.

Love,
Cathy

# Nine

Eventually I learned the consequences of careless human hunger.

I was late. I didn't tell Brad. Instead, I cornered Cathy in the locker room after practice.

"Cathy."

"What?"

"Can you come with me to CVS?"

She was rifling through her locker. She was already dressed, waiting for me so we could walk out together. She turned toward me and blushed. "Sure. What's up?"

I shoved her against the wall of lockers and leaned over her, framing her head. I needed to whisper. I didn't want anyone else to hear what I was about to say. Sound traveled across the locker aisles—two over, I could hear Ally and Mia compare the waterproof quality of their mascaras.

I pressed against Cathy and rested my mouth an inch away from her ear. A proper secret deserved proper telling. She shivered. I breathed against her lobe.

"My period is late. I need to get the test and I don't want to go alone. I'm not sure I know how to use it either. Can you come? I trust you. More than anyone else on our team." I leaned my head back but kept my body close to hers. We stared into each other's eyes. Her lips were parted. I willed her to understand what I was implying.

"Shit. Yeah. I'll come."

"Now?"

"Yeah," she said.

"Okay. Thank you." I released her. She frantically patted her curls, flustered.

"Ready?" I asked.

She nodded.

We exited the school building. I made for my car, but she plucked at my sleeve.

"I'll drive. Come on," she offered.

"You sure?" I pretended I hadn't been hoping she would ask.

"Of course, we can go together. It's, like, five minutes there and back."

"Okay." I let her pull me to her car. I clambered into the passenger seat, throwing my backpack and swimming duffel in the back without care, the textbooks and wet towels landing on the floor with a thud. Cathy frowned.

"What?"

She sighed. "Nothing." She placed her own bags carefully on the backseat and swiveled to the front, turning the car on.

As we drove, I wondered how a pregnancy would affect my

swimming. It was unlikely I'd be able to practice with a two-month baby bump. I'd have to quit. We were close to our sophomore year's end-of-season regionals meet, the most important meet of the year, and a baby would destroy my swimming dreams. Jim had pulled me aside a few practices ago to tell me there would be college recruiters in the stands, and though my own recruitment would not start until junior year, it was never too early to make an impression. I could get an abortion before regionals, but I'd likely need time to recover. Besides, would my parents have enough money for an abortion? How much would the procedure even cost? Again, I was struck by the recognition I was worrying about human problems—problems mermaids were free of—and my anxiety shifted into frustration.

"Ren, a penis is no replacement for a female friendship." Cathy was chewing her bottom lip as she stared ahead at the road.

"I need a pregnancy test and you're worried about female friendship?"

"Well, maybe I'm trying to take your mind off it."

"Hm. So, you miss me?" I teased.

"Yes. I do."

"Aren't you hooking up with Rob?" I asked.

"Yeah, but hooking up with him isn't the same as hanging out with you. We haven't been talking as much since we started seeing boys," she said.

"True. I mean, we're both busy. But the phone works both ways."

"I've tried!" Cathy slammed her foot down on the brake in front of a red light. We jerked forward.

"Cathy! Drive carefully, please."

Cathy sniffed. Was she crying? I couldn't tell.

The light turned green. We inched forward.

"Okay. You're right, you're right. I'm sorry." I apologized without comprehending why Cathy was so upset. "At least we're hanging out right now," I offered.

Cathy wiped her nose with her sleeve. She hiccupped.

"So why am I coming along, and not Brad?" Cathy asked.

"Cathy. Don't be stupid," I said.

"Fine."

"I should be more careful. Pulling out isn't always successful. But it's hard in the moment, y'know?"

Cathy snorted. "No. I don't know."

"You and Rob haven't fucked yet?"

Cathy gasped. "Ren!"

"What?"

Cathy was crimson.

"Guess not," I said.

We arrived at CVS, and Cathy grabbed my hand as we perused the aisles, passing shelves of lipstick tubes, nail polish, and sugary snacks Jim wanted us to avoid. Cathy's hand was cold and damp. We passed faces topped with hair in a rainbow of colors, smiling at us frozen from their paper boxes of hair dye, making a mockery of my anxiety.

"Here it is." Cathy came to a stop and pointed to a row of pink boxes reading FIRST RESPONSE PREGNANCY: OVER 99% ACCURATE!

I grabbed a test and exited the aisle without glancing back at her. No need for sentimentalities. I dropped it on the counter of the register, where a pimpled teenager stood, waiting. I studiously avoided eye contact.

"Seven ninety-nine," he said in a long drawl.

I dug through my pocket and opened my wallet—no cash. I didn't want to use my credit card—my mother monitored the monthly statements, searching for an inaccurate charge to explain the high total, any reason to call the credit card company and request a refund.

"Here." Cathy had snuck behind me. She rested her chin on my shoulder and passed the clerk a wadded ten-dollar bill. She placed her forehead against my shoulder, nestling it in the crook like a baby bird finding its mother.

I shifted so her head fell off. She snapped her head up and glowered at me.

I gave her a small smile. "Thanks."

"No worries."

The clerk gave me the test in a plastic bag, the pink box visible through the plastic. Our fingers brushed as I took it, but he did not glance at me. Was he judging me, did he consider me attractive, did he notice my muscles? I wondered if I could seduce him right then and there. I could get on my knees behind the counter, unzip his fly, and open my mouth. It would be so easy.

Cathy jerked her head toward the bathroom. "Want to use it here? Get it over with."

"Okay." I turned away from the clerk and nervously massaged the plastic bag between my fingers.

"I'll wait for you." Cathy plopped down on the red bench outside the bathroom entrance.

"See you." I entered the bathroom, which had a scent of dried urine mixed with ammonia. I breathed through my nose. The stall doors hung open; no one else was inside.

I barricaded myself in the stall closest to the door and rested the plastic bag atop the sanitary receptacle. I rustled through the plastic bag and ripped open the test box. I read the directions twice without comprehension. How was I supposed to put my hand under my own urine stream? I was disgusted with myself, and with my mistake, and with the entire scenario—begging Cathy to come along, Cathy paying for the test, not telling Brad, peeing in the ammonia-drenched CVS bathroom. I shoved my pants down, and holding the end as described, I let loose the bladder I had been keeping shut since practice ended. The warm pee splashed off the test and onto my hand; wincing, I kept it there despite the itchy feeling I was perverting my own body. Resting the test atop the plastic bag, I held the pee-drenched hand aloft like it was bleeding and pulled my pants back up with the other in an awkward shuffle. I rushed over to the sink and scrubbed my hands up to my elbow, then went back into the stall to peer at the test. An indecipherable smudge was forming in the circle where the directions said the results would appear. What did a smudge mean? According to the box, lines would reveal the answer; a smudge was not indicative of anything.

Fuck.

I peered out the bathroom door, turning my head left and right before alighting on Cathy, who had remained sitting on the bench, staring down at her sneakers.

"Psst. Cathy." I whispered her name, then when she did not hear me, again, louder. "Cathy!"

"Hey!" Startled, she jumped up and rushed over. "What happened? Is it positive or negative?"

"I have no idea."

"What do you mean, you have no idea? Doesn't it tell you?"

"Get in here." I grabbed her and pulled her inside the bathroom. The door swung closed behind us.

She reached out to hold the stick, but I slapped her hand away. "Ew. Don't touch. I peed on this," I said.

She giggled. "Yes, but we literally swim in each other's pee and sweat every day. And it's not like I haven't touched something covered in your bodily fluids before. Did you forget I helped you with your bloody tampon once? Honestly, a peed-on pregnancy test is nothing."

I grudgingly gave her the stick. She brought it close to her eyes, then compared it with the directions on the box, resting atop the mirror ledge.

"How much water did you drink?" she asked.

"A ton. I've been holding it in since practice."

"Okay. Well. I can't tell either. My guess is you might have drunk too much water, so your pee is diluted, and the test can't give an accurate diagnosis. You're going to have to take another one." She threw the test in the trash can. "Stay here. I'll go get you another." She exited the bathroom, without waiting for my agreement.

I turned to my reflection in the bathroom mirror. My under eyes were dark and wrinkled. With the tip of my soft pointer finger I traced the contours of my chapped lips. I didn't brush my hair after practice, too worried about the results of the pregnancy test to pay myself any attention past dressing in the requisite clothes. My mother would chastise me for my sloppy appearance. She believed in saving face and staying quiet. We never discussed sex, or babies, or condoms. Those R-rated topics remained off the table, even if they were present on the television screen when we watched old Wong Kar-wai movies together. If we didn't speak of it, then it didn't exist—perhaps why my parents always talked about money.

How many chairs would Jim throw at my head at the baby

shower? Would Brad even admit the baby was his? Would it come out of my womb with more hair on its eyebrows than on its head? I didn't care about the baby, or myself, or anyone who might have a reaction to my pregnancy. I cared if I'd be able to swim, and fast. I slapped myself, and in the mirror, my head jerked to the right. My eyes were wild and glassy. My nostrils flared. The ammonia burned my nose hairs. My cheek grew a red handprint where my hand had landed. I willed myself not to hyperventilate.

The door swung open. Cathy had a bundle of pink in her arms— she had brought back three boxes instead of one. She examined my face.

"Did you slap yourself?" she asked.

"Ignore it, please." My cheek was stinging where the handprint had emerged.

"Um, okay." She hesitated, then chose to move on. "Can you pee again?"

"I feel empty. But I'll try," I said.

"Okay. Here you go." She ripped open a box and held out the test stick.

I wiggled my eyebrows suggestively. "Wanna help like you did with the tampon back then? Penelope misses you."

She blushed. "Uh—"

"I'm kidding." I laughed humorlessly, then reentered and locked the bathroom stall door, pulling my pants back down.

Cathy cleared her throat.

It was too soon after the first test. I had no urine left.

"Cathy—I can't go anymore."

"Ren, you have to try."

"What if you go buy me some water?" I suggested.

"No. I'm out of cash," she said. "And you don't want pee that's too diluted, remember?" Her voice was disembodied, mouthless; only her feet and the bottom of her calves were visible from under the bathroom stall door. "Hmmm. Okay. I have an idea. Ready?"

"For what?" I asked.

"Drip drip drip drip. Drop drop drop drop. Water, ocean waves. Stream stream stream. Water, flowing. The pool, water hitting our skin. Chlorine. Water, water, water, drip drip drip—"

"What are you saying?" I asked, giggling.

"I'm trying to help you think of liquid! It'll help you pee, it's like the oldest trick ever. Okay, bodies of water, fluids, drips, drops, rivers, oceans, water, babbling creeks—"

My trickle of pee hit the test with a tinkle. I giggled as I let loose, remembering this was not the first time Cathy was hearing my bodily fluids. How many times would Cathy be waiting for me outside a bathroom stall door as I struggled with Penelope's issues?

"Okay. Here's the second." I stepped out of the stall and gave the test to her without rinsing. She had touched the first, so I figured she wouldn't hesitate to touch the second.

She peered at it while I washed my hands again. "Ren, it's reading as one line. I'm sure of it."

She offered it to me, but I shook my head—my hands were already clean. Instead, she placed it on the sink counter, next to the other two boxes. We leaned over it, our heads bumping, to observe the small narrow line. We were close enough I could smell the chocolate-chip Clif Bar Cathy had eaten off her breath. Her hair was still wet from practice and pressed coldly against my clammy skin. "Yeah. I guess you're right."

No joy. No disappointment. Merely flooding relief I would not have to miss practice or a meet.

For once, my human body had done well. I patted my stomach. No baby, all abdominal muscles.

Cathy punched my arm. "Lucky bitch."

I gasped in mock horror. "Cathy! You said 'bitch'!"

"I'm sure Penelope is overjoyed to not have to push out a baby."

I shuddered. "Too far."

I picked up the negative test between my thumb and pointer and threw it in the trash can, onto a bed of used paper towels. We manned different sinks, and the faucets whined as the water flowed out from their heads. Cathy pumped the soap dispenser, a squeak accompanying each spritz.

"Ready to go?"

"Yeah."

We exited the bathroom. The slumped clerk didn't see us leave, too busy tapping at a game on his phone. We headed back to her car, treading across the parking lot in large bounds, more leaps than steps—we were buoyant from the negative result and the gorgeous sunset, the sky unveiling its long strands of pink and purple. I breathed in. I breathed out. The cold winter air puffed out, visible. I whooped with glee and turned to Cathy, who was grinning, her face lit up by the parking lot lights, beautiful under such glorious evening skies.


My period came three days later. During study hall, Cathy looked up reasons why periods could be late other than pregnancy, and a whole multitude of reasonable explanations popped up: overexertion, exhaustion, stress. All of which I suffered.

Such depressing symptoms, when remaining human.

I decided to get an IUD after the pregnancy scare. Terrified of anything hormone-based, I chose the copper IUD despite the many warnings online of heavier and more painful periods, which to me was impossible, as the pain and the flow were already too much to bear. How could the months get any worse?

When the OB-GYN doctor first attempted insertion, he spent half an hour poking around my cervix before declaring me too tense, too tight, and too narrow for the procedure. He prescribed me some pills designed to loosen me up. When he tried again, a week later, I was drowsy from the pain-reduction pills, but angry at his incompetence and at how I had to miss practice twice, so close to regionals, just to protect my body from Brad's overexcitable sperm. I was half-naked, feet in stirrups, wildly exposed in a way I had never been with Brad. The bald head of the doctor whose name I could not recall shone as he dug between my legs, his beige palette a stark contrast next to the room's colorful Tyrannosaurus rex wallpaper. A strange silver contraption held me open.

"Please relax," he said, his breath ghosting over my thighs. I trembled, took a deep breath.

"You are not relaxing," he said, frustrated, impatient, as he continued to thrust what must be the copper IUD inside of me, though it cut more like a bayonet—the pills were not working.

I screamed, once, twice, crying from the pain and the labor of trying to remain calm when nothing about the situation inspired it.

The doctor sighed and sat back. "Did you take the pills I told you to take?" he asked, annoyed.

I was a puddle of pain. I nodded.

"Okay. You need to relax then," he said. He stroked my thigh.

I fought the urge to break his fingers. When he reinserted his face back between my legs, I visualized lifting my foot and kicking open his ugly skull, smashing his tiny brains to a pulp.

He dug deeper, bringing a sharp pain, and I prepared myself for the afterlife, as I was sure I had just died a brutal, violent death, convinced he had broken through my cervix, my stomach, my skin, and the copper IUD was sticking out of my belly button like an impaled sword, but instead the doctor shouted in triumph and patted the lower half of my stomach in a misguided attempt at comfort.

"It's over!" he declared, snapping his gloves off.

I was sobbing, and the doctor was bewildered at our opposing reactions, him joyous, me devastated.

"Uh—whenever you're ready, come up to the receptionist counter and the lady there will check you out." He left the room as soon as he finished washing, shaking his hands in an attempt to air dry, unwilling to stay close to a traumatized girl for longer than necessary.

I lay there, alone, half-naked, cold, my stomach throbbing, waves of nausea washing over me in great tsunamis as my body shook in the leftover earthquakes. My brain pounded at my skull, gnawing the bone like a baby teething. Though the entire procedure had been consensual—hell, my own idea—I cried for my violation. Jim was furious I was missing another practice and I could feel his white-hot anger branding my skin even when he was miles away. My mother had not wanted me to get the IUD, as it would mean her precious daughter was either having or thinking about having sex, but she had consented to drive me to and from the appointment. I could see her through the walls of the doctor's office—she'd be clutching a

Tupperware of sliced fruit as a surprise and consolation for the loss of my birth-control virginity as she sat in the waiting room on a broken vinyl chair, magazine covers showing glamorous white movie stars with hair-sprayed ponytails stacked next to her, American soap operas depicting fake amnesia on the television screen above—for them, amnesia was a plot point, and for me, amnesia was a method of tolerance, a method for getting through every headache, through every medical procedure, through each doctor's office visit.

I hated all doctors as a human girl.

The concussion doctor had failed me. He should have recognized I wasn't fully healed yet. He should have refused to let me lie.

My primary care physician had smirked suggestively as he reminded me to pee after sex. I tested positive for a UTI a month after Brad and I started fucking, and my insides were steamrollered by trucks every time I tried to pee. I told my mother I most likely contracted it from using a dirty tampon I found on the locker room floor. More lies. My mouth swished around fallacies like soda, the rottenness decaying my teeth.

The UTI wasn't from the locker room, but I did pick up toe warts from its concrete crusty floor. The podiatrist I went to told me Asian female feet were his favorite kind of feet because he could see the lingering effects of foot binding in the later generations. He had stuck his fingers between my toes and wiggled them like worms. And once Luke's pediatrician dad told me at a swim meet how he always wanted to adopt an Asian baby girl. He massaged my shoulder as he told me my muscles were beautiful for an Asian.

Then came the bald gyno, ripping open my insides, blaming my body for his own incompetence.

How was I supposed to trust any of them?

Brad remained unaware my period had been late, and he was ignorant about the IUD and the UTI too. Even if I had told him about these things, he wouldn't have the information for what the letters stood for and wouldn't have taken the time to look them up.

Cathy had been the one to call me after the gynecologist appointments. Cathy had been the one to buy me cartons of cranberry juice in an attempt to flush out the UTI. Cathy had been the one to help me pee on the pregnancy test.

Cathy said Brad had a dirty dick. Brad never knew shit.

Ravenous hunger, wanton sexuality, and the consequences thereof—how exhausting to be constrained by mortal biology.

# Ten

With the end of the sophomore year season came the beginning of my true uncovering. The catalyst for my brain to scheme how I could finally leave my human body behind.

I had done well at regionals. Jim was proud of my performance, telling me he had seen the Ivy League recruiters in the stands nodding and pointing at me in approval as I swam. He was sure they would reach out to me in the final months of the upcoming junior year, and later come to watch me during the next regionals meet. When I passed along the information to my mother, she squealed and seized my hands, swinging me around the kitchen, the most excitement I had seen her express in years. Getting recruited for swimming would mean, at the very least, a scholarship and guaranteed acceptance. Best of all, these were not state university recruiters interested in me but the Ivy League—anything less, and she would have refused their patronage.

Many of us had surpassed Jim's expectations at regionals. We swept the competition and won the meet by thirty points. Jim was ecstatic about our results. Our success deserved celebration—and so we convened at Rob's, like every year, for our annual end-of-season party, the culmination of months of self-restraint. We were sick of discipline and ready to rave, especially after this season's triumph. Even the freshmen got drunk—Rob's parents trusted in the motto *out of sight, out of mind*.

Rob hosted all our team parties, and we loved his massive back-yard with the bonfire pit, the six-foot-deep pool, and the diving board, surrounded by tacky tiki torches. Rob's house was the most luxurious house on the team, paid for by his father, a financial advisor with a copious number of military medals, and decorated by his mother, a yoga teacher with a boob job. Her boobs were notorious among us.

Cathy and I drove to the party in her car. I spent the entire ride there complaining about Jim's summer practice goals for me, Cathy patiently listening without input from her side. Jim never felt the need to specially train the slower swimmers like her. My excitement over my success at regionals had dimmed upon learning Jim's plans. I was getting tired of constant swim practice, of hyperfixation on improvement measured in milliseconds, of swimming back and forth in the same twenty-five yards. What would it be like to swim for pleasure instead, in a wide-open body of water not man-made?

When we arrived, we combined our strength and used all four of our hands to pull open Rob's heavy oak door, blinking in the soft golden light from the fake diamond chandelier above, the ostentatious sign of nouveau riche suburban family. Inside, clumps of fake mistletoe hung from the wooden banisters unfurling from the top floor to the bottom of the foyer. A strange choice of decoration, as it was not the holidays but the beginning of April, the same time as always for our end-of-season party. But Rob, ever the extravagant host, liked to hang mistletoe at parties because the point of mistletoe was to exist as an excuse. He kept a few bunches around for the inevitable romance: *Look, mistletoe! Let's make out.* A wink and a seductive smirk, leading to a passionate kiss with tongue and multiple head rotations as fireworks explode above the sky, the warbles of Bocelli's "Time to Say Goodbye" cueing in. A tragic, star-crossed love story, a lovely fantasy never actualized, as we all preferred the lighthearted pressure of Truth or Dare or Seven Minutes in Heaven—heaven being Rob's storage shed filled with blunt rakes and punctured donut inner tubes.

It was these games, the mistletoe, and the alcohol buzz specific to underage hormones that spurred our inevitable hookups at these parties. We dubbed the phenomenon swimcest. Our confessions and performances grew into fantastic legends of parties past, whispered around in locker rooms years later.

"Cathy! Welcome!" Rob's mother walked through the garish hallway with her arms opened.

"Oh, hi, Mrs. Johnson." Cathy grimaced as she was squashed into a hug.

"Oh please, I've told you to call me Julie! I'm so glad you're here. Rob's father can't wait to see you again. He's so happy you two are dating!"

Cathy winced against Rob's mother's body. I opened my mouth to rescue her, planning to suggest we were starving and needed to get to the food right away, likely a table overflowing with buffalo chicken dip, pasta, chicken wings, mac-and-cheese balls, marinara sticks; the key feature of athletic parties, more important than alcohol or the guest gender ratio—we could rely on Rob for choosing the finest microwavable snacks along with gallons of brand-name soda to mix with the inevitable vodka and rum. But I was too late—Mrs. Johnson let Cathy go to attack me instead. I was crushed against her rock-hard boobs, each breast crafted by a reputable local plastic surgeon and covered in sweat-wicking, breathable, four-way stretch spandex. One square inch of the fabric cost more than my entire outfit, one implant cost more than my car. I squirmed out of her arms, making a face at Cathy, who was stifling giggles at Mrs. Johnson's enthusiasm.

"Please go enjoy the party. Everyone's already here, either outside or in the living room! There's plenty of food for everybody." Mrs. Johnson waved her pointy, ruby-red acrylic nails toward the ajar door on the other side of the foyer, where the drifting din of our teammates' laughter echoed against the gold floral wallpaper. "Cathy, I'm going to go find my husband so you both can say hello."

Mrs. Johnson walked off, her high heels, the same gaudy red as her nails, clicking against the marbled tiles. I marveled at her wearing such impractical shoes inside the house—my mother and I wore slippers—and turned to Cathy, who was frantically pulling me through the foyer. "Ren, let's go! I really don't want to see Mr. Johnson."

"Okay, okay, I get it." I looked at her. "Why are you and Rob even dating anyway? You two don't even act like you like each other."

"I like Rob! And his mom is fine." Cathy stopped pulling me and crossed her arms. "I just don't like Mr. Johnson."

"Valid. He's scary. Don't worry. I'll protect you." I wound my left arm through the crook of her right, and together we walked toward our reveling teammates.

We played Truth or Dare like we always did, tipsy, sitting around the bonfire while snacking on the massive bags of sourdough pretzels, peanut M&M's, and sour cream and onion potato chips overflowing the patio table, the bright, crinkly plastic obscuring the bottles of Svedka Blue Raspberry Vodka and Mike's Hard Lemonade.

It had been two rounds of the game already. I was unbalanced from alcohol and the heady sense of hormonal youth at unsupervised parties. Though I abstained from alcohol during the swim season, I did enjoy drinking, the way it cleared my head of pain and made me stop thinking about the copper rod in my body, the mermaids, my mother alone in our house without a father to keep her company while I partied and swam. My body was flushed with Asian glow, causing Cathy to call me her siren. The nickname made me blush harder, adding to the redness of my skin. Cathy meant a siren like those on top of police cars, but I secretly nourished the idea that when she called me a siren, she referred to the Sirens in Greek mythology, who lured sailors to their rocky, watery deaths with their haunting songs.

Cathy had been dared to lick Rob's feet, to the hoots of Luke and Brad. Ally and Mia had been dared to make out, and they had done so with great amounts of tongue, to the ecstatic applause of the boys. So far, I had been dared to shove four jumbo marshmallows in my mouth, rather tame, and so on my second round, I again chose Dare, hoping for something slightly spicier.

"Seven Minutes in Heaven meets Truth or Dare. I dare you to go into the storage shed with Luke for seven minutes." Ally, wicked, nefarious, scheming. Though Ally had long crushed on Luke, it was okay for me to do the dare with him, because she knew Luke would never actually consider me a viable person to date.

Everyone snickered at the dare. Everyone was jealous. After all, Luke was our star. Everyone wanted a piece of him, whether it was a high-five after a race or a blowjob in the storage shed. He was disgustingly fast; he had broken and rebroken the state record, his own, in the 100 backstroke every year, setting the bar higher and higher for anyone who dared follow his legacy. In ten years, he would resemble his father, bald and big-nosed; Luke's blond hair was already thinning at the top, a sign of things to come. He was not attractive, but he had a wingspan stretching across an entire lane. And, let me mention again, because this was what mattered most for swimmers like us: He was fast. Haven't I said already, the pretty ones were always fast, and the fast ones were always pretty? He had led the team as captain two years in a row, nominated not because he was kind to the underclassmen but because he was fast. He was a winner who did not understand how to lose, the most dangerous kind.

Luke wiggled his eyebrows. I was nauseated. My stomach gurgled. I glanced at Cathy. She looked intrigued and bored. The corners of her mouth were tilted downward. The flicker of the bonfire spun her eyes into black holes.

"Wanna go?" Luke stood up and held his hand out to me in a fake show of chivalry. "Tonight could be your one chance before I head off to Yale." He pouted, a fake show of sadness at his solid future. The Yale coach had called him at the beginning of his sophomore year to give him an offer he could not refuse, a rare occurrence designated for the most talented young athletes in the United States. Of course Luke committed, as university signing day was the twenty-first-century manifest destiny for athletic superheroes. We expected Luke to go somewhere with a bigger swimming name, like Berkeley, Jim's beloved Penn State, or even Georgia, but Luke had surprised us all with his shrewd foresight—Yale would be an appealing mark on his résumé. Something to fall back on for the inevitable day his swimming skills failed. It also helped Yale's men's team was reputed to be the biggest partiers in the Ivy League. They had an infamous scrapbook ranking the looks of the female Ivy League swimmers, updated every year.

I stared at his outstretched palm. I could feel the eyes of my teammates watching me, shocked I did not grab it. Like Yale, none of them would have denied him; he always got everything he wanted— so was the power of a top-ranked time. Cellos, violins, violas of crickets, and the crackle of logs accompanied our motionless drama.

Luke frowned, his hand still out. "Let's go."

I peeked again at Cathy. I couldn't read her face. It was too dark, and I was left groping my way through, unsure of how to act, where to go, what to say.

"Stop it."

There were thirty seconds of more stunned silence from me and the teammates as Cathy's "stop it" lit up my path like a sudden lighthouse through the fog; the gloom lifted as the nausea in my stomach upchucked, up and up and up until it vomited out of my mouth as a weak mumble: "Yeah, stop it. I don't think the dare is funny. Not sure I wanna go."

Ally scoffed. "Cathy, shut up. And Ren, c'mon. It's a dare." She turned back to Luke. "I'll time you guys." She whipped out her phone, the screen illuminating a careless leer.

"Hurry up," Luke said impatiently.

The team wolf whistled. I could hear Brad's whistles coming through clearer than anybody else's. He was either compensating or truly excited I could have the chance to hook up with Luke so I could then pass on the winning genes to him.

"Do I have to?" I whined. I used a tone of voice I hoped would imply I found the entire situation quite funny.

"Ren doesn't have to. Ally, stop it," Cathy said, so quietly my ears wondered if they had been tricked.

I glanced at her. Her eyebrows, darkened by night, were furrowed so deeply they matched the wild lines of the curls on her head.

I sighed. I didn't want to ruin a fun night, a night in which Cathy and I had both been accepted as part of the team. Besides, what could Luke do to me in seven minutes? We were teammates.

I stood. My towel dropped to the grass.

"I'll go," I said.

I was wearing my blue triangle bikini. I kept it secret from my mother, who deemed bikinis too skimpy, by pushing it between the slabs of my bedroom dresser. My body was a burnt amber, reflecting the bonfire, the alcohol I had drunk, and my teammates' scrutiny. Every muscle crease of my arms and shoulders was outlined by fire.

I took Luke's hand. His hands were the size of dinner plates, effective oars through the water, easily enveloping mine. He winked at me. I suppose he thought it was charming. I stumbled as he dragged me off toward Rob's storage shed. The thinning patch on Luke's skull sparkled in the firelight. We melted into the darkness in the direction of the storage closet. Our teammates were laughing, immersed in drunken nonchalance that had already moved on to the next dare.

———

I am sure you would like to read about what happened next in the storage shed. Humans often forget their curiosity has malicious intentions.

You want every detail so you can make appropriate judgments on the participants of such ambiguous events. You would like to decide whether I deserve your pity. You want all the information so you can properly decide whether what happened that night was my fault or not. Everything must be outlined in depth before I am believed—what I was wearing, what I said, how many times I said no, if I said no at all.

You already have key information: I wore a skimpy bikini, I was drunk, and I agreed to go to not ruin the party.

My conclusion, based on these above stated facts, is that your sympathy will be hard-won, no matter what happens next.

Let me guess some scenarios in your head:

Luke pushing me against the wall, shoving his fingers up inside me while he licked my neck like a panting dog, leaving trails of drool pooling into my collarbones, me screaming, *no no no Cathy help*, Luke hearing *yes* despite the many times I screamed *no*, because the word *no* did not exist for a golden boy like Luke, his life had been and would be a series of *yes yes yes yes yes*, yes to the promotion, yes to the loan approval, yes to any girl he propositioned, whether it was for a one-night stand or a lifetime of marriage infidelity. This is the scenario that would garner the most sympathy from you. Unfortunately, I am beholden to the truth, and I can assure you this did not happen. I did not scream. I never clearly said no.

Or, and let me subvert your expectations: Me pushing Luke against the wall, a dominatrix in the making, holding my forearm against his windpipe and his arms above his head as I tugged and tugged, until he came all over my stomach and blue bikini, me laughing at his inability to control himself. This scenario is impossible because I was merely a girl in high school, too young to understand how power dynamics could be turned on and off consensually, depending on the parties involved.

Or, if I was telling a gentler coming-of-being story: Luke, respectful, saying I didn't have to do anything at all, a true gentleman performing the modern-day chivalrous equivalent of holding open the door by not sexually assaulting me, Luke inviting me to sit on the floor next to him snacking on a bag of jalapeño-and-lime tortilla chips he had snatched off the table as we made our way over to the shed, ridiculing Ally's atrocious intentions and Cathy's savior complex as we waited for time to be up. This is a derisive scenario. You must know by now my mermaid tale is no such joyful narrative. And you would not be interested in this story if it were.

I'll tell you what really happened:

Luke had pushed me up against the storage shed wall and slobbered all over me. He stuck his fingers down my bikini bottom, sending it to hang at my ankles, and I pretended to moan in pleasure, when in reality I was staring at the scene from a perch on the storage shed shelf, next to the bottles of gasoline and cans of paint, marveling at how my body seemed to enjoy the experience while I mentally did not. I never said yes, but I never said no, and the indefinite limbo of maybe is where regret and doubt and confusion reside as neighbors, forever reduced to the monotony of a clouded memory, the mind traveling in never-ending cul-de-sac circles. I stayed quiet that night and the days after. I never pushed him off, and I never accused him of anything.

———————

Brad broke up with me the day after the party. It was technically a breakup, but there was nothing real to break. No hearts, no love, no public relationship. Nothing broken.

He claimed he was jealous. The jealousy from watching me walk off with Luke made him so upset and unhinged, he had to end things with me. I pointed out that he had seemed to have no qualms about the dare at the party, laughing along with our teammates, and besides, what happens as dares stays as dares.

He said it didn't matter.

I tried to convince him we were never anything real anyway. We were only fucking, and I offered to keep fucking, because I enjoyed fucking.

He said no.

Whatever. I considered asking him to delete my nudes, but decided not to, because what was the point of acting the victim? Better to make him think of me as empowered.

When Brad said he was jealous, I closed my eyes and smelled Luke's Cool Ranch Doritos–laced breath against my cheek, heard his hard breathing, felt his fingers working down my stomach, pressing hard enough to make me vomit up butter-snap pretzels.

# Eleven

Sophomore year ended. Summer came. I grew listless like the air, buzzing heat waves lying low. Though we didn't have class, we still had swim practice. I dreaded each new day. I didn't want to see Brad or Luke, and I began to avoid Cathy, whose simpering eyes made me feel disgusted for the timidness she had shown during the party—a party I refused to refer to as *party* any longer, because *party* implied joyous delight. *Funeral* was a more apt term.

When I thought about that sophomore end-of-season party— excuse me, *funeral*—and what happened with Luke, I pictured a rotting coffin cradling the corpse of Cathy's and my friendship, borne by pallbearers named Shame and Loathing and Apathy, escorting us into the cold, cruel earth; a somber funeral march–like remix of Eminem's "Lose Yourself" playing; myself spitting on the tombstone, its epitaph inscribed: *Here lies the reaping of Cathy's silence.*

The state of Pennsylvania decreed I was finally old enough to get a job, and though my mother said I didn't have to work, that she'd prefer me to spend any summer break time studying when I wasn't at swim practice, I signed up to be a lifeguard at the outdoor community pool, open for the summer, located a one-mile walk from my house. I figured floating was my sole marketable skill, and I could waste away the summer days by making minimum wage and walking two miles round-trip to work. I couldn't bear staying at home when I wasn't at practice, with only my mermaids, headaches, and the memory of Luke's fingers clamoring to keep me company. Cathy tried to sign up, too, when she heard about my summer plans, but to my relief, there were no open positions left.

I was shocked by the conditions of the outdoor community pool. The pools I was accustomed to were for competitions: uniform lane ropes partitioning the water into perfect sections, neatly painted floor tiles, and identical starting blocks at the head of each lane. I had never been to a pool so run-down, with chipped paint decorating the sides, dead bugs floating on the water, uneven concrete cracking the deck. We repeatedly hollered at kids to walk, not run, conjuring bullhorns from the bottom of our lungs, so they wouldn't trip over a fracture and enable their parents to sue management for negligence. The hired landscaper never came to mow the lawn, and spiders wove their heavy webs wherever the broken deck chairs' legs emerged from behind the green wild stems.

The outdoor pool even smelled different. Not a horrible scent, but bizarre and unfamiliar. During work orientation, the head lifeguard noticed my wrinkled displeasure at the odor and informed me the outdoor pool used bromine instead of chlorine.

Despite the seedy conditions, I enjoyed working as a lifeguard.

The kids liked me, dropping off pool toys like Torpedo Bandits and Watermelon Balls at my feet, begging me to play with them. My skin glowed with a healthy summer tan. I perched in the tall lifeguard chair to daydream about mermaids using clamshells to surf tsunamis and sat in the office between rotations to reread Jane Austen. I shared each shift with a fellow lifeguard named Ess, who was quiet but not timid, possessing lips more languid than functional, lips they often absentmindedly traced with the whistle hanging from their neck while they sat slouched with their legs wide open in the lifeguard highchair. They were twenty years old and a college dropout. They were neither a swimmer nor an athlete, which was new and exciting, and altogether much less perilous.

I had signed up for the last shifts of the day because of swim practice in the mornings. Ess had signed up for the last shifts because after the pool closed for the day and all the patrons went home, they could use the pool to skinny dip and smoke weed in peace. The first time I smelled the vapors of their pot, I mistakenly searched for a skunk, checking underneath the lawn chairs and in the pool gutters, suspecting one had snuck into the pool area to let loose its protective spray. When I realized the odor's source was Ess and not a black-and-white ball of fur, I was agog at the easy rule-breaking; I had never considered a life where rules were discarded like ripped swim caps. A life lived for fun and not for swimming.

"Here. Try it," Ess said, motioning to me to take the blunt in between their long fingers. We were sitting on the edge of the pool, the water up to our calves. Late-summer evening air in Pittsburgh embraced fragrances of mown grass tinged with sunscreen, soundtracks of unseen birds chirping in the gentle breeze. Tiny bugs danced around our heads, unbothered. A broken branch drifted past our legs. We were too lazy to do our job and use the butterfly net to clear the pool of nature's debris each night.

"Don't inhale too much. Take it slow," Ess said.

I took a drag and choked, coughing on the bitter smoke. The air restriction was worse than choking on chlorine, the lung burn worse than a sprint race with breath held. Ess laughed at me, but I didn't mind. They weren't malicious. I liked the tune of their laughter.

Ess patted me on the back. "You'll get used to it," they promised as they blew smoke into the cooling night air. We were sitting with our thighs touching, and the scent of their skin reflected our surroundings, a mix of marijuana and bromine. My own skin was still smothered with chlorine and sunscreen.

"Can you believe Michael Phelps was caught smoking weed once?" I asked, mesmerized, watching Ess twirl their hair between their fingers while coolly holding the blunt aloft.

"Who's Michael Phelps?"

"Oh—you don't know him?" I was caught off guard, and rather proud of myself for showing off my pop culture intelligence. No wonder Cathy had a superiority complex when she explained things to me.

"He's an Olympian," I clarified. "A famous swimmer. One of the best."

"I don't follow sports. But that's cool of him."

"He got into trouble for smoking weed. I think he might've lost a sponsorship," I said.

"I'm sure. Everybody smokes, but no one wants to admit it publicly. There's still a stigma," they said.

I scratched the two bug bites on my arm I had gotten earlier during our shift. I had swatted the mosquito as it sucked my blood, killing it, and its crimson nourishment and guts smeared across my skin, reminding me of Cathy's hands when she had first helped me with Penelope.

"He used something called a bong? It was at a party. The paparazzi caught a photo, or maybe it was his friend who shared it with the press. I'm not sure how the news broke," I said.

"Sucks for him he was caught. Shitty friend, if true. But it's cool he smokes." Ess flipped their hair over their shoulder.

"Hey, I have a bong back at my house. You can come over and try it sometime," they said, tapping the muscle divot on my thigh. My quadricep trembled, the skin warm where they touched me.

Weed made me feel unearthly, out-of-body, floating. When I smoked, the ever-present headaches ceased. Was the assistance in numbness the reason why Michael smoked too? I wondered what pain a decorated Olympian would need to appease.

The combination of Ess's attitude, a drugged high, and the summer sun relaxed my muscles to the point of forgetting I had spent so many years of my childhood building them up to be stronger than the day before.

The constant bettering had been exhausting.

I was burned out.

With Ess, I finally relaxed.

I liked them. I liked their unhurried and quiet manner, so different from the rest of my teammates always jostling for attention. I liked the lackadaisical way they dragged the lifeguard buoy over the ground, not caring if it snagged against rocks. I liked the way they didn't care about anything at all. I myself cared too much, about swimming, about my grades, about my body, that to wrap my thighs around their sunburnt waist as I leaned backward, floating atop the water, was an act of omission. When we made out, I hoped their un-concern would transfer to me by way of saliva. I wanted to be more like them. Uncaring. The cicadas would scream around us as our bodies merged in the bromine, the empty lawn chairs as our audience. Then we'd pass the blunt back and forth dipping our toes in the navy pool, silent.

One day Ess showed up at work with their long, wavy brown hair dyed into shades of turquoise and aqua. Their hair was a gradient, beginning with the roots at the top still dark brown, shifting into beautiful shades of blue effortlessly, like a gorgeous waterfall had attached itself to their head. They twirled around me and laughed at my enamored reaction.

"Like it? I wanted mermaid hair," Ess said, giggling, bobbing their head so dramatically the office's dreary wooden surfaces flashed blue.

"Mermaid hair?" I asked, dazed. I gently massaged a strand of Ess's hair, the blue running through my fingers. Their hair was coarser than the day before from the bleach and chemical treatment, but still soft. I grabbed a larger handful when Ess stopped dancing and rubbed their hair across my cheek.

"You like it, huh?" Ess winked at me. They drew me closer, and we began to slow dance, their hands around my waist, mine grip-ping their hip and crook of their shoulder. Their fingers pressed into my skin, and though I was ticklish, I held my laughter back, the moment too soft for loud humor. Our hair intertwined, black with blue, and in the muggy humidity, the strands clung to our skin. We swayed to the twangy country song playing on the lifeguard office radio, the laughter of the pool patrons twinkling in tune with the song's banjo. Though we had never practiced slow dancing before, our feet instinctively stepped in sync.

"I love it. I didn't realize blue hair was mermaid hair," I said.

"It's not just the color deeming it mermaid. It's what the hairstyle in general is called—long waves, plus any sort of aqua-toned colored hair. It's a fun look, isn't it? I used drugstore dye and it turned out much better than I thought it would!"

"It's beautiful."

"I can help you dye your hair mermaid-style too," Ess offered. "It would be hard with your black hair, and we'd have to use a lot of bleach, but we can try."

"Does it hurt?" I asked.

Ess hesitated. "Yes. The bleach burns. Especially near the scalp."

I rested my chin onto the angle where their shoulder met their neck, breathing in the weed and bromine. The country song on the radio ended, shifting to a mournful love ballad. The crooner sang of July grass stains on white dresses, secret love behind campus bleachers, denim cutoffs, cans of cold beer. Ess began to hum along, their skin vibrating.

"If it hurts, then no," I murmured, my voice muffled by the closeness of our bodies. "I can't handle more pain."

Some nights, after we had smoked, skinny-dipped, and had sex, Ess would invite me to a party at their house. These parties were never the type of raging parties I saw in the movies but were understated basement affairs with other stoners and tattooed people who called themselves artists—they were a new social circle for me. Ess's friends passed blunts and strummed melodic nonsense on their guitars. I was fascinated by these stoners, and they were fascinated by me, a swimmer. An athlete. Though I didn't belong with them, they made me feel comfortable, and though I still coughed when the blunt came to me, they never skipped my turn. I appreciated them and laughed with ease far greater than I had ever laughed with my teammates.

Ess's friends asked me why I did what I did, why I kept swimming. I said I wasn't sure. It was true. I forgot all my reasons for existing. It didn't matter. We were high and I wasn't hurting.

My performance at practice had started to suffer, and Jim was angry at me. I had never disregarded his rules so blatantly before. Though I always made sure to brush my teeth and shower so I wouldn't smell like weed when I got to practice, I could tell he suspected I was no longer his pure, innocent swimmer. When I swam at practice, it was like I wasn't even in the pool, my mind elsewhere, like I was out-of-body, a similar sensation to when Ally dared me to go in the storage shed with Luke. My muscles were working, but I had no say over their performance.

I still had to share a lane with Luke that summer, which made me recoil before every dive in. But even when I was half-high and corrupted with leftover lifeguarding sun—even if Jim thought I was slacking off—I was as fast as the boys.

I realize now Ess, and by extension, those months of summer break, saved me. Ess, with their mermaid hair and easy laughter and unplucked eyebrows and sunburnt cheeks with soft fur like peach skin.

What happened with Luke, and by extension, Brad and Cathy's uncaring, and Jim's ever-increasing pressure, had weighed me down. Thanks to Ess, I learned none of the past really mattered in the end. Ess never asked me any intimate questions, yet we shared intimacy far greater than discussing how we were doing, or how swimming was going, or how our parents were. Ess owned a body more a vehicle for their own pleasure rather than a body carrying scars on its surface. From them, I learned I could seize my body back from those who sought to destroy it.

I never told Cathy about Ess. To be frank, I forgot to tell her—I drifted away from Cathy that summer. My life with Ess seemed separate from everything else. I'd enter the community pool in my red lifeguard swimsuit and forget about the swim team, Cathy, my swimming times. Ess would lick my neck and I'd blank.

Like all good things, we ended too quickly—August and junior year sprinted in faster than the final leg of a relay; the trees had already begun to drop autumn-flavored leaves into the water when the community pool closed for the season. Ess and I hadn't skinny-dipped together for the entire last week of it being open, the evening air with a foreboding chill due to the lack of sun. We were unaware our last time alone together was the last time. I wished we could have given it more ceremony rather than splashing around the pool, stoned. But Ess did not show sentimentality about it, so neither did I.

I learned unconcern from them too.

School started, along with the real swimming season. I waved a sad goodbye to the stoners and Ess.

My tan faded in days. But the realization my body was ultimately mine did not. I was happier, and my attitude showed it. I promised Jim I would do my best during junior year, a year fraught with high-strung and weighted expectations: I was expected to take the gold medal at regionals in the 100 butterfly, win our team many points, qualify for states, and then there, make it in the top three. If so, and if I swam fast enough, I would get an early acceptance to whichever college I wanted. My parents wanted. Harvard. The Ivy League.

Jim sent me daily text messages of encouragement:

*The harder the battle, the sweeter the victory!!!!!*

*The pain you feel today will be the strength u feel tomorrow!*

*No more sex, no drugs, no alcohol, no sweets. Get ur head in the right place.*

*I love u. Ur mom loves u. WE LOVE U.*

Jim had called my mother when the school year began and invited her to his office, a bouquet of daisies sitting on his desk. He made sure to shower in advance so his office would smell of flowers and soap instead of cigarettes, an earnest attempt to make a respectable impression to convince my mother to relinquish the reins to him. Using a whiteboard to visually chart the path forward, he outlined for her, in no uncertain terms, my potential. He drew arrows to connect each step, from the Pitt pool to the Harvard pool to the Harvard career center to the ideal job or postgrad university. *Whatever Ren wants! Whatever you want! We can have it all! I'm already getting calls from college recruiters about her. Yes. Including Harvard! Junior year is when recruiting begins; we need to be ready!*

When my mother heard the Harvard coach was interested in me, any worries she had about my excessive swimming faded away. She told me to focus. Study hard, but practice harder. Listen to Jim. He knows best.

I agreed, because there was something bigger coming for me, on my own terms. Though I wasn't aware yet of how I would break free, the time would come, and soon. I was patient. The mermaids would wait for me. Rightful brethren always did.

Twelve

## CATHY

Dear Ren,

In regard to my last letter, I hope you're not angry about me sneaking into your room. And I hope you don't think my apologies are inauthentic or weak. These apology letters are all I can offer until I see you again. If I could apologize in person, I would. I'd get down on my knees and bend my forehead to the floor if it meant you would forgive me. I'd grovel until you bless me clemency. I'd do anything.

I still have more things to apologize for. This new letter is once again filled with my apologies.

First, I'm sorry I didn't say anything more at the bonfire. You said it was fine and so I stayed quiet. And then when you stood up in front of the fire, you looked so beautiful in your bikini, I was struck silent, too busy admiring your muscles to hear your silent cry for help. You were so strong. If I laid you down in Rob's backyard lawn, I would have been able to measure the angles of your muscles, obtuse and right and acute, far better than any rhombus on my geometry worksheets. Acute, acute, cute. I wanted to run my fingers over your definition, discover where the lines met.

But then the darkness swallowed you and Luke. You both disappeared and we moved on. You never told me what happened. I guess I never asked. To be honest, I didn't want to know the details then, and I don't want to know now—but you could've told me. I would've listened, I promise.

Afterward, you kept avoiding me all summer. I suspected it was because of the bonfire, but it wasn't me who assaulted you, it was Luke, and I couldn't understand why you blamed me. To be honest, even today, I am not fully sure why. What could I have done? How could I have stopped Luke from doing what he did second best—swimming first, hooking up with girls second, like a young Jim protégé? Drag you back to the car, step on the gas, and drive away from the mess of the party? Tackle Luke into the fire so his skin would char, let his body burn while Ally cried?

I could've done those things, but it's useless to stew in alternate realities.

Nevertheless, I'm sorry.

When junior year arrived, you came back to me. I was so happy and relieved you decided to mend our relationship. I shoved the irritating notion that I hadn't done anything special to deserve your forgiveness out of my mind. I committed myself to supporting you, protecting you, in whatever ways I could. Jim didn't pay me any attention like he did with you, but I was convinced severe abstinence was a bonding activity we could do together. I, too, gave up dessert and late nights watching TV in exchange for an apple after dinner and early bedtimes. I even gave up excess at pasta parties, settling for palm-sized scoops of whole wheat noodles with less sauce and bigger portions of dressing-less salad. I knew you wouldn't be able to bear watching me eat cookies while you had to settle for carrot sticks. I ejected sugar from my lunch every day, throwing out my Hershey's Kisses and settling for grainy Red Delicious apples from the cafeteria instead.

You never thanked me for my sacrifices. Did you even notice what I gave up?

Thanks to these actions, I did start swimming well. It was the first time I ever qualified for regionals in the 100 breaststroke. You were so proud of me, never bitter that you weren't dropping time drastically like I was—you were always more generous to me and to our teammates than we deserved, although in this case, I guess it helps you were already fast. Close to the threshold of your body's ability. Tsunamis of seconds waved off my times while your own milliseconds ticked down like droplets. I heard you chant your ideal 100 butterfly under your breath during study halls and cafeteria lunches and practices and travel meet bus rides: 56.00, 56.00, 56.00, 56.00, 56.00, 56.00, 56.00, 56.00—like saying it over and over again would make the achievement come true.

My sudden improvement caused me to entertain the romantic idea of us getting recruited to the same college—a silly notion, as my grades wouldn't match up to yours. But I secretly nourished the idea of us being dorm roommates, long nights spent partying in future frat houses with each other for protection and company. I still regret this never came true.

The beginning of the junior-year season was the happiest time of my life. Brad and Rob and the many wedges between our relationship had been forgotten. You joked around with me and stayed by my side at school and at practice. You helped me memorize physics equations at study hall and I texted you daily pictures of cats stuck in strange places. On weekends, we shared salads and beds at travel meets, gossiping about our *Fuck, Marry, Kill* choices during the bus rides and cheering for each other at the ends of our lanes.

Ren, I truly believed you were okay. It seemed to me like you were handling everything fine. Sure, you'd arrive at school and swim practice looking scary with uncombed hair and wild eyes, brandishing another invasive text from Jim, but the entire time you were joking around about it, bragging about how many nights in a row you hadn't slept because of schoolwork and joking about how Coach Jim was a better ex-boyfriend to you than Brad, with his obsession over you and your body and your mindset. You kept talking about the future too—how we could visit each other during college summer breaks, how fast you would swim at regionals, how you couldn't wait to chat with the Harvard coach. You talking about that future indicated to me you were thinking about that future—a future where you were still human, where you still existed in our world. My world. I never saw you chug ibuprofen either, and you never asked me to sneak you some from Jim's first-aid kit. It was like you had weaned yourself off the pain-reliever pills because the headaches had naturally stopped. I saw you laughing with Jim in his office too, him using the dry-erase marker from his whiteboard where he usually wrote down our next set to draw on your skin where your muscles needed to get stronger and improve. He left long streaks of ink all over your shoulders, chest, and arms, and you were laughing the whole time!

These signs pointed toward you being okay. How was I supposed to predict what would happen? How was I supposed to foresee your evolution when you wouldn't warn me?

*Again, I'm sorry.*

*Again, I wish you would've shared your secrets with me. Why did you stay quiet?*

*You could've told me you were mad at me because of the bonfire. You could've told me you were stressed. You could've told me the homework, the practices, Jim's touch—all of it—was too much. You could've brought me an extra spool of thread and explained your plan in detail, and maybe I would've joined you. We could've been together right now, both mermaids. I already have red hair like Ariel. It wouldn't be too far of a stretch for me to ascend like you did.*

*Okay. There's not much more on my mind other than what I've written. I've been having trouble feeling excited about anything since you left. Nothing's new with me, back here in the domain of humankind—it's boring. Every day is the same.*

*I'll leave you with my regrets.*

*Love,*
*Cathy*

# Thirteen

In the many months before the regionals meet, I presented myself as others desired me. My mother saw me studying and swimming. Cathy saw me laughing and sharing stories. Jim saw me obeying his practice sets and prescribed daily diet plan:

4:30 A.M.: Fuel for morning practice. One cup of raw oats mixed with one cup of unsweetened applesauce, with a sprinkle of cinnamon for flavor. An ibuprofen.

7:30 A.M.: Post-practice breakfast before class. Two scoops of flavorless whey protein powder resembling chalk, shaken with an overripe banana, three raw eggs, and four cups of water.

10:00 A.M.: Snack time. Two hard-boiled eggs and a smattering of almonds.

12:30 P.M.: Lunch. Chicken and boiled broccoli, accompanied by a copious layer of peanut butter slathered on lentil sprouted bread. An apple. An ibuprofen or two—or three—depending on the severity of the headache instigated by morning practice and morning classes.

3:00 P.M.: More hard-boiled eggs. Chug water.

4:30 P.M.: Pre-practice fuel. More almonds, plus an apple or banana, maybe some berries if my mother allowed a splurge at the grocery store—a pint of blueberries cost more and lasted shorter than a bunch of bananas, but was significantly more delicious, and so my mother let me buy a carton every few weeks.

6:30 P.M.: Post-practice. Wolf down an energy bar wrapped in a white plastic wrapper with strange chemical ingredients written in marker. The bar tasted like a mash of gravel and oatmeal, and was peddled to the team by Jim, who was sponsored by the company. Double-fist the bar with another protein shake, two crushed ibuprofens mixed inside.

7:00 P.M.: Arrive home and, at my mother's insistence, grudgingly eat her dumplings, noodles, or fried rice. Grudgingly, because though my mother's Chinese food tasted much better than athletic fuel, Jim insisted dinner should be another chicken-and-broccoli meal—more protein, less carbs.

11:00 P.M.: Eleven almonds before bed. Jim asserted a small amount of protein before sleep made the muscles recover faster.

On the outside, my body consumed and performed what was expected of me.

Inside, my brain conspired, its mermaid mechanisms hidden in my skull, fighting headache demons while planning a future escape from my human body.

My loved ones did not suspect anything. They saw what they wanted to see.

Humans, ever foolish.

The last home meet of the season was scheduled three weeks before junior year's regionals meet, where the Harvard recruiter would come watch me swim. The home meet was in the evening after school, and I had packed an extra portion of lentil bread and peanut butter to sustain my energy levels.

At 8–0, we hadn't lost a meet yet, and Jim was looking forward to yet another undefeated season record. The last home meet was against our rival school district, one of the few able to put up a fight. On the girls' side, they had a fast butterflier, a few good sprinters, and a decent 4x100 freestyle relay.

For competitive home meets, swimmers like Cathy were relegated to the sidelines, while swimmers like me were slotted into our top events. I was to swim the 100 butterfly and the butterfly segment of the medley relay. If I won both heats, which was expected, I'd win enough points for our girls' team to declare victory. I hadn't lost a home meet race my entire high school career. I had swum against the opposing team's butterflier before and beaten her easily. Her impact was so negligible that if I was threatened with eternal exile from the pool unless I listed some details about her, I wouldn't even be able to recite the first letter of her name.

My uterus sensed the upcoming meet was important, and so, like most needy children, it announced itself at the most inopportune of times. It started shedding in my eighth-period math class. I sneezed when Mr. Morris scrawled a set of integers on the chalkboard, and when my snot ejected, my vagina did too. My stomach rumbled and the cramps loomed. I congratulated myself miserably on selecting black granny panties and dark-wash jeans. The knives and forks began to stab. The meal commenced.

I raised my hand. Mr. Morris nodded at me, giving me permission to go to the bathroom. I stumbled into a stall and heaved myself and my head into the toilet, emptying out the contents of my stomach in a waterfall of mushy chunks: lentil bread, raw oats, applesauce, carrots, chicken, ibuprofen.

Trembling, I stood at the sink and watched a bead of sweat drip from my forehead to my chin. I was paler than usual, my skin washed out, even paler than Cathy's. I winced and clutched the edge of the sink as another cramp tore through me. Turning on the faucet, I splashed cold water over my face, ignoring the drops spilling onto my shirt collar as I cursed my bloody, monthly fate. It was already difficult for me to practice through period pain; competing would be worse.

But I had to do well that night. My team depended on me. Jim depended on me. I had to win, or Jim would scrutinize me further. I could not handle any more pressure from him. My muscles, now sore and swollen from menstruation, were barely functioning under the daily onslaught of his abuse.

Instead of heading back to the classroom, I descended the stairs to the pool locker room. With the cramps, I wouldn't be able to sit up straight, and I didn't want to be yelled at—Mr. Morris had told us on the first day of school he hated students with bad posture. Clearly, he had never inspired enough trust in his students for them to explain to him the effects of monthly bleeding.

I clutched the stair rail for balance as my insides were ravaged.

I mimicked the Hunchback of Notre Dame—I was the Hunchback of the Swimming Pool.

I debated what to do. I wanted to go home, but there were only two hours left in the school day, and it would be a waste of gas and energy to drive home for such a short nap.

I settled on an abbreviated version of at-home period care. I entered the locker room, which was empty, and tugged open my lock to take out my heating pad and a bottle of Pamprin from the top shelf. The heating pad and the pills were my salvation each month. I threw back three pills with a dry swallow and a fleeting concern that the added Pamprin might be too many pills for my ibuprofen-infected system, but I shook the worry away when another cramp tore through my insides, and I reassured myself I'd already thrown up the medication. I put the bottle back in my locker and exited the room into the pool area, peeking my head out first to confirm no gym classes were swimming laps. The chlorine was pristine, untouched.

I stepped into the supply room connected to Jim's office, which he always left unlocked, and grabbed an exercise mat. I lugged it and my heating pad to the back room behind the pool, where Brad and I had sometimes hooked up. Nobody ever came in except to abandon broken lane ropes, damaged flippers, and strapless goggles. I didn't need to worry about Brad either; I had forced him to promise he'd never use the room after we ended things, using the threat of his dick pics to force his verbal agreement.

Amid the discard of swimming dreams, I lay atop the mat and closed my eyes, resting the heating pad on the lower half of my stomach. Weary from blood loss and internal pain, I fell asleep, lulled by the faint scent of chlorine.

————————

I woke up disoriented, to intense shouting and shrill notes. I recognized Jim's whistle and my teammates' voices.

*Where is she?*

*Somebody call her mom!*

*We did! Her mom says she's not home.*

*Her mom is as confused as we are.*

*I texted her but she didn't respond!*

Cathy's voice came clearest to me. *What will we do without her?*

I grinned. Yes, what would Cathy do without me?

My tailbone ached. There was an intense heat radiating from my front lower half and a cold puddle of sweat under my back. I stretched, disturbing the pad balancing on my abs; it fell to the side with a muffled thump. The pills, heat, and nap had worked—my cramps and exhaustion were gone. The lone evidence of my body's earlier violence was a warm moisture in my underwear and an itchy lower stomach, the skin inflamed from prolonged exposure to the heating pad. I stood up, my muscles protesting. They were never allowed enough rest.

I rolled up the mat and my pad into one soft burrito and placed them neatly next to the door. I exited the room, checking first to make sure no one looked my way. I didn't want anyone to see me come out. The room was my little secret, a place to nap and hook up without disturbance during school and after practice.

"Hello." I sidled up next to Cathy, already in her swimsuit, tapping her bare shoulder. Behind her, Luke's and Jim's eyes widened at the sight of me. Luke rubbed his chin, confused.

"Where were you?" Cathy whirled around and hugged me. "We were searching for you! We can't win the meet without you." She stepped back and examined my face. "Hang on."

Cathy pressed her palm against my forehead like she was checking for my temperature. "Why are you all sweaty? Do you have a fever?"

I shook my head and her hand fell off my face. "No. I'm fine. I was—uh—in the locker room the whole time," I said, coughing to cover up my fumbling excuse.

Cathy furrowed her eyebrows, thinking. When she concentrated, she resembled a cute furry red ferret. "No, you weren't. I was there. I checked all the showers. Ally was also in the locker room searching for you, and she checked the bathroom stalls. Neither of us saw you," she said, frowning.

I shrugged. "You must've missed me."

"How is that possible?"

I avoided her gaze. "I dunno? Maybe you were being careless."

Jim interrupted. "Ren, get your suit on and let's go. You gotta warm up. The meet's about to start. You feelin' okay?"

I untangled myself from Cathy's embrace, ignoring her wounded pout. I gave Jim two thumbs up. He was a touchy-feely kind of person and listened best when body language was used.

"I'm feeling great. I'll go change. See ya later." I saluted them and marched off toward the locker room to change.

"Weirdo," I heard Luke mutter.

With my 100 butterfly heat up next, I stretched behind the block, muttering under my breath the words of my end goal: *first place first place first place*. The pressure was high. My teammates weren't swimming well. Only Luke had won his heat so far, and the opposing team had some new decently talented freshmen Jim had never heard of, and therefore did not account for in his calculations. But I wasn't worried. I would win the race and earn the points we needed to catch up. My warmup might have been cut short, but I was well prepared, and both opposing butterfliers in the lanes to my left and right were puny in comparison to my muscles. I ran through my typical stretches: the streamline, the flamingo, the toe touch. I was thrusting my hips forward, stretching my hip flexors and groin, when the heat ahead finished.

The swimmers climbed out of the pool. It had been a close race. I moved aside to give Rob, who had won his heat by four milliseconds, enough room to pant. He was always overly dramatic after his races, whether he won or lost. His skin was flushed red, and his chest heaved from exertion. He bent over, his hands resting on his thighs, as if standing straight up against gravity cost him too dearly. He looked like he was about to puke. I refrained from mocking him and snapped on my goggles instead.

"Good job." I shoved an underhand palm underneath his face.

He nodded, tapping my hand before dropping his arm, lacking the energy for a real high-five.

"Good luck," he wheezed, the two words barely audible.

I pressed my goggles further into my skin with my palms. I jumped up and down, my feet slapping my butt, prepping my muscles for the struggle of the swim.

The official blew his whistle.

I stepped upward, onto the blocks. I bent forward. My feet moved into position: right foot forward, toes wrapped around the edge; left foot back, on tiptoe.

My hands dangled, fingertips framing my right foot.

*Take your mark.*

I gripped the block, my feet as springs.

BEEP

My muscles leaped, I dove forward, I was in the water, undulating my body furiously, my arms squeezed tight against my ears in streamline. I broke into the air with a hard stroke, my arms spiraling, and my chest dove back down into the water as I lifted my head for a quick breath, my legs kicked powerful buckets, there was the wall, I was nearing my first turn, I touched the wall and threw my body backward, my head came up and I saw Cathy, leading the cheer at the end of my lane, it was hard to discern her face but I recognized it was her because of the red hair and who else cared about me enough to stand there?—A roar of encouragement thrust into my eardrums before I tipped back and pushed off, entering the cool silence of the underwater. I undulated, streamlined, I chanced a slight look to my left from underneath my biceps and saw no one, I was alone, everyone was behind me. I was in the lead. Winning. Like always.

The second wall came, and I repeated my turn, the cheering quieter on this side of the pool. My arms started to burn. I lifted my head out more times than Jim and I had agreed on before the race, but I needed air, I needed oxygen, and I was in the lead anyway. I kicked harder: The third lap was always the toughest. The last turn with Cathy's red hair and indiscernible cheers for a split second, then the fourth, final lap: I gathered whatever steam I had left and shot my arms forward, plunged my legs downward. I flew. Cramps? What cramps? I was on fire, surrounded by water. My vision was tinted purple—my goggles gave everything a purple haze, but victory always had a colorful lens; though I could not see them, I could sense the lengths of my competitors' bodies behind me the way a hunter senses prey.

And there. The final wall. I drove my hands into the touchpad, the abrupt stop to my momentum forcing my body back a centimeter. Then I whipped my head up, hand gripping the gutter edge, at the scoreboard. 59.28. It was not my best time, but I was in first place by three seconds. I slammed my hand on the water. The parents and my teammates roared in delight. I whipped off my cap and goggles and sunk the back of my head into the water to let my hair fan out.

The rest of my heat finally finished. I tipped over the lane rope next to me and stuck my hand out for the girl next to me to shake—proper behavior for swimmers, regardless of victory or loss. The girl glowered at my outstretched handshake, barely brushing it before hauling herself out of the pool. I smirked—I could tell she was bitter over my clear victory. I pulled myself out with the bottom bar of the diving block, hopping up and down a few times to rid myself of the water in my ears. I was abuzz, I was awake. I wasn't weak like Rob, who acted as if every race nearly killed him. I was tougher than those dumb boys, I could bleed out my vagina and still win first place. I searched the deck for Jim. I was supposed to check in with him after each race to learn how I could improve in our next.

"Excuse me."

I whipped around. There stood the wrinkled old man who officiated all our meets. He held a clipboard and frowned. I was familiar with faces like his, but not his specific name. Swimming officials were exact replicas of each other, like a scientist had cloned his grandparents out of a test tube—turtle chins, wasted muscles, white, old, and retired, with no plans except to relive their glory swimmer days while wearing ugly white polos and navy Bermuda shorts. They all had miserable attitudes, spending their free time disqualifying and disappointing young swimmers.

"You're disqualified," he announced.

"What?"

"You're disqualified," he said again.

"WHAT?" I cried.

"You're DQed. Dee, Queue," he said, enunciating each letter like I was learning how to read. "It didn't show up on the scoreboard because we had to discuss and confirm with the official handbook."

"I think you have the wrong person." Furious, I spun away, my wet hair sprinkling the official's white polo. I spotted Jim, waiting for me in front of the officials' table, his mouth set in a firm line. He had taken his baseball cap off his head and placed it over his heart, as if grieving.

I stomped over. My feet splashed in wide puddles. The officials sitting behind the table glared at me, chlorine droplets splattered across their papers.

"Jim, what the hell? The officials say I was disqualified."

He pursed his lips and thumped me on the back, using enough force to tell me his action was not a comforting pat but a hit meant to hurt and impart his anger. "You are. Your legs were coming apart in the final lap. Your feet were wide apart."

"What are you talking about?"

"Your butterfly kick. I think you got tired and let your legs relax too much. There's a basic rule saying your legs and feet must stay connected. Ren, are you stupid? What the fuck happened? We're going to have to spend some more time in the water practicing your kick. You need work."

I reared back in shock. I willed myself not to cry. My exhaustion slapped me in the face.

"I've never heard of that rule," I said.

"Well, amateur swimmers do it, so it never gets brought up at your level," he said.

"Are you calling me amateur?"

"Ren, it's your fault."

"I guess we didn't get the points," I said. I trained my eyes on my toes. I couldn't bear to make eye contact.

"No points," Jim spat, his voice shaking, hoarse and deep, anger woven through every syllable. If we hadn't been at a swim meet with officials and parents nearby to control his behavior, I would've ducked—Jim's tone of voice indicated he was furious enough to throw six chairs at my head.

He pushed me. I stumbled forward and caught my balance before I landed on my knees.

"Go stretch and get ready for the relay. Don't fuck up again." He spun away from me and started to scribble on his clipboard, no doubt taking notes on Luke's absolute perfection of form. Luke was swimming his second individual race of the meet, and he was already an entire lap ahead of everyone else.

I stormed away, pushing aside a mix of my teammates and the enemies, who were milling about the side of the pool watching Luke's race.

Cathy had followed me. "Ren, what happened? Your winning points weren't added to the counter," she panted, sliding in the puddles on the floor as she tried to keep up. She pointed toward the scoreboard. "See?"

"Leave me alone," I gritted through my teeth. I slumped onto our team bleachers. What the hell had happened? What an idiotic rule. What an idiotic swimmer I was, addled by menstruation pain and gold medal hubris. My uterus, fallopian tubes, and winning attitude had conspired against me, leading to my doom.

But perhaps it wasn't me. Perhaps the opposing team had paid off the official. There was no way I could have committed such an offense and paid for it so dearly. Either the official had been bribed, or he was racist. Yes, he had probably targeted me because I was Asian, because he had some sort of personal vendetta against anyone who wasn't white—

"Way to go, Ren." Mia shook her head, stretching her pectorals by leaning against the tiled wall with one arm in a high-five position. She braced against the edge of the bleachers for balance. "DQed for your butterfly kick? Pathetic."

"Shut up," I said, though I was not offended. Nobody could make me feel any worse.

Cathy had taken a seat on the row ahead of me, and when Mia began to speak, she turned around, her eyes darting between us like a ping-pong ball. She opened her mouth as if hoping to mediate the conversation.

I interrupted her. I couldn't bear to be defended for my mistake. "Cathy, it's fine. Mia and I are getting ready for the relay. You don't need to stay." I twisted my torso to let the lactic acid barrier in my abs and shoulders break down.

Cathy shut her mouth, then opened it again. "Okay. I'll be cheering at the end of lane five. I'm here if you want to talk before or after." Cathy leapt up from the bleachers and hurried away, glancing back over her shoulder at me.

"She's, like, obsessed with you or something." Mia snorted. "No way Rob and her actually dated. How'd he put up with her?"

I wrung my hair over Mia's toes in response.

"Hey!" Mia jumped back, glaring at me. "Bitch. You better not fuck up our relay," she said, shaking her toes like a wet dog, the chlorine droplets hitting my ankle. She moved into the hamstring stretch. Her leg kicked up next to me on the bleachers. Her foot was an inch from my thigh. The sole was wrinkled and pale, soaked for too long in water.

"I won't." I pushed at her heel with a finger, disgusted. "And get your gross feet away from me."

We lost the meet. It was close. If I hadn't been disqualified during my individual butterfly race, we would have earned enough points to win. I had swum my heart out during the relay, keeping my legs slammed shut, emerging from the pool as visibly fatigued as Rob did for all his races. My efforts there paid off—we beat the second-place team by five seconds. But the relay points weren't enough to make up the gap from my disqualification.

Jim was enraged he did not get his perfect season, and the team was devastated they had lost. They blamed me. Whenever I walked into the locker room, the girls would slam their lockers shut and scurry out. During team stretches on the pool deck, I sat alone, separate from everybody else. When we rested in the shallow end of the pool between sets, my lane mates floated on one side of the lane, I alone on the other. But I didn't need their shame because I shamed myself in their stead. I had never swum so horribly, and in the days after the disqualification, I stopped existing, stopped studying, stopped having any sort of facial expression other than stoic. I stopped eating. I sat immersed in the chatter of the cafeteria and offered my lunch to Cathy. What she did not eat, I threw away.

I could tell she was worried, but Cathy did not press. At home, I scraped my dinner into the trash can when my mother wasn't looking. I withered.

On Sundays, with no school or swim practice, instead of studying or hanging out with Cathy, I stayed home to watch and rewatch *Chungking Express* with my mother, like when I was a child. I cried every time Faye Wong reappeared at the bar in her flight attendant suit dragging her suitcase of missed connections behind her. I cried so much during and after the movie I had to change my pillowcase twice before falling asleep every night. My cheeks became scratched and tender from my tear tracks. Whenever I submerged myself in chlorine, my face burned with somber penitence. My tears dripped off my eyelashes, down my cheeks, and into my mouth. I began swishing peppermint mouthwash to alleviate the never-ending salty water of sorrow. My eyes were so swollen I wore sunglasses to school. My teachers didn't ask me to take them off for the same reason they did not bother me when I fell asleep during their lectures: I was a swimmer, a star athlete, a straight-A student. No need for their admonishments. Sometimes I cried so much at practice, I had to stop at a wall during sets to empty out my goggles. I cried because of my abject failure, because I had let Jim down, because real mermaids never failed to swim like I had. I was beginning to wonder if I would ever embrace mermaid at all.

Once, during a freestyle set at practice, I crashed into Luke's back because I couldn't see. I had been crying so hard my goggles filled and fogged up. Luke slapped the part of my cheek where I was most red and raw, and yelled at me to get out of the way or get out of the pool. Nobody defended me. Not Jim, who wanted to watch me suffer for my mistakes. Not Cathy, who, as always, was too timid to speak up in front of the entire team. I was the most hated swimmer on the team for losing the meet, and everyone wished they could slap me the way Luke had.

In my mental state, I was neither human nor athlete, but Jim still insisted I come to practice. To ensure I never made the mistake again, he forced me to bind my feet together in practice with rubber bands during butterfly kicking sets. At first the binding felt abnormal, uncanny; I endured rather than enjoyed. It was even hard to float.

Eventually, after a few practices, my body became used to having more of a tail rather than legs. I kicked butterfly faster and more comfortably with my legs tied together. To be unshackled and separate was to be incorrect. I was unrestrained when I was bound. Free. More like me.

I didn't want to face any teammates in the locker room after practice, and I wanted to be in the pool alone at least once every day. I hid out in the back room, shivering and damp among the junk, waiting for Jim to shut the pool lights off. Once everyone went home, I'd dive back into the pool, relishing the silence and the cool water crashing against my hurting head. I preferred the pool late in the evening when the chlorine was navy and the pool surface glassy. I'd come to rest atop a lane rope, my spine balanced on its line of disks, staring up at the ceiling, chlorine for company. These moments after practice, in the dark, alone, were sacred and divine. Though I believed in neither God nor organized religion nor Jesus, I imagined I was in church, experiencing my own sort of baptism. I'd pray to the Pool Gods and Poseidon as I reclined on the lane rope, my body half-submerged, inhaling the embrace of chlorine like it was the last drop of water left in the oasis before I died parched in the desert. I'd float alone in the dark, silent pool for hours until the school janitor entered and yelled at me to go home.

After a few days of giving up my lunch, Cathy caught on to my depression diet. She informed Jim, who already suspected I was not eating. Without regular intake of calories, I had lost quite a bit of muscle, and Jim could tell, especially considering he had mapped out every inch of my body ever since I was a child. Jim was already upset with me because of my endless crying, and so, frustrated at my lack of self-care, he told me, a week after the home meet, to leave and not come back until I was ready to swim fast and work hard.

I lied to my mother yet again, claiming practice was canceled because the pool needed to be cleaned, so she didn't ask why I came home straight after school and locked my bedroom door. Again I had tricked her into thinking I was studying, but instead I was lying in bed, the sheets coarse against my skin, craving the smoothness of water, staring at the mermaid shrine I had hung up against the far wall of my bedroom.

I started avoiding Cathy. I hated her pity and I hated her tattling. During the lunch period, instead of sitting in the cafeteria with her, I huddled in the library with the stacks of books I used to love. Friends I had given up in favor of the pool.

After four days of avoiding Cathy during lunch, she came to the library to find me.

"Hey." She walked directly to my desk. When I caught sight of her entering the library, I immediately gazed down at my textbook, pretending I hadn't seen her, freezing in case any flinch on my part would quicken her pace toward me. I cursed myself for taking off my sunglasses so I could read better. I had placed them in my backpack at my feet, far from arms' reach. My tear-crusted, red-rimmed eyes were exposed.

"Hey." I didn't look up from the integers in front of me. I was reviewing for my calculus test the next day.

"What's up?" she asked tentatively.

I held up my book, tapping the title with my finger while hiding my tear-crusted eyes, hoping she would take a hint.

Instead Cathy pressed against the edge of my desk. She wore our team sweats, and the excess cotton fabric spilled over the pressure of her body leaning on the wooden surface. She pushed the top edge of the book down, revealing my face. I dropped it back onto the desk in defeat.

"You're still crying?"

"How'd you guess I was in the library?" I asked by way of response.

"Of course you're here. You love books, right? And we're allowed to eat lunch here."

I ignored her.

"You look like shit," Cathy commented. "Like you haven't been using the fancy skincare lotion from Japan you and your mom are obsessed with." She lifted a hand, as if to brush my cheek. I shifted out of her reach.

Cathy dropped her arm by her side. Her fingers drooped. "Your skin looks like you were in a fight with a raccoon. And your eyes are swollen and bloodshot. You look so tired. Have you even slept?"

I sniffed, annoyed at her gentle care disguised as an insult, turning a page in my textbook as loudly as I could in the hope she would get the point I was too busy studying to have a conversation with her.

"Here. I brought you something." She rifled around in the duffel bag slung over her shoulder and pulled out a plastic bag. She turned it upside down, dumping its contents onto my desk.

I jerked backward with my book in hand to avoid the projectiles, wincing when the top of my neck hit my tall chair backrest. I rested my textbook spine down on my thighs, marking the page. I squinted at Cathy's ammunition and saw wrappers with white rabbits and Hello Kitty cats, boxes with sticks dipped in chocolate, rice crackers covered in sugar spots like snow. The snacks lay around me like my burial shroud.

"You brought—Pocky?" I asked in disbelief. I had anticipated Cathy yanking me out of the library by my ankles, or at least sitting with me until I got annoyed enough to push her out, but these gifts were unforeseen and rather appreciated, leading me to forget my commitment to a frosty attitude.

"Surprise!"

"Where did you get these? How did you know what to get?" I asked, amazed.

"I asked your mom to come with me to the Asian grocery store downtown. She showed me all your favorite snacks. We had fun! I told her it was a thank-you gift for helping me study for my biology test, which of course, thanks to you, I aced." Cathy winked and clapped, then dragged the vacant chair at the adjacent desk over to mine, depositing herself across from me. The chair legs screeched against the linoleum floor, and the librarian scowled at us from the entrance desk.

"I tried a few," Cathy said, poking around the snacks. "I like these Chinese fruit gummies the most." She held up a small shiny wrapper with a grape illustration.

"Those are Japanese," I corrected her. "The character lines are curvier."

Cathy brightened—she was unashamed about her mistake, and even my lackluster reply was better than none. "Well, there's more where those came from. We should go to the store together. It'll be fun."

"Nah."

"Why not? We can pick something we've both never tried before," she offered.

"I'd rather not," I said.

Instead of answering, Cathy picked up a snow rice cracker. She pulled the plastic wrapping off and began to lick the cracker, on the side with the hardened sugar spots.

"Are you still upset about the disqualification?" Cathy asked while lapping at the cracker, her pronunciation of each word twisted with her tongue out.

"What do you think?"

"Ren, please, I'm going to be blunt: You need to get over it." She shoved the cracker in her mouth and swallowed without chewing. "It's not your fault we lost the meet. We all swam terribly. Except Luke, but he always does well." She flapped the air, banishing Luke's consistent and insufferable excellence out of our conversation. "Besides, everyone's moved on already. No one's going to avoid you in the locker room anymore. We're too stressed for regionals to stay mad," she assured me.

"Wow. Thanks. How comforting," I said sarcastically.

"You're welcome." Cathy beamed. I softened. I could never resist her sunny disposition too long.

"The upcoming regionals will be my first one, remember? I finally qualified. I'm so excited to swim at the meet with you," she said. "I want you there. I need you there. I'm nervous for it. You'll be my regionals meet guide, okay?"

I grunted.

"Come back to practice?" She reached out and tucked a stray piece of hair around my ear, too fast for me to jerk back again. "Our team isn't the same without you."

I looked away. Her gestures, pleading, and gifts made me feel genial, a sensation I hadn't suffered in days. What was I without swimming, without the water, without her?

I sorted through the snacks and picked up a White Rabbit candy, one of my favorites since childhood. I unwrapped the sheer blue-and-white wrapper and placed the white rectangle on my tongue. The papery coating melted into a puddle of honeyed milk, coating my tastebuds.

"Fine," I huffed, the sugar and her generosity rendering me agreeable.

"Fine what?"

"Fine, I'll come back to practice," I said.


Jim greeted me with a butt-patting hug when I returned to practice. He hadn't yet forgiven me for my home meet disqualification, but we both knew he depended on my wins for regionals. I needed him; he needed me. It was a parasitic relationship neither of us could escape until its college recruitment conclusion.

I had one week left until regionals. I had already wasted two weeks crying. I exchanged my saltwater tears for chlorine pools. At practice, Jim recommenced the foot and leg binding. Using the heavy-duty, widest rubber bands he could find from the office supply store, we welded my legs together by rolling the bands up and around my ankles, my calves, and my thighs. I performed hours of butterfly kick in streamline, my bound legs propelling me across the pool with efficiency. I became so powerful kicking with my legs bound, I could beat most of my teammates who had free use of their arms and legs. My bottom half experienced a wrenching loss at the end of each practice, when I had to unroll the tight rubber bands down my legs—after such exhilaration in the water, it was unnatural to walk on solid ground unfettered. In the locker room, the rubber bands placed carefully in a gallon-size plastic bag, I'd massage my legs to remind the blood to flow, kneading the red streaks left across my skin like whip marks.

Jim had confirmed the Harvard recruiter, and a few others, would come to regionals to watch us perform. To watch *me*. Jim reminded us that their attendance did not assure recruitment. There were always other swimmers elsewhere to recruit, at different regionals meets, in southern or eastern or northern Pennsylvania, across the state border into Ohio, across the country. We were so easily replaceable, and for those of us who weren't in the top 0.01% of exceptionality for early recruitment like Luke, this was our one chance to show the judges what we could offer. The pressure was intense, with everybody anxiously discussing in the locker room before and after every practice about which recruiters wanted them. Yet I was calm. Focused. I did not trouble myself with locker room gossip. My head pounded at random intervals, and my legs threatened to disobey, yet I still reigned supreme over my agitated teammates. I had existed my entire life under a sort of pressure far greater than anything they could comprehend. This addition was nothing I couldn't swallow. And though I had taken two weeks off from training to lament my failure, I was ready. I had been ready since the very beginning.

Life became the absence of anything worth living. Broccoli, brown rice, chicken breast, homework, swim practice, anxious sleep. Instead of paying attention in class, I visualized victory. Not the race— Jim had warned us visualizing the actual race caused paralyzing anxiety on the day of. It was better to focus on the destination, not the journey.

I imagined the weight of the gold medal hanging from my neck, the thump of it against my breastbone. I imagined Cathy cheering for me at the end of my lane. I imagined the recruiters' astonishment, Jim's weepy pride, my parents'—*both* of my parents'—joy at the inevitable acceptance letter in the mailbox.

My brain no longer accepted a reality in which I would not win first place and drop time.

As regionals drew close, Jim insisted we go back to the beginning if we wanted to achieve greatness. He forced us to do technique drills, diving drills, flip turn drills, dryland drills. He said if we reviewed and remastered the basics, then we'd thrive in the real competition. "If, then" statements composed an athlete's life: If I spent hours practicing, then I'd drop seconds in the race; if I eschewed any sort of earthly pleasure—from food to sex to staying up late—then I'd find pleasure in the inevitable best time. And if I were to succeed at regionals, then I needed to go back to the beginning. If I wanted to win, then I'd need to go further than anyone else.

I'd need to go back to the very, very beginning. To why I started swimming.

I recalled why I had begged my mother to take me to tryouts—because of the book of mermaid mythology. I came home from practice each night and gazed at the mermaid stories and illustrations I had hung up on my bedroom wall years ago, torn from the original book I loved. The words and colors were faded with age, but everything was still intact, the paper pristine.

I traced my fingers over the sentences and faces composing my wondrous mermaids. The little mermaid who changed into air and light. The mermaid with the rainbow armor. The two water-snake-girlfriends. How effortlessly these mystical creatures swam through the pages of the book and back into the forefront of my consciousness. Mermaids were beautiful, and was I not also beautiful? Alluring? A creature of the water? Not of salt like the mermaids in the book, but of chlorine. Perhaps I could announce myself as the first. The first chlorine mermaid, to win first place in a pool. Fitting. I was always in first. My legend, cemented—humans would pass down my story through the ages, whispering around campfires in awe and fear. I'd be memorialized in athletic record books and folktale collections, and maybe, in the future, I'd even inspire a young girl like me to transcend too. And it dawned on me one night, when the rubber-band marks were vivid across my skin and my eye bags were dark and haggard, that mermaids would never be disqualified for their legs coming apart, like I, a girl who couldn't even keep her legs together for her best swimming event, had been. If mermaids, the most successful swimmers of all, owned single tails instead of two legs, then wouldn't chlorine mermaids carry tails too? I frantically schemed how I could achieve this conquest. How I could become.

I realized I would have to force my body to *embrace pain*, one of Jim's favorite mantras.

I thought of the sewing kit nestled in my mother's desk drawer. I mused over my mother's unyielding stitches when she repaired my clothes, hemmed my pants, constructed a new tablecloth.

A tight seam. Like how my legs should be.

I asked my mother if she could teach me to sew. She agreed, because we hadn't enjoyed an activity together in a while, and she was lonely with a husband in China and a daughter in the pool. We practiced sewing with *Chungking Express* playing in the background. Faye Wong labored at the fast-food fryer while I stitched sloppily. At first, I couldn't sew in a straight line, and my stitches were too far apart. My hands shook from fatigue and my eyes ached from squinting. I had to redo more stitches than I made. But I was a quick, disciplined learner, faithful that repetition would bring perfection—a mindset cultivated from endless laps in the pool.

I was soon able to make tight stitches. I moved from cotton shirts to thicker denim, using the thrifted clothes I had outgrown and stuffed in the back of my closet, and then to chiffon and velvet. The more slippery the fabric, the harder to sew.

Exuberant over my quick progress, I researched medical stitches, the next step in my sewing journey. I settled on the lock-stitch suture, used in intestinal surgery, where the needle was passed through the loop of the preceding stitch. The stitching variation, allowing equal tension throughout, would be stronger than a simple quick pass.

I moved out of the living room and into my bedroom, with the door locked. My mother was disappointed I left her side so soon, but my sewing forays required privacy. I sewed and sewed and sewed. I practiced and practiced and practiced some more. I gave up sleep. When my eyelids began to droop, I'd yell *GO GO GO JIAO YOU JIAO YOU JIAO YOU ADD OIL ADD OIL ADD OIL*, the commands echoing in my head, taking on Jim's scratchy baritone voice instead of my own, and it was the shift in pitch compelling my eyes to jerk open, my fingers to tighten on the needle and continue weaving the pointed silver instrument through the fabric. When I needed my body to commit to an action, I commanded myself in Jim's voice, an effective technique.

My sewing never caused me pain. As an extra precaution, I added another pill of ibuprofen to my diet plan before I began the stitches each night, but the pain in my head outshone any pain I felt on my body. Loose strands of threads covered the floor of my bedroom like a threadbare rug. There was no fear of my mother finding out—I had demanded she stop entering my room so I could concentrate on studying, and she agreed, terrified of doing anything interrupting a potential A+ and the diploma she fantasized was already framed above our nonexistent mantelpiece.

When my fingers started to throb from the needle, I would then take breaks to worship the mermaid folktales and illustrations, kneeling underneath the pages hung up on my wall, bending my forehead to the floor, my tears puddling underneath my cheekbones, praying to the Mermaid Gods to guide my path. I begged Nüwa to sculpt me a beautiful mermaid tail with the same magic she had used to sculpt human beings. I implored Ariel to spare me her curse of stabbing knife pain whenever she set foot on land. I reread the Passamaquoddy tale until I could repeat it word for word, chanting each sentence under my breath as my needle moved forward. I craved those two water-snake-girlfriends' adventures. All day long, they splashed and swam outdoors together; they were wanton, witchlike girls, liking eccentric and forbidden ways, relinquished of their stupid earthly conflicts. I pleaded for a partnership like theirs.

Eventually, weary from the intensity of my prayers, the pages of my mermaid book began to wrinkle and fall off. I crumpled the fallen paper into balls and shoved them in my mouth, chewing and swishing the damp tatters around my cheeks. Upon near dissolution from my saliva, I then swallowed the remnants of the stories, cherishing how the sludge felt sliding down my throat, swaying to the rumbles of my stomach when the ink-depicted tails hit my gut.

This was my solo version of a pre-meet pasta party. My pre-victory banquet. My digestion of my girlhood dissolution. Other mermaids consumed into me, nourishing my own, soon to burst free.

# Fourteen

The time before big swim meets was always rife with tension, both exhilarating and tiring. We'd roughhouse more than usual, punching one another in an effort to oust the tension, but the energy would merely move from one's fist to the other's bicep, then circulate within our team like hurricane diagrams. Our bodies were wound with pre-meet jitters, made ethereal with the lack of lactic acid, then ejected by the week of rest. In case any lactate lingered, we lay on the floor with our legs pointed upward against the wall, hoping the acid would follow gravity's directions and flow down through our muscles and out our pores. We wanted to be pure and clean.

The tension culminated on the day before the meet. We never did much at practice, a few dives here and there to time our reactions, some half-pool sprints to remind our muscles of speed, yet Jim would throw more chairs than usual, and our captains would bark encouragement more disheartening than motivating. When Jim let us go, with a few tense directives about getting enough sleep and controlling how much we should eat at the pasta party later, we split into two groups, girls and boys, to congregate in our respective locker rooms for the final night ceremony.

I looked forward to the ceremony every year. I loved the rousing speeches, the jittery shaving, the steam of the hot locker room showers, the proximity to other girls' naked bodies.

We sat cross-legged, dripping wet, on the tiled floor of the communal showers, the shower heads hanging above us like temple deities. The area was the one space in the locker room large enough to hold all of us sitting in a circle. There was Ally, Mia, Cathy, the rest of our teammates, all of us as one. During these speeches and shaving parties, we became a part of something bigger than ourselves. A team. We were to rotate clockwise and read whatever inspiring words we hoped would encourage victory for the next day.

Cathy had recited Eminem's "Lose Yourself," specifically the part about Mom's spaghetti, because the plan was to go eat our moms' spaghetti at the pasta party afterward. She remixed the lyrics to end on a more uplifting note related to swimming: *the best time will come out, the competition's chokin' now, best times for all, blaow!* She had excitedly practiced with me during study hall, asking me with wide eyes after every bar if she had gotten the cadence correct. To me, her speech was basic and uncreative, as "Lose Yourself" was every swimmer's classic hype song, but her enthusiasm was cute, especially because it was her first year qualifying for the regionals meet. I refused to dampen her excitement.

I had debated reciting a basic popular speech from Michael Jordan, the classic *I've missed more than nine thousand shots in my career.*

*I've lost almost three hundred games. Twenty-six times I've been trusted to take the game-winning shot and missed. I've failed over and over and over again in my life. And that is why I succeed.* I loved Jordan's speech because it reminded me of my many failures—the disqualification, the concussion, the Truth or Dare game, the summer of my stoner brain— and how these traumas would help me succeed into mermaid. But Cathy had reminded me Ally used the exact quote last year, with the girls going wild, slamming their palms down onto the tiles, thunder echoing around the cavernous showers. I couldn't copy Ally's performance—I was better than her, both in intelligence and in swimming, and therefore would need to come up with something more appropriate to my standards.

The idea for my speech had burst through to me at three A.M. the night before, while I was sewing. I had immediately dropped to my knees in front of the mermaid shrine and kowtowed in blessed thanks for their divine inspiration.

I refused to tell Cathy what my speech was, despite her endless badgering at study hall earlier. It would have to be a surprise, or else the effect would fall flat. I sensed she was nervous on my behalf— she hoped to waylay any potential teasing from our teammates by dissuading me from speaking in Chinese proverbs or reading some medieval ballad from a book of poems. Perhaps if I didn't have my sewing plan, I would have confessed my speech to her, or at least recited it once under her watchful ears and eyes. But with the recognition of my mermaid tail soon to be, I no longer cared about whether my teammates would make fun of me. They were unimportant humans with tiny minds, and I was more expansive than they could comprehend.

I insisted on going last, as the climax, and because I was a fast swimmer, they let me. My speech was marvelous, almost too grand for the tiled, crusty locker room in which we sat, and too bold for the cowardice latent in my teammates' bodies, their ears anxiously cocked toward me. I spoke of being caught between ambition and duty, between the darkness and the light:

*Why, our ambition makes us one. 'Tis too large for one mind. O God, we could be bounded in a nutshell and count ourselves queens of infinite space. Our dreams are indeed ambition, for the very substance of the ambitious are the shadows of our dreams. And we dreamed of touching the wall first, of breaking records, of reaching our best times. We hold ambition so airy and light, so deep and still, that we will dive into the water and become monarchs and outstretched heroes.*

I sat back down and stared at them, expectant, but I received neither applause nor thunderous palm floor slamming. Everyone was silent. Cathy tapped the tiles with her nails in a timid show of support, a sound more like scuttling insect legs than enthusiastic cheering.

"Let's start shaving," Mia announced, interrupting the awkwardness. Mia grabbed the new razors and shaving-cream cans bought by our parents' swim team association and began to distribute them, while the rest of us coupled off.

"Wow. Nice speech, I think," Cathy, my shaving partner, said to me. We didn't need to ask; our pairing was assumed.

I sighed. "Nobody got it. I edited it from a conversation between Rosencrantz and Hamlet. It's supposed to stoke ambition. I love the line 'I could be bounded in a nutshell and count myself as a ruler of infinite space'—there's a lot of hope in those few words. Like I am bound, but I can envision myself infinite." I left unsaid the way in which I would become infinite.

I sorted through the pile of shaving paraphernalia Mia had dropped off next to us and picked up the shaving cream. I squirted a wiggle of foam into my palm, lathering it between my hands, covering my legs with the soft white bubbles.

"Shakespeare?" Cathy asked.

"Yes," I said. I frowned in concentration, my razor streaking over my calves. I had to be careful over the shinbone, where the bone edged the skin, with less muscle and fat to protect it from the razor blade.

"Was it a happy ending?"

"*Hamlet?*" I asked, incredulous, eager to capitalize on an opportunity to explain a cultural reference to Cathy, no matter how outdated, but her question and its framing made me pause. "Maybe. Depends on how you define happy endings."

We had turned on the showers to assist our shaving, and steam rose from the tiles, cloaking us in translucent robes. The water's pitter-patter hit the tiles with the thud of a rainstorm, the kind coming on suddenly, bursting through the clouds with the force of hail. We lathered our bodies in shaving cream, suiting up in hefty layers of foam, running the razor over legs first, then tops of feet, then arms, then hands, each finger carefully mown, then armpits, then vagina. The back, shaved in pairs, last. For most of us, our back hair was invisible to the naked eye. But invisibility did not mean it wasn't there—it was merely cloaked, and it was necessary to shave off even the hint of it, along with the dead skin accumulated since last year's shaving. We had no shame at shaving parties. The ritual eased the knots in our muscles. We had to make room for new cells, to make the skin feel like a shark's, ready to chop through chlorine-infested waters. We dipped our razors into the caps of shaving cream turned upside down, filled with water, where ditched hair and remnants of shaving cream clouds floated on top. We emptied out the dirty liquid and replaced it with clean shower water after each razor drag—one inch of leg clogged the blades past usability. It had been months of abstinence, after all. We left no square millimeter of skin unshaved. Accuracy was crucial for a sport measured in milliseconds.

We allowed ourselves one concession: Though Jim insisted using shaving cream led to a lower-quality shave, it was too painful to go without. The sharp razor blades would draw blood if we didn't protect ourselves. The goal was not blood but victory—though Jim insisted they were identical.

"You ready?" I asked. I would be shaved first, our partnership's traditional order.

Despite the steam rising from the showers, Cathy shivered without the blanket of her body hair.

"Yes," she said.

I unleashed my arms from the straps of my swimsuit, wiggling it down to rest at the lower half of my belly. Even in the shower steam, my ab lines were visible and defined. I sat on the tiles, knees up to my chest. My breasts were pressed flat and hidden against my thighs. With the can of shaving cream, Cathy drew two upside-down U's, then an inverted triangle, connecting the shapes into a heart. Then: her hand against my spine, rubbing the heart into a rectangle.

Cathy shaved in silence. I pretended she was an artist wielding a paintbrush, drawing delicate lines of the female form on a canvas of skin, me her muse. She ran the razor up, down, side to side, across my back—an effective shave meant moving the razor opposite of its growth direction, and because back hair grew fierce, without rhyme or reason, our razor would dance wild too. It was slow and intimate work, the back exposed to a blade held in a teammate's hands. Did other girls, non-swimming girls, ever shave their bodies communally, the way we did?

I shivered with each new stroke of the razor.

"I'll never get used to this feeling," I said.

"Really? I love it," she said.

In my peripheral vision, Cathy dipped the razor back into our shaving cream cap where my discarded back hair floated atop the water. The debris reminded me of the many branches and dead flies in the pool Ess and I had once shared.

"It feels like a cold egg is being cracked down my back," I said.

"It's a unique feeling. And I like doing it too. The shaving, I mean," Cathy said.

I dipped my head forward to rest on my forearms, encircling my legs. "It's your first time at regionals tomorrow—are you nervous? Do you feel ready for the 100 breaststroke?"

"Yes," Cathy said.

"Yes that you're nervous, or yes that you're ready?" I asked.

"Both, I guess," Cathy said as she carved another rectangle in my back.

"You've trained hard all season. You're going to swim well."

"It's fine if I don't. Swimming isn't as important to me as it is to you."

I hesitated into the protective cocoon of my tangled forearms, as though I were about to confess a great truth kept hidden from her for years.

"Lucky. I always wished I was more like you," I admitted.

She snickered. "What do you mean?"

"Well, no offense, but you're a slower swimmer who isn't thinking about swimming as a way to get into college, or to get ahead in life—the way I am."

She didn't respond. My lungs began to constrict, and the steam choked my airways. Our teammates' laughter and the water droplets beating the tiles spun in my eardrums, turning demonic, and I pressed my palms against the floor, seeking an anchor. I rose my head out of my arms and gasped, desperate for air, the cap on the pressure I had bottled inside me bursting open.

"Cathy, I'm so nervous. I feel like I can't breathe. I feel like I've been breaking down all year. Like my body is a machine I haven't been able to get fixed. I'm constantly thinking about fucking up. About not getting first place. About gaining time. Did you hear the Harvard recruiter is coming tomorrow? Jim is freaking out. He says tomorrow's race is my best chance to get in. I didn't even tell my parents. No need to make them get all excited over something I might fail at."

She gave a noncommittal grunt. "You'll do great. You can surprise them with your success," she said.

I was stunned by her brevity. Had I offended her? Perhaps Cathy was unwilling to agree with a characterization of an ingroup and outgroup based on talent, though this very distinction had always upheld the social fabric of our swim team.

I twisted my torso around to face Cathy. The sudden movement of my back and neck forced her hand and razor to make a zigzag pattern in the cream, ruining her methodical lines.

"Hey! Watch it. I could've cut you." Annoyed, she sat back, dropping the razor blade-first into the water cup to indicate she would not continue until I turned around.

"Listen, don't tell anyone, but I'm going to do something tomorrow to ensure I get my best time and wow the recruiter. No one's ever done it before, and it's not in the referee handbook, I checked. There's no way an official can disqualify me." I bared my teeth, my lips drawing back, the pulse of my heart in my throat. My cultivated ambition, made up of thread and mermaids and shimmering water, threatened to spiral out of me. I widened my eyes, trying to express my plans for tomorrow with my gaze. I wanted Cathy to understand. Where I was going. Who I would become. *What* I would become.

What I already was in all but form.

The steam collected in puffs around my mouth as my chest heaved.

"Are you sure?" Cathy's face was screwed up in concentration as she tried to understand my intentions. The crease between her eyebrows was so deep the water dripping from her hairline rested there precariously instead of trickling down. "I mean, they never test us for anything. But what if it's bad for you? Don't forget about those breast enhancement rumors," she said, crossing her arms.

Cathy believed I was talking about some kind of performance-enhancing drug. Some of the wrestlers at our school were rumored to be taking steroids, and Rob had warned us if steroids were taken without exercise, the pectoral muscles would droop and cultivate fat, like real breasts. Cathy's and my breasts had been flattened long ago by the tight spandex of our swimsuits, and so we joked that perhaps after swimming was over and we could laze about in peace, we could try steroids to regrow the womanhood we had lost.

My heart, no longer beating fast from the venting of pressure and the exhilaration of confession, pulsed sluggishly with disappointment. I didn't bother correcting her. Cathy never understood me. She would remain oblivious, misinterpreting my hints.

"Don't be ridiculous. It's not toxic. It'll hurt, but you miss one hundred percent of the shots you don't take, blah blah blah, suffering is optional, pain is weakness leaving the body, blah blah blah," I said, and winked, and she let out a small giggle. My jokes were references to our past team T-shirts, which had phrases like PAIN IS WEAKNESS LEAVING THE BODY and SUFFERING IS TEMPORARY BUT GLORY IS FOREVER screen-printed in blazing orange letters on the back. Both these prior slogans were at least better than this year's T-shirt: SO YOU'RE SAYING I HAVE A CHANCE? The question riffed off the *Dumb and Dumber* scene where Jim Carrey insisted even a one out of a million chance was still a chance to get with a girl who repeatedly said no. A classic Jim joke. The parents got the reference, but we didn't. We were too young to have seen the movie or understand the humor in nonconsensual sexual quotes.

I turned back to the locker room wall and faced away from her. My senses righted, sharpened with the clarity of failed interpretation.

"Look, I got all the supplies already. Don't tell anyone, okay? I wanted to tell you because you're my best friend on the team, and it feels more real to tell someone," I said, my fingers curling over my calves.

Cathy brought the razor to my back again, tracing the creases of my lats. "I won't tell," Cathy promised, scraping white foam off my back the way a painter's knife slashes a ruined canvas.

To Cathy's annoyance, I skipped the team dinner. I went home directly after the shaving party, shivering in the absence of body hair. My convulsions and goose bumps were eager signs of the impending regionals meet. My *Hamlet* speech had flopped, but I didn't care. I was queen of my own infinite space.

I prepared for my solo pre-meet ritual by sliding on headphones and taking eight deep breaths. I had developed the eight-based routine when I was eight years old and followed it ever since, eight being a lucky number in Chinese. The meditative actions soothed me, centered me, calmed my nervous mind, and ensured I'd never forget anything vital like goggles or my swimsuit for the meet.

"沉醉" by Faye Wong blared through my headphones. I sifted around our hallway closet and grabbed two towels: a fluffy bath towel for drying off, and a long beach one for sitting on the bleachers. I folded them against the floor of my duffel as a base. I tucked my folded team warmup jacket atop the towels, patting the pile of fabric eight times. I tucked my racing suit, the most delicate, vital, and expensive of my swim bag items, into the crease between the towel and my jacket. Layers for protection. Then I nestled my head armor—my cap, my goggles, and my quickly emptying bottle of ibuprofen—into the arms of my jacket, wrapping the sleeves around each other like lovers. I stroked the bundle eight times.

My gold earphones matching our team colors went into the duffel front pocket. My razor rested in the left pocket for the last-minute shaves. I rubbed eight clockwise circles on both pockets.

However, that night before the fateful juniors' regionals meet, I made one change to my ritual. After the earphones and the razor, I opened my duffel's right pocket and slid in my mother's Shi Ba Zi Zuo vegetable cleaver, the caiduo, thinner than her meat cleaver, because it was meant for more careful work—and what required more care than my tail-to-be?

Next to the knife, I placed a small metal tea leaves box stolen from my kitchen cabinets. Inside the box were five ibuprofen pills, a spool of black thread, and my needle. The box interior carried the lingering odor of jasmine green tea leaves, and I hoped the thread would absorb the aromas so I would smell of tea fragrance and chlorine. I tapped the pocket eight times after zipping it closed. I placed the duffel bag by the door leading to the garage.

I kissed my mother good night eight times on each cheek.

I stomped upstairs to my bedroom, hopping eight times on the top step.

I undressed.

I kneeled in front of the last few mermaid pages stuck on my bedroom wall, saved from my swallowing by the sheer strength of their old tape and pushpins. I touched my forehead to the floor eight times. I repeated my thanks eight times to the mermaid deities for their blessings.

I got into bed.

I visualized: the gold medal, the recruiters' acceptance, Jim's victory, my parents' glee. Cathy's pride. My legs. My metamorphosis. My tail.

I fell asleep smiling, the first night of true rest in weeks.

# Fifteen

I sat with my legs splayed out on the floor of the single shower stall second to left. I had been to the university pool enough to memorize which stalls' nozzles had the best water pressure. Once, Ally and Mia had wrestled for the right to use the stall I now sat in, and Mia slipped, hitting her head on the floor. She was diagnosed with a minor concussion, and I instructed her to obey her doctor, or else— my head had twinged in agreement when the advice left my mouth.

Today, my head was calm. Blissful. Ready.

It was quiet enough inside my stall, allowing me to concentrate on the task ahead. I could still hear traces of the other few girls in the locker room, fumbling around their bags or flushing the toilet. One girl was sitting on the bench sobbing to her teammate about her failed race, but crying swimmers were such a common occurrence at high-pressure swim meets that grief blended indistinctly into the scenery. Though the tumult of the swim meet outside was suppressed within the stall doors, I could distinguish the occasional chirrup of a coach whistle and the low beep of the starting horn, reminding me where I would go after I transformed.

I turned the shower to the highest heat setting. The water hit me in a concentrated target, a dull thud. I would achieve my physical goal more easily if my skin and surroundings stayed dry, but emulating a mermaid-like watery environment would carve an easier path for my mental transcendence. Swimming had taught me the best results came when the mental and the physical worked together.

The knife, needle, pills, and thread lay between my thighs. I had ditched the metal tea box and cloth outside the stall. I threw back the pills, catching water in my mouth to help swallow. I inspected the gleaming sharp needle tip. I picked up the thread and brought it to my nose: odorless. I was disappointed, but not dissuaded, that the thread had failed to absorb the scent of tea. I threaded the black string through the needle's eye without pause or mistake. I had practiced the movements for many nights.

I was calm. Years of swimming had taught me to remain undisturbed in the face of great anticipation and adversity. My hands were steady. Pain would not come from sewing my legs together. Pain came from Jim's 8x200 butterfly descend red punishment set. From disqualifications. From concussions. From losing.

Pain came from remaining human.

I was already wearing my competition swimsuit. Cathy had helped me slide it onto my body before warmups. It took nearly ten minutes to wrap the straps over my shoulders, and she had noticed my suit was too small, tentatively asking if I wanted her help in stretching it out before my race. I snapped at her. *Are you stupid? It's none of your business.* I had specifically bought a suit smaller than my regular size so I could wear it for longer, as I suspected I wouldn't have time to change my clothes before leaving to find my mermaid family after my swim. And my mother had agreed to buy a smaller size, not because she knew I was planning to leave but because when the suit inevitably stretched out, I would still be able to use it, instead of spending the money on a new one.

I regretted my outburst when I saw Cathy's lips tremble, like she was about to cry. I had wanted her to have a fun experience at her first regionals meet, and I cursed myself for making her upset. I hoped when Cathy saw my tail, she'd forgive me—mermaids and myths were given more leeway than girl friends.

The Fastskin LZR's straps dug into my shoulders as I hunched over on the floor. If I lifted the strap, I'd spy permanent indents. I poked at the fat, skin, and muscle spilling out from the thigh sleeves. I had no choice but to prick through the suit's sharkskin-mimicking nylon. I'd ruin the compression, but my mermaid tail would be faster than any swimsuit anyway. I would transform into the first mermaid with a Fastskin LZR top instead of a shell bikini top—much more practical for the water.

*Sorry for ruining the suit, Mother,* I thought. I giggled out loud, catching some shower water. I choked. I spat it out, along with some of my saliva.

I began.

Near the top of my inner thigh, with my left hand, I pinched a centimeter of flesh between my pointer and thumb, then expanded my fingers into an L-shape, stretching out my skin to create a smooth path for the cleaver. When stretched this way, skin did not look like skin, but like the still waters of the pool, waiting for a diver to ripple and break its smooth surface.

I gripped the knife with my right hand, then positioned the blade onto my stretched skin.

I sliced.

I winced, more a performance than a reaction, because nothing hurt. I was numb.

My skin fractured open like an earth fissure, a crimson canyon, from which burst forth foot-high poppies, pulsating gently to the tune of my heartbeat. Scarlet petals oozed from my carved thigh. Each poppy followed gravity, forming a river eroding my skin, running downstream. The blood swirled with the puddled water on the shower floor, a garden of diluted pink blooms. I was thankful I kept the shower running, washing the blood away so I could see my carving. Yet the metallic odor of blood remained, mixing with the sweaty, moldy smell of the locker room, the faint chlorine tang leftover from the endless swimmer bodies who had showered before in this stall.

I had purposely slanted the knife, creating a skin flap rather than a clear incision. I flipped over the flap, looking inside my cut. If I squinted, I could nearly see faint globes of something white and yellow wiggling amongst my bloody inner thigh, like maggots squirming around rotten slabs of meat—I wondered if this was the fascia Jim had always lectured us about when we were stretching, the web of connective tissue vital to keeping our muscles limber and loose.

I dropped the knife and picked up my needle, piercing it through the skin flap as easily as my mother would cut through the sponge cakes from the Asian grocery store downtown. Human skin was nothing. A delicate layer of false protection. So light. So thin.

I pulled the flap over gently to the other thigh, then drew the needle and thread through my muscle, tying the knot, beginning the first stitches. I picked up my knife again and cut another skin flap, warm blood gushing out only to whirl down the shower drain. I drew the needle through this new flap, then pulled it to the other thigh again.

I watched my hands move, mechanical. I was the third party, the observant bystander. The teammate on the sidelines.

Slice, pierce, pull, slice, pierce, pull.

Left leg, right leg, left leg, right leg.

On I went, working methodically down my thighs like they were another biology multiple-choice bubble-sheet exam with easy questions. The steam from the hot shower began to rise, obscuring my vision, and I began accidentally pricking my needle into the wrong spots on my fingers and legs, tiny rubies of blood joining the poppies. I waved the air, dispersing hot clouds, and the rubies went flying, splattering the shower walls with crimson spots.

I worked down my legs, leaving mermaid tail in my wake, though my hands were getting tired and shaky from the careful work, the needle imprinting into my finger pads from my tight grip. It did not help, as I moved farther down, that my shinbone grew close to my skin surface. I stabbed myself too deeply multiple times, the reverb of needle-striking-bone coursing up my arm. It hurt. Like sea urchins had punctured me up and down my lower legs, the sharp pain traveling through my inner network of nerves, up to the left side of my chest, then down again to my fingertips.

I shook. Paused. Slapped myself on the cheek, imprinting misty red marks on my face. Pushed myself to keep going. Reminded myself I had chugged pain relievers before embarking on this journey. How dare I feel anything but salivation for glory?

The black thread tightened. My legs welded shut, and the crossed thread began to resemble overlapping diamonds. My mermaid scales, my tail, emerging inch by inch. My long black hair dropped out of its bun, splaying its strands down my back and around my face. I could no longer distinguish between my hair and the thread. They were made of the same color and thickness, and so my mermaid scales were made of me.

I stopped when the needle reached my ankles. I tied a neat knot to ensure the stitches would stay in place. Bending my top half farther down, I ripped off the dangling extra thread with my teeth.

I sat back on my hands and admired my embroidery. I knew that my scales, so intricately formed from flesh and thread, were sophisticated enough to make any mermaid I admired in the book profusely complimentary.

I left the bloodstained needle, knife, and near-empty spool of thread in the stall. I'd return for them after I swam—I had inherited my mother's habit of zero waste, from drying plastic baggies to reusing food scraps, and there was no need to waste any of her sewing materials. I kept the shower running, hoping the water would wash out the bloodstains from the thread and the floor. I didn't want to bother the janitor.

I gripped the stall door and heaved myself up. I hopped, experimenting with my balance. My mermaid tail coursed with pleasure. The two sticks I once owned, those measly human legs, had vanished. How had I survived my seventeen years balancing atop such sluggish mortal twigs? I suspected if I ever grew feet again, I would indeed be thrust with sharp knives with each step.

I moved out of the shower stall toward the locker-room door, leading to the pool deck. My tail shimmered with my undulating gait. With its emergence, I was clunky on land, but I didn't mind. It was worth the clumsy hopping. I'd become elegant as soon as I dove into the water.

The noise of the swim meet resurfaced.

Cheers of the parents in the bleachers.

The coaches' whistles.

*Swimmers, take your mark.*

I snapped on my swim cap. The pool auditorium roared, its brightness disorienting after the darkness of the locker room. I heard gasps, and I saw minuscule people rushing out of my way, clearing my path forward like commoners would for royalty.

I sniffed the air for chlorine—I was so close.

A few more inconsequential heats.

A dive off the blocks.

Then I would be home again, in the water, where I belonged.

# Sixteen

## CATHY

Dear Ren,

I think you haven't been reading my previous letters, because I haven't received any responses from you. I refuse to accept the possibility you would read my letters and ghost me afterward, so I'm choosing to suspect my messages in bottles are getting lost along the way. Maybe the creek washes the bottles ashore before they can sink. Maybe the caps of the bottles weren't sealed well, and every word I wrote was waterlogged into indecipherable black splatters of ink. Or, maybe mermaids don't read letters on paper, and you communicate via bubbles instead. I'm not sure.

But writing to you has helped me feel better after your absence. It feels like a conversation with you, albeit one-sided. So I'll keep going, for now. Send me a sign if you can.

*I keep reliving the moments after you sewed your legs together. I sift through my jagged memories, hoping to find some sort of clue that will show me where you've swum off to, or if there was anything I could have done differently. I've rewound the tapes in my head so many times now, I'm not sure I can notice anything new.*

*I regret I didn't see you come out of the locker room first. Maybe, if I was the first, I could've run up and swept you away in my arms, and we could've escaped straight from the meet, avoiding all the bullshit afterward. But alas, I was sitting on our team bleachers, alone and distracted, half visualizing my 100 breaststroke race, and half searching for you in the pool. You had disappeared without warning, and I wondered if you were warming up, having switched lanes without my knowledge.*

*I'm still angry that Ally, instead of me, was the first teammate to see you. She stood directly across the locker room entrance. When you came hopping out of the locker room, Ally nudged Luke, who was stretching his quad and standing next to her, as usual—later, after you were carted away by the ambulance, Ally said in hushed tones you were hopping out of the locker room like a bunny, ignorant of the blood trails you left behind in your wake.*

*Then Luke nudged Jim, whose face was engrossed in his clipboard checking the upcoming heats. Jim dropped his clipboard in shock when he caught sight of you and your legs. Later, I found his pages wet and clumped on the damp pool deck. The black ink announcing heats and swimmer names mixed with the chlorine and the red of your blood, rendering both unintelligible, as if the upcoming races understood they would not happen, and so sought to destroy any record of their existence.*

*It was Coach Jim who stopped your race before it began.*

*I'm sorry.*

*I should have tried to hold him back.*

*But Jim is a heavy man. Even with my swimmer muscles, there's no way I would've been strong enough to contain him.*

*Thanks to Jim, you never swam at regionals with your legs sewed together. You never had the chance to prove whether what you did was right or not. I still muse over how fast you might have gone that day. It was always a joy to watch you swim, how your movements were never stilted, but smooth like real ocean waves, the way you lapped your opponents in any event longer than eight laps. With your legs sewed together, I bet you would have flown off the blocks and into the air, out of the auditorium, away into the sky, swimming through clouds by way of their tiny water droplets.*

*Before the announcer could whisper into the microphone, Jim roared at the officials to stop the race with his fiercest big belly voice, the voice he used when he wanted to terrify us most, the voice warning us he was going to throw a chair warmed from his ass at our heads. The officials were shocked, never before interrupted in such a fierce manner. They complied.*

*Jim barreled from his end of the pool to yours, his sneakers squeaking and sliding on the pool deck, knocking over four swimmers from other teams in the process—on purpose I bet, because Jim was always searching for an excuse to harm our enemies. He scooped you up, your body squirming, and he carried you from the blocks to the aluminum bleachers, where I was sitting in shock. He laid you down like an offering before Poseidon, placing your head tenderly on the sacrificial table of my thighs. You were so heavy. Sometimes when I'm sitting down, I feel a heavy weight on my thighs, and I look down, expecting to see* your head, but there's nothing, just my skin, and all the muscle and bone and fat it hides—you've become my phantom limb.

You were jerking around, twisting your body, flopping up and down the shaking bleachers like a fish out of water; terrified, goaded on by Jim's panic, I reached down and wrapped an arm around your neck in a headlock, with my other arm around your waist, trying to keep you still, but you kept squirming, your arms waving wildly, reaching for the pool, your hands clutching at air, aimed toward the water. I remember staring aghast at the flaps of flesh that had slightly come undone from your thrashing, crimson pooling in your scale grooves until it overflowed and dripped onto the vibrating bleacher seats, puddling underneath my thighs, my suit soon wet and warm from both the pool water and your blood. The smell of chlorine mixed with blood made me nauseated, as did the sight of your gory tail, but I smothered my rising vomit and looked away, desperately searching for help in the form of a parent or another coach.

What I locked onto was the recruiter.

He was clambering up the auditorium stairs, on his way out instead of coming to check if you were all right. From my angle below the auditorium seating, he was as small as an ant. I had entertained the notion before I saw him that the recruiter would be a giant, at least with a body size representative of the power he wielded over you, but he was puny. What a stupid man.

You were gasping from my chokehold, and I loosened my grip enough for you to start moaning, My tail, my tail, my tail. Not in pain, like everyone believed. I understand now you were moaning in desire, in need, in yearning. To test the new mermaid tail. To drop time. To show the recruiter you belonged.

*I wasn't strong enough to hold Jim back from stopping your race. But I was stupidly brave enough to hold you back from freedom. And for that, I'm sorry.*

*Luke called the ambulance. It arrived, sirens blaring and tires screeching, within four minutes, coming from the university hospital a mile away across campus. Jim called your mother, who was at home, the only parent to not come cheer us on at regionals. Between your screams, I could hear your mother's panicked voice crackling from Jim's cell phone—first she asked if the ambulance was in-network, and then she asked if you were okay. Jim yelled at her to drive to the university hospital on Dithridge Street, hung up, then hurried to join us. Neither I nor Jim escaped being targets of your flailing fists, until Jim finally seized your wrists, pinning them to the hard metal bleachers until the EMTs sprinted inside and took over.*

*Ren, when you told me about your plan at the shaving party, I didn't expect something so visceral. I wasn't prepared for the sight of your legs bloody and knitted together in diamonds, skin pulled taut. So how could I stand the sight of your thighs, calves, and knees fused together? Especially when those thighs, calves, and knees were part of a girl I loved?*

*Ren, I loved you when you were girl. I admit it, freely.*

*And I love you now when you are mermaid.*

It's okay, you'll be okay, *I whispered to you, my arms locked around you, my eyes fixed resolutely on the pool ahead.*

*You quit your chant of* My tail, my tail, my tail. *You began to whisper,* Let me go, Cathy. Let me go, Cathy. Cathy, Cathy, Cathy . . .

*My name. Nobody has ever said my name the way you do. A breathy exhalation after the hard C, a tongue dragging across teeth for* thee.

Every time someone calls my name, a fist clenches over my heart, yearning to hear it from your mouth instead.

Every night before bed, I try to recall your voice. A lullaby of sorts, to soothe myself to sleep. Yet restful slumber eludes me. I remain exhausted. Worse, I have nightmares—Ren, I've never dreamt so vividly in my life since you've left:

At first, in the days after you sewed your legs, these nightmares were about swimming. I dreamt about everything that could go wrong—of miscounting my strokes during the 100 backstroke and crushing my head against the wall while attempting to do a flip-turn, my brain leaking out of my ears; of misaiming my hand during the 100 butterfly, catching the lane rope instead of the water, the plastic rings shredding my skin to pieces; of missing my alarm for morning practice, pressing snooze three times too many, and then arriving so late practice had already ended, Jim throwing a chair at my head in retaliation, knocking it clean off, my head sitting on the pool floor staring up at my headless body with a worm's eye view; of ripping my $300 suit in the crotch right before I bent over for my dive; of swimming the 200 breaststroke, raising my head to breathe, and seeing nobody stood at the end of my lane to cheer me on.

These swimming-specific nightmares left me gasping for air when I woke up, like I had just swum a mile at sprint pace. I'd roll over in bed, pull the covers over myself, and try to fall back asleep to no avail. I'd stare unseeingly in the darkness fabricated between blanket and mattress and ponder all the vicious images my mind had just conjured. How could I have enjoyed a sport so malevolent and easily twisted? The nightmares made me realize just how much I hated swimming. Not the water itself—I never told you about that one week my family and I went to visit my grandmother in Florida, during the summer we weren't talking, when you were working as a lifeguard and I was wallowing in an emptiness inspired by your neglect. During that visit, I spent hours in the Atlantic Ocean, lying atop the waves, letting my body move with the natural shape of water. My skin never burned when I was immersed in that nonchlorination. Instead I felt nothing and everything at once, a nonbeing in nonexistence. Sometimes I'd even gulp the ocean down, relishing the bite of salt on my gums, swallowing smooth. How I loved that body of water. How I loved that sensation of floating.

Ren, I hated swimming, the act of it, and I hated how I would never become a star athlete like you or Luke. I lacked the delusion: Star athletes had to be delusional enough to think they could withstand physics and gravity enough to fly up onto the first-place podium and shine with the sheer force of athletic ability; there was nothing more bold than a star, after all, visible with the human naked eye despite its death eons ago. To be a star there could never be any room for self-doubt, which was where people like you and Luke thrived, as you both were larger-than-life characters who kicked out any lingering whiffs of insecurity by the sheer volume of your egos; me, on the other hand, I had enough self-doubt to fill a million pools.

My love for you had convinced me to ignore my festering wound of hatred, to endure it for you, but with you so brutally changed, I began to think clearer: I hated everything about swimming. Everything! I hated the unhealthy, crippling competition, the bullshit Jim forced us to do, the overwhelming sense of insecurity. I hated the wet hair, how as soon as my red locks air-dried, they had to go back inside the latex cap that ripped off the baby hairs near my forehead—my hair hasn't grown more than an inch in years. I hated the dry, burning skin, how my face flaked off in dandruff ashes. I hated shaving parties and I hated shaving cream and I hated shaving razors and I hated all the sheer shaving accompanying swimming for the sake of shaving seconds off a time that I never managed to manifest. I hated the dullness of moving in a confining 25-yard space. I hated having to dodge the long wingspans of boys who had hands like bludgeons. I hated my bottomless hunger. I hated my teammates. I hated Jim.

And I hated what swimming did to you.

I want you to know I hated it all. I hate it all. My hatred is as dark as the murky depths of the deepest oceanic trenches. Maybe this is why we are destined to never be together. Because I hate swimming, and you love it. Depend on it. Thrive on it.

Since you've left, my nightmares have shifted into wet dreams. Not the fluids of sex, but the fluids of the pool, of the athlete. Chlorine. Sweat. Blood. My nightmares have become wet dreams, centered around you. The idea of you as mermaid. I dream of Ren the mermaid, pulling at my feet as I try to escape to the pool wall; of Ren the mermaid holding me underwater without air, drowning me; of Ren the mermaid lying naked in a pool of blood with hair swirling down the drain. In my dreams, Ren the mermaid is Ren the girl from belly button up—the same sturdy biceps, bulky deltoids, ropey lats. Until I look down and see those legs, sewed—Ren, I realize now the mermaid I was dreaming of was always you. But I didn't understand then. I interpreted my visions of Ren the mermaid as harmless figments of my haunted imagination.

I wake up wet from these wet dreams. It's sweat and something else. Something sticky. Gooey. The liquid concentrates under my lower back and butt, and to be honest, the feeling reminds me of the blood and chlorine puddle that had formed under my thighs when I was holding you back from the pool.

I reach down between my legs to find a sticky mess of clear goo. I do not understand why such liquid expels itself from my body every night, and why it seems so natural to bring my hand to my mouth to take a deep whiff. A small lick.

Ren, have you ever tasted yourself down there?

I haven't told anyone about my nightmares—I don't have anyone to talk to. Nor do I try any of those silly remedies like popping melatonin or meditation. I prefer to believe my insomnia is my penance. Punishment for my previous apathy. Me, your tortured lover, a sleepless death.

Once, I drove downtown to the Pitt pool, returning to the scene of your beginning, of my ending. I idled in my car outside the building for hours, debating re-entering, to trace my footsteps around the shower drain where the sewing had occurred, or to sit on the bleachers where I held you down while you screamed, but I knew it would be hopeless and counterproductive. If I entered the memory, I would not have the strength to exit. I would want to join you. To conjure a needle from thin air and stab it into my thighs.

Ren, would you want me to try? You know I hate pain—and now you know I hate swimming—but I'd suffer for you. Then we could be together with our tails, a congregation of similar beings, a mermaid clan of two.

I'm sure you have a clan of many. You've probably made a lot of new friends down there in the water. Up here, where I am, I'm alone. My mother tries to convince me that I should socialize with new people, especially since I quit the team, but what's the point? Nobody can replace you. I'm a permanent swimmer yet an ex-swimmer, and because the circles of these two categories never overlap, I float aimlessly in between. I sit alone in the cafeteria and walk alone through the hallways. I keep my head down and avoid any spaces where swimmers congregate: around Luke's locker, around the stairs leading down to the pool, around Ally's car in the school parking lot.

I am alone. A-lone. A-, a prefix meaning "without." I am without you. I miss you.

Love,
Cathy

# Seventeen

Even when I was frantic, flailing around in Cathy's lap after Jim carried me away from the blocks, I trusted her to save me. I believed after Cathy said her goodbyes, she would let me go and roll me over, off her lap and off the bleachers, into the pool where I belonged. I hoped Cathy understood me and my desires, but as always, I expected too much from her. I was too focused on the race, and the recruiter, and the possibilities afterward, to think I would be thwarted by two people who were always on my side: Cathy and Jim.

Betrayal comes too easily to humans.

I was thrashing so hard when the ambulance came, they were forced to sedate me, then later, I came to myself woozy, unsure of time and place, tucked in a white bed—a hospital bed. Panicking, I immediately fumbled to feel my bottom half, relieved to find my tail still existing and intact. I tried to move it, lifting it up one or two inches, before it fell back onto the sheets with a thud; the scratchy, thin blanket hiding the iridescence of my scales remaining immobile. Gravity and air were too heavy. My tail needed water to be graceful and effective. I clutched at my throat—for mermaids, oxygen was more suffocating than chlorine, than $H_2O$, and though we could breathe all three, I had to remind myself how.

I was sore all over my body, especially on my tail, which itched for the water, and on my knuckles, purple and blue bruises blooming from my fights to get away. Instead of calling for the nurses, whom I doubted I'd be able to depend upon (human as they likely were to be), I forced myself to revel in the physical pain; after all, wasn't pain weakness leaving the body? If so, I was the strongest I'd ever been before. I hoped I would not forget the stinging. I committed to memory the stabbing swords, the licking flames in the crevasses of my scales.

When I was a human, my brain preferred to forget—a skill learned from swim practice, from strenuous races, from the teasing of my teammates, from Jim's inflicted emotional scarring. I suppose deletion was my chosen method for putting myself through repeated torture. I had to forget how painful a 100 butterfly sprint could be, or else there was no way I would let myself do it again.

But mermaids—mermaids relish pain. Mermaids embrace pain. Mermaids accept the pain of discipline is far less than the pain of regret. And it showed: when I woke, my head was mentally clear in ways it hadn't been in years. My headaches, the remnants of the concussion I had suffered the year prior, had vanished, leaving one clear goal pounding through my brain:

*Get to the water.*

I had tried, already. And failed, in part due to Cathy and Jim. Yet I was not the irresponsible type to rest blame entirely on others—

I had been misguided all along. I should have known the water I needed to reach was not of chlorine. Hadn't chlorine always burned me? Forced my skin to peel dry, crack into useless scales, irritate into shades of red—chemical burns, because chlorine was, in the end, a chemical, merely a tool, an additive, for humans to control the water. Chlorine mermaids were not in the folklore book because *chlorine mermaids did not exist*. If I remained in chlorinated pools, I, too, would be controlled by humans, doomed to suffer as a chained mermaid until I sought to turn back human or die. I had to go to water untouched and untamed: open water, saltwater, fresh water.

As the realization of chlorine's punitive damage dawned on me, the nurse poked her head inside and realized I was awake. She called for the doctor, who soon entered the room with my mother in tow.

I had imagined a play-by-play of our parent-child reunion in the nights leading up to my sewing. I had envisioned the absolute adoration on my parents'—both my parents, my dad actually present—faces upon my mermaid transformation, and the subsequent recruiter call. But only my mother walked in, and on her face I saw human physiological reactions indicating sadness, anger, and confusion: wild eyes, messy hair, red skin slashed by newly sprouted lines of wrinkles, concentrated above her eyebrows and on her forehead.

My mother stopped a few feet away, out of arm's reach, as if I had a contagious disease.

The doctor came closest to my bed. I avoided his gaze and looked up to the ceiling tiles. There was a stain the color of milky coffee in the corner of one of the rectangles, a shade similar to Jim's teeth. The doctor cleared his throat, indicating I should look at him, but I refused. Like all the other doctors I'd known, his competence was fake, his knowledge unimaginative, and, as a mermaid, I now had the wisdom to ignore what he would soon impose onto me, a power I had lacked as a girl.

The doctor's thin lips were a flat line, skin-colored, nearly non-existent.

"I'm Dr. Smyth. I'm here to help you. Please hold your questions until after I am done speaking. I do not like interruptions. Now, it appears you've sutured your legs..."

He droned on and on about my legs, ignoring the fact I had a mermaid tail, not legs, reinforcing his ineptitude. He understood nothing.

My mother interjected with questions, sparking Dr. Smyth's obvious irritation, yet I only heard them all as if I were underwater, swimming a race, their voices filtering to me in a distorted roar, but I understood enough of the garbling to tell me the ugly doctor was not asking me *why*. Why I had sewn my legs together, why I had chosen to transform, and he did not ask either if he could help me work through these whys.

The doctor was telling me *what*—this is *what* you did. What you did was horrible. What you did needs to end.

I watched my mother's head move. I watched her keep her gaze on her own nails, bitten down past the skin, bare and colorless. Her nails matched mine. We didn't care for manicures. Why would we waste time in salons built upon the burden of hunched Vietnamese women breathing in chemical fumes? I related more to the Vietnamese women than I did my white teammates who received manicures from them. My teammates would come into practice with perfect, almond-shaped, red nails, but the manicures would chip and crack as soon as they dove in. A ridiculous money suck to me, a worthwhile beauty endeavor to them. Swimming appeared a gentle sport, all waves and soft water, but this was a patent illusion, because no manicure, no styling, no *body*—no matter how hardy—could survive Jim's practice unscathed.

The doctor fell silent. He had asked me a few questions, but I did not answer, I could not answer.

He left. Without the doctor's presence, my ears unsealed. My mother hadn't moved from her faraway corner, her eyes down on her fingers.

I waited for her to initiate. I refused to be responsible for the tone of our reunion.

She spoke, her voice hoarse. "Why?"

I was silent, sure this one-word question expected an extensive answer. A short give, a long take. But what was there for me to say, other than this was who, *what*, I had always been?

"Why did you do it?" she asked again.

"You don't understand me," I answered. What mother would?

She sniffed, and I braced myself for her tears.

"The doctor wanted to take the stitches out right away, when you were still unconscious, but I thought"—she hiccupped; I willed myself not to crumble—"I thought you would want to be aware of this decision. Awake for it. And I wanted to know why you did what you did, before it was undone. But you won't tell me. You never tell me anything," she accused, ending her plea in anger.

I was grateful for her delay. But I lacked the explanations she wanted. So I did not respond. How could I have woven my many-years-long tale for her, there in the hospital? I did not have that much time. *We* did not have that much time. No mother-daughter ever did.

"Baba has already landed at the airport," she continued. "He's on his way. I wanted him to be here, too, before I made any big de-

cisions; clearly, by myself . . . I never know the right thing to do—"
she whimpered, and in my periphery I saw her hand rising to dab at
her eyes.

"Daughter, it will be okay," she said. "Dr. Smyth said yours is a
special case, one he's never seen before. They'll have to conduct some
tests before getting your stitches out. But they can start as soon as
we allow, and he's confident everything will be fine, especially since
it's been less than twenty-four hours. The procedure will be easy.
He said you'll be able to walk afterward."

She closed the distance and wrapped her arms around me. Mermaids love their mothers, no matter how impassable, and so I allowed myself to kiss her cheek and pat her back.

"Mom, I'm a mermaid. You can't take my tail away."

Her arms tightened, then she let go, her eyes wide. She stepped
back again. Away from me. Though the weather outside the open
hospital room window was cloudy—Pittsburgh's ever-present state
of being—there was enough light strewing in that I could trace the
tears falling in the divots of her wrinkles and count her many sun
freckles and moles peppering over her saggy cheeks. She hated the
dark spots on her face, and my dad had once promised to take us
both to Seoul someday, the capital of plastic surgery for East Asian
people, to remove them, but the promise had evaporated long ago.
We used the plane ticket and procedure money for swimsuits and
travel meets.

"What do you mean? You want to stay mutilated?" My mother's
voice was hoarse, feeble.

"No."

"So you want the stitches out?"

"No. I mean I'm not mutilated."

My mother hesitated, careful to choose her next words. "Okay. You are right. Not mutilated. But we can remove the tail, right?"

"Then I *will* be mutilated."

A pause. My mother's confusion, clear on her face. I spoke again, to make myself clear: "I'm keeping my tail."

"You can't."

"Yes, I can."

My mother stared at me. I stared back at her misery-lined expression, and if I had been a weaker-willed being, I would have opened my mouth then and there to beg for her forgiveness, because she did not deserve both a husband and a daughter who abandoned her—

My father burst into the room, the door banging into the opposite wall, startling my mother and me. The door swung wildly forward, hitting his arm, yet he stood there, chest heaving, ignoring the heavy panel. His clothing was disheveled, his shirt skipping two buttons and his pants unzipped, and he did not carry luggage with him—I guessed he flew here from China immediately, hopping on the first flight available when he had heard of my transformation. His face was unshaven, and above the stringy black patches across his chin and upper lip, I saw mysterious tear tracks. I had never seen him cry, not even when we got the call years ago about nai nai's death.

My mother ran to him, and they gripped hands, an intimacy that suddenly reminded me of my teammates, and of Cathy, the way we would high-five and handshake before and after races. I had never seen my parents hold hands, or even kiss on the cheek—we did not display affection in public. Had there been a seismic shift in how my parents showed face when I shifted body?

My dad stomped forward, as if to take charge, as if his presence were enough—often it was, because he was in a permanent state of absence, and his mere presence was surprising enough to make us pay attention. *Who is this man?* We never had time to take him or his directives for granted. Whenever he was around long enough that we could remind ourselves he was the father, and he was here, in America, to assert his dominance, he'd leave again for China. So now I, too, would leave, and it dawned on me then: the main similarity between humans and mermaids was that both are always leaving the ones they love.

He did not say hello. Did not hug me like my mother had. Did not ask me for my reasons. Instead: "Ren, ai ya, ting wo shuo de hua. Get rid of the stitches and then we can all go home, hui jia. Hao?" His voice thundered through the small room.

I chuckled, the tenderness I had felt upon seeing him dissolving at his aggression. "Dad, go home to where? What is a home? *Whose* home?" My voice came out sharper than I expected, no longer fuzzy from sleep, the mucus magically cleared away. My deadened senses had reanimated with the return of my father. Mermaids love their fathers but hold them to low standards they can still never jump high enough to fulfill.

"Ai ya, sha bao bei, what are you talking about?" My mother stood up and wrung her hands. "Why?" she asked once more. "Why, bao bei? Who are you? What are you doing to yourself?"

"I am Ren Yu," I said. "Still your daughter. But a mermaid now. And if you had paid attention, a mermaid always."

My mother flung her arm out against my father's chest, stopping him from barreling to the side of my bed to slap me. She spoke. "Ren, we are your parents. Your ba ma. You must unsew your legs. You must accept the surgery."

"No."

"You are not a mermaid. Listen to us," my mother begged, dropping to her knees with a crack. She began to bawl fountains of saltwater, the tears creating rivers in the canyons of her wrinkles. My father began to cry, too, fat tears misting his glasses that still slid down his nose—he had been too busy scheduling meetings and pitching ideas all these years to find glasses that fit correctly—collecting at the edge of lens and frame, then following his previously laid tear tracks, catching in the stringy hairs of his face. He opened his mouth and began to loudly wail, his screeching more haunting than any siren song documented from rocky coastlines.

I closed my eyes, the audio of my father crying terrible enough that the added visual would have cracked me open, would have been convincing enough to grab the nearest surgical knife and chop off my tail if it meant my parents' agony would cease. I would've done anything to please them. But I had to remain strong, remain in my mermaid ways.

I hadn't properly considered my parents' emotions in the consequences of sewing my legs, too busy charging ahead without thought, but my bullish actions could be blamed on Jim—to be reckless was how he had taught me to live. To dive straight in without a plan, so by the time my muscles realized how icy cold the water was, it would be too late. I'd be moving already, swimming without stopping.

I spoke, my voice hoarse, barely audible over the din of my parents' sadness. "I must go back to the water, to stay there for eternity. You cannot stop me."

My parents did not respond in coherent words.

I continued, more gently. "Ba, ma, I would rather return to the water with your blessing than leave without it. Can you grant me your permission, at least?"

My mother keened. Grasping my father's hand, she pulled them both forward to embrace me. Their hug hurt my sensitive scales. They were both heavier than I remembered, as if their sadness had materialized into solid weights onto their shoulders, but it is true that what humans call intergenerational trauma has always been heavy, sinking to the gloomy abyss of repressed memory to be mined for so-called wisdom later. I was newly aware my parents were people who carried their burdens on their bodies rather than within themselves—this was my doomed inheritance.

I stroked their hair, my tears falling onto their black strands. The droplets glistened underneath the hospital room's buzzing fluorescent lights. We sobbed together, loving each other, despite and because of everything that had happened, and would come.

In popular legends and retellings, mermaids do not treat their families well. Mermaids leave home to seek out new lovers, to have grand adventures impossible from the safe confines of their family homes. Mermaids do not regret leaving behind mourning parents.

But I must urge you to consider where these stories come from: Would a mermaid who stays at home, much-loved, with two beautiful parents and loving sisters who share everything, be worth memorializing?

No.

Humans and monsters both understand stories about magic and marvel and myth are made interesting by their stemming from trauma and violence and blood. How can one grow without pain?

Nüwa was surrounded by nature's beauty but still devastated with loneliness before she decided to carve humans out of clay, cementing her legacy. Her loneliness was the catalyst for her mythology.

And the forever unfaithful Ariel ditched her sisters, disregarded her father's advice, and threw herself under the curse of the evil witch, all for a man and for two legs, the most unworthy of trades in exchange for her magical being.

Remember, I am no Ariel. And I am no Nüwa.

I am my own mermaid, with my own tale. My own tail.

Understand I loved my human parents. Understand they loved me. Everything we did for, and to, each other was out of love. Even our farewells.

My tail-removal surgery was scheduled for two days after our family reunion. My father tried to push for sooner, but my mother insisted I needed some mental recuperation before something I so clearly valued was seized from me.

She always tried her best to keep me happy even when she tried to destroy me.

My parents did not come back to visit me in my room. I suspected they were too scared of another cathartic confrontation. Yet they still returned to the hospital to drop off what they hoped would make it feel more like what they perceived as a home: the blue fish vase from my bedroom, a bag of my favorite Chinese snacks—a reminder of when Cathy found me in the school library after my disqualification—and a stack of novels. These gifts were brought into my room by the nurse instead of them.

They never explicitly accepted my transformation, or me leaving humankind. But at the very least, through their actions, I sensed they forgave me. Forgiveness without acceptance. For me, from them, that was enough.

The nurse also brought in get well cards and clumps of balloons, leaving them within arm's reach, as if the proximity of written prayers would infiltrate my mermaid dreams and force my body to heal itself. I shuffled through the cards from my teammates, grimacing at the note from Luke and his family, a simple "feel better!" in a near-indecipherable doctor scrawl above an illustrated frog with a thermometer in his mouth.

My tail pulsed with fury when I landed on Jim's at the bottom of the pile. I didn't want to read his note. Every pen stroke of his, whether it was crossing the t's or dotting the i's, slashed my heart with both ferocious anger and wretched, unwanted affection for the diabolical man who had controlled so much of my human fate. He was always doing questionable things; by now, in the hospital, I interpreted his actions as wrong and inappropriate, but it was too late to stop him, and back then when he might have listened, I had been too young—and too human—to understand the harm the man's thousand small cuts would do long-term to girls like me. Instead, I had laughed, conceded, even enjoyed. Wasn't this cordiality what all the men wanted? A genial concession to their advances, to keep the door open for the possibility of their future creeping? Jim had tried to be my father figure, and I had unwittingly allowed him, so much so that I bestowed unto him the position of *being* my father, and I his adopted swimmer daughter, because my real father was always absent and Jim was always there. No love existed as strongly as that of a coach for his athlete.

It was true my swimming performance was inevitably intertwined with Jim—my victories were his, and my disappointments were his too. Reliance was a feature of any close relationship, as were desires. A proper education, a predictable curse, a classic trait of girlhood: to be forever confusing your desires with that of an older man's. And the folklore book had shown me even most mermaids were not free of this—I would never forget those Chinese mermaids, stranded on sand or stolen for marriage, dependent on the goodwill whims of men.

I swore to myself, as I ripped Jim's card into shreds, that I would break the curse and write my own legend.

There were no cards from Cathy. I double and triple checked each envelope and signature to confirm. I missed her. We spent so much time together at meets, practices, school, and all the times in between. I had adjusted to a life with her consistent presence, and to spend so many hours lying immobile without her was a malicious act against my nature. I had trouble focusing on the television, or on the book I was holding, because my brain was too busy conjuring sepia-toned fantasies of Cathy lying in the hospital bed with me, or of cuddling Cathy in a musty hotel room during an away meet. Whenever Dr. Smyth came into my room, wielding an evil leer, my parents' permission to saw me apart, and the reminder that he was going to destroy me, change me back to human, and force my legs to reemerge, scale-free, I would force my mind somewhere very far away, where Cathy and I would intertwine our bodies at the edge of the ocean and sand, making crowns out of seaweed and drinking aloe water from conch shells. The need to disappear when medical professionals came was so profound, I disassociated, imagining Cathy's weight on me as the doctor bustled around, conducting whatever tests he wanted to do. When he finally left my room, I would awaken back to the cold hospital room, touching the scratchy blanket covering my mermaid tail, reorienting myself.

I could not let Dr. Smyth succeed. The brief euphoria of becoming a magical creature would never be enough to sustain me through a life reduced to woman. I had to get to the water. The fresh water. But how?

# Eighteen

A knock on the door.

A rare evening golden sun was streaming through my window, casting my room in a warm light. I had just woken up, blinking blearily in the tentative space between afternoon and dark's falling—I had been unable to sleep that night, fretting over how to escape the hospital before the operation, whether fresh water would not be as easy to swim through as chlorinated water, and if my eyeballs would acclimate underwater without goggles, until dawn hit and I finally succumbed out of sheer exhaustion.

"Come in!" I said, thinking the knocker was a nurse. My voice was guttural, low-pitched, still clouded with the grogginess of slumber.

The door creaked open, and instead of a bustling nurse came a girl with red curls, freckles, a warm smile, round cheeks.

"Hi, Ren. It's me, Cathy!"

My mouth dropped open, then I closed it immediately, my jaw snapping shut.

"Of course it's you. Who else would it be?"

Cathy grinned. She wore uncharacteristically high wedges, a denim skirt, and a tight black shirt underscoring her flaming hair, as if she had decided to dress up for our visit, a first date after a long separation. I had never seen her so dressed up, as she usually resorted to sneakers and sweatpants—leggings if feeling fancy—with some sort of swimming team gear or team spirit clothes on top. I scanned her up and down, nodding with surprised approval. She blushed at my silent assessment and leaned against the doorframe, shifting her weight from one foot to the other.

"Wow, it feels like so long since I've seen you!" I exclaimed.

"Yeah, well, a lot has happened in that short time," she replied, frowning.

I raised my eyebrows, the excitement upon seeing her leaking out of me. Cathy's expression made it seem like those happenings had been nothing but negative. "Took you long enough to stop by. I thought you would've come yesterday, straight from the pool. Honestly, I thought you didn't want to visit or something."

Cathy shook her head. "No, I've wanted to come ever since the ambulance took you away. But there are specific visiting hours, and I had to wait for Jim to leave."

"Jim was here? At the hospital?"

"Yeah. I walked in, saw him, and quickly ran out back to my car before he could see me. He was demanding the front desk reveal your room number. Throwing a tantrum like a toddler. I felt bad for the receptionist. I think your mom might have listed his name as prohibited or something."

I was reminded again of how my mother had always tried her best to keep me happy.

Cathy was watching me. "Did you want him to come? I can call him."

I wavered. I could, with Cathy's assistance, invite Jim to my hospital room under the guise of wanting him, needing him, craving him and his coaching. And then I could enact my revenge. Haven't mermaids have always possessed the ability to tempt men to their deaths with the power of their voice? If I wanted to, I could open my mouth and sing so beautifully that Jim would be convinced to smash his head against the wall, the way a man's ship would crash against the rocks. His skull would crumble like the ship's planks of wood, and his brain would ooze down the side of the wall like the ship's soggy flag. I could curse him so he would choke on his next cigarette, the way men did when they tried to breathe underwater. I could rewrite his destiny so he would fall into the pool and drown at his next swim practice, the way men did when they crawled into the ocean to meet the mermaids. Or I could suddenly beg his forgiveness and claim my previous words were simply jokes, and let Jim come close to hug me, the way he always came too close, and in the seconds before he kissed me on the cheek, I would bite his jugular with my shark-sharp teeth, and he'd suffer on my hospital blanket while I cackled at the poor mortal man's hubris. He would bleed out and die before the nurses could save him. But the taste of his skin, his neck, would be disgusting—likely Mountain Dew and preservatives and whatever cheap cologne he decided to splash on—and I had to remain clean, or else the water might reject me. Everything was pure down there and I could not blemish myself or my system with Jim's death. He did not deserve my debasement. He did not deserve to see my ethereal mermaid abilities used on him.

"No," I said. "I'd rather not."

"Okay."

Cathy stood at the entrance awkwardly, as if waiting for a proper greeting, for me to pull up a chair. She carried a pothos plant in her arms, which I recognized because my mother cultivated a copious number of these easy-to-grow plants in our own home. The pothos would soak up the rare glimpses of Pittsburgh sunlight streaming through our house windows. Pittsburgh could crush any Pacific Northwest woods in a battle of average annual precipitation and gray skies, but my mother still insisted on trying her best despite the lack of sunshine. She had gotten my own pothos for me from the hardware store months ago, thinking I could learn a green thumb out of the blue waters of the pool. I had ignored the plant, but it refused to die. Impressed with its hardy will to live, I grudgingly conceded with watering, and so its leaves and stems stretched themselves down the wall, across the carpet, and onto my bed. Some nights, I had nightmares where a mermaid with snakes as hair would pull at my feet, trying to drown me in teeming, stormy whirlpools. I'd fight the mermaid, screaming that I was a mermaid, too, simply unformed. Then I'd jolt awake, kicking my feet up, the covers floating upward like a ghost, the pothos shaking in annoyance, and I'd realize that it was the pothos touching me, not a mermaid who did not recognize me as one of their own.

The plants were narcissistic and greedy, dunking themselves in excess sun and water, but I suspected Cathy's would serve a purpose: an offering, an apology, a hello. Its leaves were thick, round, and juicy, and the tendrils snaked out of her arms to brush against my skin, a tentative greeting.

"Well, are you going to just stand there?" I asked teasingly.

Cathy smiled, as if she had been waiting for my permission. Limping, like her feet had already formed blisters, unused to the rare heel, she headed to the windowsill and placed the pothos in the middle of the afternoon sun, where it settled with a thud, the leaves shaking and already snaking closer to the window glass, where it could reach the sunlight.

Then she toddled toward my bed—toward me—and placed her arms around my body in a hug, her hair tickling the bottom of my nose. Her weight was tentative, as if trying not to crush me. I fought the urge to throw her off. She was my first close contact since transcendence who was neither a medical professional nor a wailing parent but what I could call a friend—although there had always been other connotations between us I was too tired to define—and yet because she was human, I was nervous at how my tail might react to her proximity. I remained tense, my arms stiff at my sides, curling the blanket between my fists, willing my top half to relax so Cathy would not pry into how I was feeling.

"You smell like spicy ginger," she said.

"Really? You sure I don't smell like a hospital?"

"Yeah, there's a disinfectant smell around you, too, but it's not bad."

"Gee, thanks."

"Ren, I know it's only been a day, but I missed you," she said, nuzzling her face deeper into my shoulder.

I hesitated. Then: "I missed you too." Did I?

There were differences in what it meant to miss someone. I had grown up knowing this difference. I missed many people. My dad, my mom, my self I hadn't yet met. And I missed them all differently. Missing someone out of love, missing someone out of loss—both an *I miss you, I missed you too*, but with disparate connotations. And like the unspoken implications in our friendship, Cathy and I had always carried our connotations differently.

Cathy let go but kept sitting on my bed, her butt next to my tail. "You look great."

I stared at her. "To be honest, you don't." She was close enough to me now that I could see cakey foundation on her cheeks, smeared over spotted purple and blue—petals that matched those on my knuckles. I lifted my finger and gently traced one of the bruises. Cathy winced.

"Did I do this?" I asked, hushed.

"Yes, but don't worry about it," Cathy said. "You weren't—" She hesitated. "You weren't in your right mind."

Right, wrong—I had never been more right than in my current state. I frowned. "I'm sorry," I said, not because I actually felt sorry—rather, I felt a thrill of perverse pleasure at seeing our matching bruises, proud of myself for fighting the best I could to free myself from her grip, which had restrained me from the pool. But I knew sorry was the right thing to say. Mermaids knew sometimes violence was necessary for self-defense, lover-defense. It was better to apologize afterward than allow the ferocity to fester.

"How are you?" she asked.

"I mean, there's not much to report. I've been stuck here." I shrugged and leaned back on my pillows.

She squeezed my hand, and there was a reminder of love line, lifeline, and sweat between our palms.

"So you brought me a plant?" I giggled.

"Yes. If you want, I'll bring you plants until you feel like you're sleeping in the forest."

"No, it's okay. No need. Soon I'll be with seaweed and algae," I said, grinning.

"Uh—right." Cathy looked around for a subject change, which disappointed me—did she think we would not talk about my mermaid tail at all? Why would she have come to visit if she couldn't bear to discuss our reality?

"You really made the hospital room your own," she said, avoiding my topic of a return to water.

"Give the credit to my parents. They dropped everything off," I said.

"Oh. Well, I recognize the blue fish vase—wasn't it in your room before, with dried wheat stalks inside?"

"Yes—but how'd you know it was in my room?" I narrowed my eyes. "I don't think you've ever been in there."

"Oh—uh—maybe not. Well, it looks like your parents tried to make the room feel more homey? Uh—and the stack of books and pile of Chinese snacks on the table look like our tables at study hall. I probably associated the fish vase with you and your bedroom as a guess." Cathy blabbered on, chuckling nervously, as if I were testing her, then she petered out.

I didn't respond. There had been several occasions when Cathy could have been in my room without my knowledge—a pasta party or picking up my mother to shop for Chinese snacks—and I would not be surprised if the truth was that she had broken in randomly, when neither I nor my mother was home. Cathy had always wanted to be me.

No, be *with* me.

As the silence trickled onward, I wondered at Cathy's reasons for her visit. I had known humans, and had been human myself, for too long to believe their motivations were totally pure. Did she want me to ask her to join me in mermaidhood? I could tell her to bring me a needle and thread tomorrow, so I could offer to sew her legs for her, so she wouldn't have to learn how to stitch the way I did, using other parts of the body as sacrifice. I could bend my tail in half, contort my body in the same position a human would do to get down on one knee and propose, except instead of opening a ring box, my palms would hold a spool of thread and a needle. We could swim off together into the water and ride the waves together, searching for the most beautiful seashells to turn into earrings, befriending the fish, who would be forever jealous of the way we cavorted and loved each other. But I knew this fate was not for me. I did not want to waste time indulging another's transformation when I had spent so long attempting my own. And I did not desire the type of partnership Cathy could give me. I wanted only myself, and the water, and the mermaids who had already made it their home.

Cathy spoke.

"The regionals meet was canceled after you sewed—after it happened. But we still had an end-of-season party that night, for some reason. I didn't want to go, but my mother made me stop by. It was weird, without you."

"Oh. I didn't know there was a party."

"I figured. I saw Ally removed you from our group chat. I'm hoping it was more a kind gesture on her part than malicious—she probably didn't want to bother you, since everyone's been sending nonstop texts about your condition"—Cathy quickly corrected herself—"All nice things, though. Like wishing you well, wondering if you're doing okay."

She pulled out her phone from her skirt's back pocket, jostling the bed mattress as she shifted her weight to reach behind her. "Here, check out the team photo from the party. We all missed you."

"You guys took a team photo?" I gently took her phone and rotated the screen to my eyes. The photo was slightly blurry, as if whoever had taken it had been too busy admiring the real-life people instead of the photo quality. The team was standing in Rob's foyer, some of them spilled out on the staircase, and some standing on the main floor. Everybody was slightly squashed together, arms touching arms, but between Cathy and Rob was an empty space wide enough for one person.

Cathy leaned over and pointed to the blank space.

"Look, we left a space for you. It was Rob's mom's idea. She was being sweet. We were thinking of you."

I fought the urge to cringe. I hadn't wanted them to think of me in sentimental ways, I wanted them to think of me as transcendent.

"Luke looked like shit at the party. He thinks you're haunting him," Cathy said.

"What?"

"Yeah, he's been acting stupid. He even called me last night, around three A.M., five times until I finally picked up, to ask if you were still in the hospital."

"Why?"

"He claimed that you're stalking him, or haunting him, or whatever. He said that for years, he had followed Jim's advice to stay loose and hydrated by chugging a liter of water before bed every night, and so he pees at three A.M. like clockwork, but yesterday, he somehow managed to hear someone, or something, making *pop pop pop* sounds like a needle entering skin behind his shower curtain when he peed. I ridiculed him and hung up, mostly because it was an ungodly hour and he's always been incredibly annoying, but then I lay in bed wondering if it was really you."

"Are you serious? Of course it wasn't me. I'm a mermaid, not a ghost."

"Right." Cathy coughed.

I fell silent, squinting at the photo. Luke looked the same as always, grand, taller than everybody else, a wingspan wrapped around Ally. Though I had changed, they had not, and I was slightly nauseated thinking of Cathy at a party with them, discussing my condition and gossiping about the reasons for my metamorphosis. I pinched the screen, zooming in to check if Cathy was right about Luke's state of mind—Luke's eyes were wild, evident even in the photo blur, and his blond hair looked more mussed than usual, as if he had nervously been scratching his skull instead of keeping his hair neat and gelled, the way Ally preferred.

"Do you think Luke's acting this way because he feels guilty about that night?" Cathy asked, tucking a loose strand of hair behind my ear.

I moved my head away from her hand. "What night?" I asked, glaring.

"You know. *That* night."

I did. But I had no desire to talk about the night of the Truth or Dare game. I bit the inner skin of my cheek to suppress my rising rage. "Why are you bringing it up? You've never wanted to discuss it before."

"I've tried, I swear. You never wanted to talk to me about it. But you can now. If you want." She wrung her hands. "I want to help you, Ren."

I glared at her, realizing now that she was visiting, though perhaps unconsciously, out of her own guilt. For me to assure her innocence.

Cathy bowed her head.

"I stuck up for you, remember? I said you didn't want to go," she said quietly.

"Yes, I remember." How could I forget?

"You didn't argue. I would've said more if you were clearer on how you didn't want to go!"

"Well. Thanks." I looked away, back to the window, where through the glass and the pothos leaves, I could spy the hospital parking lot. There was Cathy's silver sedan, parked crooked, one tire over the white painted line. I hadn't noticed it until now. She had bought the car as her birthday present with her parents' credit card from the slimy old salesman at the sparkling dealership by the high school; she told me she would never forget the salesman leering over his clipboard at her chest. When I heard the story, she had to hold me back from going to the car dealer to claw out his eyes so he would never leer at her, or anyone else's, chest again. I had wanted to protect Cathy, but she had ended up protecting me in certain times instead, only to fail when it counted. I was angry—so angry—at all the ways she had failed.

Perhaps I could offer her one last chance for true redemption.

"Ren, why did you do it?" Cathy asked, whispering, as if verbalizing my mermaid tail in normal tones would make its existence real.

"You really don't understand why? You didn't expect it?" I spat.

"How could I? How could I imagine you'd do that"—she shuddered—"to yourself? Think about your legs—"

"Tail."

Cathy flinched. "Tail."

"Of course you don't get it. You never have."

"I'm sorry."

"Don't," I snarled, then I reminded myself to relax. Manipulation was easier when calculated. Calm. Not angry. "Why apologize for what is right and good?" I patted my tail. "This is who I am. Who I was always meant to be. A mermaid, not a human."

"Why? Why can't you stay with me?" Cathy pleaded.

"Why would I want to?" I sniffed.

"But—"

"Cathy. Don't even try to convince me." I paused. "But it's not too late to help me now."

Cathy opened her mouth, then closed it, gaping like a dying fish. I snorted at her expression, thinking she would fit in with the marine creatures perfectly.

"Ren, please, you're upset."

"Clearly. So. Will you help?"

She paused, hesitated, and I held my breath.

"Yes," she said.

I hid my glee. She could not understand the extent of my control over her. "Okay. You have to get me out of here."

"How am I supposed to do that?" she asked, clasping her hands and resting her elbows against her knees, hunched over like she was praying to Nüwa for my recovery.

I snickered, cruel, at her posture. "I don't know how, or else I would've done it myself. But if—when—you succeed, I'll forgive you. That's what you want, right? Why you came, and why you're asking me what happened that night?"

"No, Ren, I—"

"Cathy, I'll forgive you for the past if you really can help me escape before the surgery tomorrow," I said, scoffing, reveling in the malicious glee coursing through me, invigorating my senses—was this the same rapture a mermaid would feel while she sang, luring sailors to their watery deaths?

The door swung open. We both jumped. My tail recoiled.

"Hey, Ren—oh, hello." A nurse popped her head inside, interrupting. "Are you Ren's friend?"

Cathy wiped her eyes, then nodded.

"Well, it's nice to meet you, but I'm sorry, you have to leave. Visiting hours are over." The nurse shifted her gaze over to me. "Ren, buzz me when you're ready." She smiled, then disappeared. The door clicked shut.

"You should go. Time's up," I said.

"Ren, I promise you," Cathy said, grabbing my hands with both of hers, as if her tight grip could make her promise come true. "I will make it up to you." Her breath caught, as if wanting to confess more, but I looked away, to the side of the hospital room, where the wall was a white expanse of nothing. I was tired of our conversation. I was tired of her. Tired of this human world with its petty problems and unending regrets.

Understanding she was dismissed, Cathy stood up, unsteady in her pinching wedges. She walked crookedly to the door, limping with her right foot heavier than her left. She looked back at me, pausing with her hand on the doorknob. I waved cheerily, as if we hadn't been arguing, as if Cathy hadn't promised me help I wasn't sure she could give.

She nodded, a quivery smile on her cheeks. She exited and closed the door behind her with a soft click.

I was alone. Happier, alone. My tail throbbed under the blanket, aching for the water. I petted my scales in absentminded comfort, smoothing the blanket taut. I lay back on my pillow and mused over Cathy's red curls, so much like Ariel's. Cathy had been insufferably nervous as she flitted around the room, seeking desperate new topics to replace any awkward silences. I had expected seeing Cathy would be a warmer reunion, and we'd be able to talk about what had happened, but she never asked directly about my mermaid tail, merely asked why I had done it, without specifying what *it* was. She never asked to see my tail either. If I was honest to myself, I was disappointed—rooted in the belief that, out of everyone, Cathy would not dance around the topic of my transformation.

Yet was her behavior truly a surprise? Why was I still allowing myself to be displeased by Cathy? Why hadn't I fully accepted by now that she would never act the perfect human I expected her to be? I clutched at my hospital robe, over my chest, where my heart had cracked open. I had recognized her as my last possible salvation, not out of devotion but out of necessity. Who else could I depend on now, and who else could I have depended on in the past? The disappointment, the frustration, at not being known, fully, truly, by her, even now, with a tail so clear and magnificent, was enough to sever any last tie that kept me bound to her—

Though not the strings I'd use to manipulate her.

I resolved my will.

I had achieved freedom from human bond.

What I needed now was freedom of movement.

I prayed: *Nüwa. My divinity. Keep me safe. Keep me free.*

# Nineteen

The morning of the scheduled tail demolishment surgery, I awakened to the nurse entering my room to rip open the window and its curtains. Late afternoon sunlight and fresh air washed over my face and smacked me awake. I winced at the brightness.

"You can try standing up if you'd like. Dr. Smyth says your legs need to regain their strength before the surgery later this afternoon," the nurse said as she ducked out.

As soon as the door clicked shut, I was out of bed and on the hard ground, my tail holding me aloft. I disagreed with Dr. Smyth's assertion I would attend the surgery, and that I even had legs. But he was correct in how I needed to regain strength in my bottom half after lying prone for so long. I was fidgety and impatient to find my mermaid family, and therefore would need all the strength I could garner in my tail.

My mental health had been affected by my inactivity too. Lying still reminded me of all the times I had remained sorrowful and inert in my bedroom.

I could stand, though I was rather shaky. When I put weight on my tail, I expected sharp, stabbing pain, but instead felt detached relief. As I strenuously hopped toward the open window, bracing a hand against the wall as I jumped forward, I wished the floor was any sort of liquid, instead of solids like linoleum and tile and hardwood. I wouldn't have any trouble moving or breathing in a world made of pool, of water. I'd be able to surpass anyone who tried to drown me.

I stuck my head out the window, tipping toward the sunlight like I was an extension of Cathy's pothos gift. The sky was blue and clear. The gentle wind swatted my hair around my forehead, whipping in my ears. The temperature was balmy for an early spring day. I had not paid any attention to the rapid changing of the season while preparing for regionals and staying in the hospital, too busy thinking of water and mermaids to follow nature's natural march of time. The spring, and incoming summer, would be scorching. Perhaps the water I'd eventually find would be unbearably hot too. Pittsburgh had been getting warmer each year, though the cloudy days remained. I would not be the only mermaid worried about global warming and the dying coral.

I surveyed the parking lot below, idly searching for my mother's car. I had hoped she would stop by in the hours as the surgery neared, although I rather dreaded the in-person visit—I'd end up comforting her more than she would comfort me. Such was the reversal effect of sympathy, requiring the damaged to soothe the spectator. But I wanted her to visit before I escaped, because she, and not my father, and nobody else, deserved a final goodbye, and a reassurance of her blamelessness—I worried my mother assumed teaching me sewing was the catalyst for my mermaid transformation.

"Ren!"

I heard my name called in a warbly voice I recognized as Cathy's. She recited my name differently from everybody else, with the *eh* sound extended, like she swirled my name around her mouth in delight before letting the syllable escape. I squinted toward the parking lot, raising a hand to shield my eyes from the sun.

"Down here!"

I gasped. I caught sight of Cathy waving frantically directly below my window, standing atop the hospital lawn next to trimmed hedges. I blinked, rubbed my eyes—I was sure I was dreaming her.

"Ren, it's me! Cathy!"

It was really her.

I waved back. My hair swung in the breeze like I was Rapunzel, gazing downward toward my lover, rescuing me from the evil witch named Dr. Smyth, who had locked me up in the tower.

Cathy cupped her hands around her mouth. "I'm sneaking you out. I promised. Come on." She pointed toward the long ledge jutting out beneath my window. "I've mapped out the whole process. You climb out the window and stand on the ledge, then jump down. I'll catch you, or you'll land on the hedge. Either way it'll be safe. It looks far, but it's a manageable few feet, I promise."

"Are you serious?" I hissed. "Didn't you get a C in physics last year?"

"Trust me, it'll work!" Cathy flashed me a double thumbs-up, as if her thumbs had studied the equations of jumping out windows and off ledges for years and could confirm the safety of the journey.

I brought my head back into my room and rested my forehead against the wall. I slammed my forehead once, twice against the plaster, frustrated. I pondered my options—jump out and possibly die a mermaid, or stay put and die a slow, torturous human death, with scars down my legs as proof of my expired beauty. If I had to suffer through mortality, the most fitting farewell was to go out in a blaze of mermaid scales by my own hand.

I tenderly placed the pothos onto the floor, away from the windowsill, so it would not be harmed by my escape. I poked my head out the window again. Cathy was anxiously scanning the surroundings for any bystanders, but because my window faced a side of the hospital away from the entrance, the sidewalks were empty.

"Okay. I'm coming out," I hollered.

Cathy grinned and moved forward to brace herself beside the bush. "Swing your tail out and you'll touch the ledge. It's right under you," she instructed.

*Tail.* Cathy had called my tail a tail.

My dormant hopes reared their heads.

I shifted my weight, testing my tail. Moving my bottom half no longer caused me any pain, but it was dead weight until I could submerge.

"Good job!" Cathy called while tying her curls into a ponytail to keep hair out of her face for the catch. "You're doing great! You got this!"

I had this, yes—my part was easy. Did *she* have this?

Yet what choice did I have? I had asked her to rescue me, and here she was. Hope, ever cruel.

I sat on the window ledge clutching the sides of the wall, my back to the sky. I cracked my neck. I stretched my sides in streamline.

*Swimmer, take your mark.*

I tensed. My muscles coiled.

BEEP

With a fluid jerk I lifted and revolved my tail through the window, into the air. It dangled, the bottom of my fins brushing against the ledge. I was half outside, and halfway to freedom. I lifted my butt off the sill to rest my weight on my tail, then pushed away from the window, my arms flailing. My weight caught me, and I rebalanced, upright, as Cathy clapped her hands. A clean landing, a perfect dive.

"You're almost there!" she called. "Keep going!"

I grimaced. I looked down. The top of the hedge brushed the ledge. Farther below were Cathy's outstretched arms. The perspective from my height stretched the distance into scary proportions.

"Ready?" I asked.

"Yes! Go for it!"

I turned to face the building wall and fell backward, my arms outstretched, closing my eyes, faithful the wind, the hedge, and Cathy would catch me. A trust fall, like the ones Jim had forced us to do as team bonding at the beginning of each season, where we stood on the cafeteria tables and fell back like limp rag dolls, and though I hated the activity, Cathy never let me hit the ground. I didn't rely on any other teammate for those icebreakers, especially not Ally nor Brad nor Luke. Whenever I landed onto the soft net of human flesh, the one pair of arms I recognized cradling me were Cathy's. I knew her arms by the padding of their muscles, by the plush curves of her limbs. This fall from the hospital ledge onto firm ground was the same action, same stakes, same players—we had practiced my descent for so many years. Had Jim foreseen the future? Had he predicted I would need to trust, and Cathy would need to catch?

The wind whistled in my ears as I plummeted toward the ground. My stomach swooped; my heart rushed upward into my throat. I landed with a thump in Cathy's arms. I opened my eyes—and was immediately taken aback by the sun's rays hitting her head from behind, illuminating her hair into a halo. I was awash with the illusion of having lived this already, a few years ago, on an icy winter night outside Mia's house, my head throbbing, the stars arranged in mermaid tails. Cathy, wide eyes locked onto mine, hovering over me, worrying if I was okay, though today was different from that past bleak darkness, because today was drenched in sunshine. A warm spring day, a preamble for the coming future I had fought for.

Cathy trembled, jolting me out of my dazed reverie. Her fingers tightened against the skin of my lower back and upper arm. Then she shuddered, as if she could not stand our close contact any longer. She pushed me upright. I regained my weight on my tail, wobbling to keep balance. When I left her hold, she threw her arms around me in a hug.

"You're out now!" she yelped, her face burrowed in the crook of my shoulder, hiding her gaze, the intimacy of our prolonged eye contact too blazing to continue.

I patted her back as she squeezed harder. I spat out a glob of her red hair, which had gotten caught in my dazed open mouth when she tackled me. The wind caressed us.

She let me go and grinned, keeping her hands on my elbows to help me balance. "Ren. Don't worry. I'm here." She patted my cheek. "Come on." She pulled me to her car, idling on the curb across from us.

I stumbled, and Cathy slowed her pace. She loosened her grip to let me hop at my own ability. I tilted, and Cathy came to my side, wrapping her arm around the crook of my elbow, allowing me to rest my weight on her without asking.

She opened the passenger door and gestured for me to step in, bowing at the waist and snickering as I rolled my eyes.

"Aren't you supposed to curtsy, not bow?" I asked.

"Curtsying is for girly girls," she said.

"And you are?"

"I'm a chivalrous girl," she said as she winked.

"Never make that joke again. Or else chivalry really will be dead," I said, clambering inside the car.

As Cathy climbed into the driver's seat, I glanced in the back and noticed a checkered blanket, neatly folded, with a large lunchbox on top.

"What did you pack? Did you bring me Chinese snacks again?" I asked.

"No guesses. I'm not telling." Cathy turned on the car engine.

I poked her arm, and she glared at me. "Hey! Watch it. I'm about to drive here."

"Fine. Want some music?" I fiddled with the volume knob, noting the crumbs resting inside each crease of the car dashboard. The interior of my car had been similar—crumbs in all corners of whatever transportation you chose were the price of being an athlete constantly hungry and on the move. You ate wherever and whenever you could.

"I don't mind silence," she said.

"It's lucky I was on the second floor and not any higher," I said. "I don't think I could have jumped out of a five-story window."

"Well, I would've snuck you out through the storage elevator or something. Maybe stolen one of those ambulance stretchers." Cathy tapped the steering wheel as she pondered the many possibilities. "Ooh! One of those silver gurneys they use in surgery or autopsies would have been perfect. You could've pretended to be a dead body, and I would've thrown a white sheet over you, so no one would know it was you. Easier than jumping out the window!"

"That plan is extremely morbid," I said.

"Morbid or not, I would've gotten the job done," she said proudly.

Cathy drove out of the parking lot. Through the rear window, I watched the hospital recede, a white speck ebbing into the brilliant blue sky. I considered flicking the building off while yelling out the window, *GO FUCK YOURSELF, DR. SMYTH,* but I reminded myself how mermaids did not gloat—when victory was expected, bragging was not justifiable. Mermaids were gracious, humble creatures when it counted. Instead, I lowered the car window and stuck my head out, screaming euphoric nonsense into the whipping wind, the force of its gale biting my cheeks, my hair in a tornado around my face. I was free! Free! Free!

Through the air's howls and my yells, I heard Cathy whooping in glee alongside me. Surprised at her brazen display of elation, I reinserted my head inside the car and looked at her questioningly. Her curls had fallen out of her ponytail, a messy look befitting a proper getaway driver. She smirked, then quickly fixed her face back into a serious mask, concentrating on the road, her eyes narrowed. Though the gales outside the window had been strong, she was driving at the speed limit. Cathy had always been a nervous—and frankly terrible—driver, once knocking down two mailboxes on her street in an attempt to back out of the driveway, but it was endearing the way she still insisted on driving everywhere.

I settled into my seat and closed the window, sealing off the roar of the moving car. The landscape zoomed past, a blur of various shades of green atop brown, budding trees regrowing their leaves. I realized with a jolt that today would perhaps be the last time I'd witness the coming of a Pennsylvania spring. How much had changed on this land, and how much hadn't, since I entered the hospital? How much would change, and how much would not, after I left it?

I pinched the inside of my wrist to distract myself from the poisonous line of thinking. Mermaids refused regret.

"Why'd you rescue me?" I asked Cathy. I had cruelly ended her previous hospital visit with a clear demand she owed me a rescue, but I hadn't expected her to actually try, or even be successful. By now the adrenaline of escape had settled, and I was awake to my curiosity as to how she had garnered the courage and the ideas to save me. Neither her expression nor her posture changed with my question, but I recognized she heard me by the way her cheeks blushed.

"You know why," she whispered.

I scoffed, throwing my head back, bouncing against the headrest, basking in her response—yes. I did know why.

She had chosen rescue, and wasn't the act of choosing enough?

Our choices showed who and what we loved. I had chosen water, mermaid.

Cathy had chosen me.

"Ren. Do you forgive me?" she asked quietly, her eyes fixed on the red stoplight ahead.

I didn't respond. Cathy didn't understand I had forgiven her yesterday, realizing, after she left the hospital in a sad rush, how it was impossible to hold humans up to a high standard. Cathy was fallible. I was, too, when I was a girl.

Which was why, as soon as I touched the water, I'd be gone.

I'd disappear. I couldn't keep her around. She was weak. She reminded me too much of all the ways my human life had been a falling domino line of defeat.

I would not ask her to come with me. She could try to follow me if she wanted, but I would not save her if she drowned.

The car idled. Cathy sighed, relinquishing her yearning for vocal forgiveness.

"Where to?" she asked instead.

It had been endless eternity since I had left the Pitt pool for the hospital. I had to go where I craved.

"Take me to the water."

# Twenty

We drove for two hours, leaving Pittsburgh's city limits far behind, miles out from where my mother and I had ever gone. We passed billboards with smiling babies accompanying Bible verse headlines, musty gas stations with Confederate iconography hanging off the roofs, roaring motorcycle convoys carrying bearded men in crusty leather and flapping American flags. I did not feel welcome, but I had never felt welcome wherever I went, not truly, and at least Jim, Dr. Smyth, and my parents would not be able to find me in such a sprawling rural area. Cathy took an unmarked exit off the highway, and we finally parked in a gravel lot after driving down a rural shaded road for fifteen minutes. The lot was empty but for a souped-up red pickup truck parked in the corner, with wheels as tall and wide as Cathy's car.

Before I could get out of the passenger seat, Cathy was already outside, opening the door for me and reaching out to help me steady.

"I don't need you to treat me like I'm delicate," I said. "I'm fine." I refused her assistance, but tripped as I stepped out, and fell into her. She spasmed, gripping me to make sure I had control over my balance, then gently pushed me off her, placing me to lean my weight against the car side.

"Yeah, right." She fumbled around in the backseat, collecting the food and blanket. Her butt was poking out of the open door, shaking as she reached for the blanket that had fallen on the floor as we drove. I averted my eyes and instead glanced around us. I accidentally met the eyes of the truck driver. His window was rolled down; he carried himself with an air reflecting an age somehow both twenty-six and seventy-six years old, wearing a denim vest with frayed armholes, wrap-around sunglasses, and a baseball cap pulled low. Smoke furled out of his fingers, where a cigarette dangled out the window. I couldn't decipher if he was watching me or Cathy's swinging ass behind his sunglasses. Either option was invasive. Weird men were everywhere, especially around rural Pennsylvania, and their ever-present gazes were insufferable. I turned back to Cathy, wondering if I should shield her, but she had finished gathering up our supplies into a backpack, slung on her shoulders. She held out her hand, waiting for me to take it.

I grasped it tightly. Her fingers were cool and dry. She helped me along to a neat trail I hadn't seen, tucked away next to the pickup truck. I did not have to look back at the truck window to discern the man's gaze had followed us, but I kept my eyes forward on the trailhead, inhaling the fresh air, feeling relaxed despite myself. My ears picked up a faint gurgle, and my tail itched, sensing the water was close. Cathy and I had matching paces and strides; though mine were lopsided hops, Cathy was adjusting her smooth steps to match.

"Where are we anyway?" I asked, panting from the long bedrest. I was out of shape already. I had seen enough of our swim team alumni with freshman fifteen weight gains and muscle loss who came back to visit during college breaks to accept how it did not take long for the hard swimming body to evolve into something mushy. My swimming muscles would never fully disappear, but they would shrivel and hide under layers of soft body puree.

"McConnells Mill State Park. It's named after an old, defunct mill, a few miles up the creek. I think we might've driven past, but I didn't see it. Ever been here?"

I shook my head. "No, my family's never been the type to go hiking."

"My family used to come here almost every weekend when I was younger, before I was too tired to go hiking in between swim practices. It's quite peaceful. Not many people come here, and it's a big enough park, you don't often run into anyone if they do."

"It's nice," I commented, looking up toward the fluttering leaves.

"Yeah. I like it here." Cathy hesitated, then said, "We're almost to where I want to stop. You're a bit out of breath. You okay to go a bit farther? Or do you want to take a quick break?"

I brushed off her worry. "No, I'm good. Let's keep going. The trail's smooth. It's not hard to hop on."

"Yeah, I think state rangers, or a local volunteer mountain club, clear the path every month or so."

The dirt was dappled by sunlight filtering through the surrounding tree branches. I still could not see the creek, but I could hear it crashing over rocks, in tune with chattering birds. When the creek's happy bubbling grew louder, Cathy pulled me off the trail into a slight opening between a few trees. Jutting roots and loose rocks made the going bumpier, and I leaned harder into Cathy for balance.

We emerged onto a shore about twenty feet wide and fifteen feet long, the dirt eroded over the years by the water's gentle brushing. The creek's surface was calm in this hidden spot. The water sparkled like mermaid scales, calling to me.

I broke free from Cathy's grasp, pushing her backward as momentum to help me hop frantically toward the water I thirsted for. I swung my arms, urging my body to move faster. The creek beckoned me closer, and closer, and I could nearly stretch out my arms in a streamline to prepare for a dive when a jerk near my navel pulled me backward.

"Wait! Not yet. I have a surprise." Cathy had wound her arms around my waist like the Heimlich, preventing me from salvation.

"Let me go!" I wiggled and twisted my body, my mermaid tail twitching, but I could not break free of her iron grip. The back of my tail pressed against her warm stomach. How dare she thwart me again?

"Ren, wait one hour," Cathy pleaded as I thrashed.

"No!" I screamed, many birds bursting from the treetops to flee into the sky, startled by my outburst. "I have waited too long!"

"Ren, please. I got you out of the hospital. Can you please let me say what I need to say? I'll let you go afterward, I promise."

I stilled at hearing her promise. I would let Cathy have her farewell if it meant I could leave without further fuss, though my tail disapproved of the delay. Besides, at regionals, she had never promised anything—merely helped Jim foil my plans. Perhaps this time, a spoken promise was worth something. Perhaps her promise would be kept. She had helped me this far, after all.

If not, I resolved to not hesitate in unleashing my mermaid powers against her.

"Fine."

Cathy loosened her hands, tentative, as if expecting me to dive away as soon as she let go. After a brief pause, her fingers tracing my waist, she untangled herself and stepped away, flattening the picnic blanket onto the ground.

I plopped down, impressed by the surrounding nature's tranquility despite my reluctance to spend more time than necessary out of the water.

"Nice, right?" Cathy crouched onto her haunches next to me, unzipping the lunchbox.

"How'd you find this place?" I asked.

"It's a secret."

"No, seriously. How? Online?"

"I told you: my mom used to take me here, before she got all prissy. Believe it or not, before she became the perfect housewife, she did like to hike and be outside. She found this hidden shore one day when she was off-trail, following some birdcalls. We always came back. Until we didn't."

"Huh. Wouldn't've guessed," I said.

"Yeah, well, sometimes people surprise you."

"Like when you showed up below my window. You're my prince." I nudged her with my elbow, and she overemphasized in mockery, capsizing and laughing.

Cathy unpacked the lunchbox, pulling out containers and cloth napkins, placing the napkins under a rock so they would not fly away in the breeze.

"Cathy! You didn't!" I gasped.

"Yes, I did! I went to the right place." She tapped the edge of her forehead with her finger, commending her brain. "Costco, freezer section, microwave." She opened the containers and the sweet smell of defrosted, American-made dumplings and egg rolls wafted toward me. "Your mom's specialty. My favorite pasta party dish."

Cathy picked up an egg roll and gestured toward my mouth. I leaned forward and ate it off her hands, wrapping my lips around her finger, licking the traces of oil off her skin with the tip of my tongue. She blushed. She watched me suck.

I leaned back and chewed, inwardly smirking at her red cheeks.

"Yum. Thanks." I wiped my mouth with the back of my hand. Cathy stared at me in a daze. I licked my lips. Her eyes traced my tongue.

"So you came here with your family?" I interrupted her lustful gaze, raising my eyebrows, unwilling to delay my escape any longer in deference to her want.

Cathy spasmed, startled. "Yeah, we picnicked here every time we hiked." She gestured to the swaying orange flowers planted behind us. I hadn't noticed them until she pointed them out. "See those? My mother taught me a trick about them. You should try squeezing the bulbs."

"Why, is it poison ivy or something? Are you trying to trick me?"

"No! How could you think I'd prank you? Try it. It's fun, I promise."

I scooted closer to the bush and wove its stems around my fingers as I brought the cone-shaped flowers closer for examination. The flowers were trivial, benign, gentle, not ostentatious like the dahlias my neighbors grew, so heavy their drooping stems could not hold their weight, and not perky like sunflowers, proudly arching toward the heavens atop thick stalks. These flowers' petals were a gradient of orange and yellow, with spots of red like blood splatters across the surfaces, reminding me of the evidence I left on the locker room shower stall floor. A faded green stem poked through the middle of each flower, with tiny white tubers attached to the end. The flower seemed harmless—how could I think Cathy would hurt me after all this time?

With my thumb and pointer finger, I squeezed a bulb—I squealed and fell backward onto my elbows in surprise as a pod jumped out onto my shoulder.

Cathy was laughing as I sat back up and dusted myself off, trying to rearrange my features into annoyance, but I was amused by both the flower's and Cathy's reactions.

"What attacked me?" I asked grumpily.

"They're called jeweled touch-me-nots! Or jewelweed. Well, technically, jewelweed is the real name—but I like to call them jeweled touch-me-nots. Has a nice ring to it, right? Like, don't touch me or else I'll fight!" Cathy raised her hands and curled her fingers in mock claws. "And their weapon is raining seeds and flowers down on you." She reached out to the bush and squeezed the flower next to the one I had, giggling as the pod released and jumped into her hair. "They grow by creeks and other wetland. I think they're technically a weed, but I love them."

"Touch-me-not," I murmured. "I like the name."

"I do too."

"Wish I had these flowers around when people didn't ask permission to touch," I said.

"Jim deserves a bouquet of touch-me-nots," Cathy said.

The sun had started to set. Shadows drawn by the overhead trees grew longer, darker, but it was warm even in the widening absence of sunlight. We sat in silence as we munched on the dumplings and egg rolls, using our fingers instead of silverware, our skin growing greasier with each gulp. A pill bug scuttled across the blanket. The jeweled touch-me-not leaves nuzzled my back, waving in the gentle evening breeze.

It was time. I was sated from the snacks and impatient to swim. I braced my hands against the dirt, preparing to propel upward. My stomach was rested, and though full, would not cramp with heavy action. I planned to slide into the water as soon as Cathy reached for another egg roll. I wasn't sure if she would cheer me on or pull me back again. I would have to go as fast as I could, leave while she was distracted, so she wouldn't have a chance to beg me to stay longer. And I couldn't allow myself to hear her begging again. It would make the farewell harder.

I understood why my father never looked back when we dropped him off at the airport.

Cathy lifted a hand, aiming it toward the egg roll container. I tensed, my elbows bent, but Cathy interrupted before I could spring up. Her hand landed on top of my tail instead of the food, in a cautious hold.

"Ren, are you really a mermaid?" she asked.

"What do you think?" I parried, annoyed at the delay.

"I'm not sure. Why—" Cathy paused, then closed her mouth.

"Just ask me."

"Why—why'd you keep swimming for so long, when frankly, so much of it was torture? It made you a"—Cathy swallowed and stammered—"a-a mermaid." She shifted uncomfortably on the blanket. "It wasn't like you were going to make it to the Olympics," she added, as if repeated failure were a valid reason to abandon the sport.

"And you were?"

"Well, no. I wanted to quit every day, actually. But the actual act of quitting something so ingrained into my identity was terrifying. Who would I be afterward? I couldn't do it. I was scared. All my friends—well, you—you were a swimmer, and if we didn't have swimming in common anymore, what would we do or talk about?" Cathy rested her chin on her knees, drawing her legs up so that she curled into a ball. "Would you have even been interested in me if I wasn't a swimmer?"

I snorted. "Of course. But we wouldn't have been as close."

"Why not?"

"Because human lives are situational. Humans think they have free will, free agency, but really, they follow the push and pull of whatever happens. Take us, for example. We were pushed to swim, then we followed Jim's instructions, which pulled us together. Pulled us close."

"I get it."

"Do you?"

"Yeah," she said.

"Well, that's why, as a mermaid, I'm taking charge of my future. No more pushing and pulling from others." I steeled myself. My tail twitched, and I nervously stroked the upper half, cooing to it in my head how we would go to the creek soon. "Cathy, I'm leaving. You can't keep pulling me back."

There was no need for elaboration, or explanation. Our relationship had progressed past the verbal. Cathy glanced at me, her face partially obscured by the jeweled touch-me-nots.

"I figured," she said.

Through our conversation she had inched closer to me. We were near enough I could see all her freckles despite the dimming sunlight, and with my eyes I traced the outline of her curved nose, so different from my flat one, to her lips, slathered in the oil from the microwavable food, pursed as if in deep contemplation. I closed my eyes. I anticipated what was coming. I had done it enough with Brad and Ess. I would do it with Cathy. I'd allow myself one more human mistake.

How deeply I desired this last mistake. How surprising, this desire.

Cathy kissed me, and the action began as a gentle push against each other's lips, then the passion sloped like a pool from shallow to deep. My hands skimmed her warm neck.

It was over. We parted. My cheeks were hot, prickling. Cathy was flushed red. Her skin matched her hair.

Cathy stood and began to strip.

"Uh. Moving a little fast, don't you think?" I laughed.

"Relax. You've seen me naked before. I'm going swimming in the creek. No one's around." Her voice was muffled as her head fumbled, stuck in her shirt.

I stared at the dirt in shock as Cathy's clothes hit the ground, thrown off guard—I didn't expect she would go into the water before me. She jogged toward the creek, clutching her breasts to avoid the ache from running braless. Her pale body shimmered through the setting sun like the shiny necklaces I used to secretly admire in my mother's jewelry dresser. I'd let the metal strands run over my fingers like silk, and pinch the clasp between my thumb and pointer, relishing how the metal dug into my skin.

I had a burning desire to do the same with Cathy's body.

"You coming?" she asked without looking back.

I gaped, amazed.

In the woods, Cathy was freer than I had ever seen her at school or at swim practice. As she neared the creek, her red hair shook behind her, and she moved unconstrained by the tight swimsuits we forced ourselves into. She waded into the water, yelping as the cold nipped her ankles, and I smiled at the thighs flashing against nature's muddy brown and green camouflage. Despite the chilly temperature, she dove in headfirst without fear when the water reached her knees. Cathy's head popped up from the surface a few feet away from where her body had first entered, a dot breaking the navy glass. She waved, offering a white flag of surrender.

I waved back. Strange loneliness coursed through me. I planned to swim in the opposite direction of Cathy and embark on my mermaid journey alone. The water was vast, the world endless, the heavens infinite. I had much to see, much to travel, much to find. Yet despite my desire to ditch humankind, the left side of my sternum pounded in pain. My heart was breaking before I even left.

I wasn't sure what our picnic meant to Cathy. A farewell? Closure? An innocent trip out to nature? How could I interpret our kiss? Part of the healing process perhaps, though I was unclear whether the healing was for me or for Cathy. I had already crossed into mythology, evolved out of a girl and into an aquatic creature, so interrogating the motives of Cathy seemed out of my reach. Though human motives already confused me, I suspected I would not forget my human memories so easily, both the good and the bad, for the bad was always mixed with the good: our team huddles, speeches, and bus rides; the times we helped each other put on our performance suits; the body hair we shaved; the cheers we yelled at the ends of our lanes. As Cathy swam back and forth in the creek, I grieved, not for my girlhood or the swim team or the failed races, but for losing *her*, for losing the chances I could have had with her, and for my memories forever tainted—such was the price of transcendence beyond human.

Cathy ducked her head back in the water, flipping for a handstand, her feet popping up where her head had been. I stood shakily, using the tree trunk for balance. The swaying touch-me-nots cheered me on like pom-poms. Cathy reemerged, her curls wet but still voluminous, undeterred. She paused in her lazy backstroke to holler and splash the top of the water, encouraging me, louder than an audience of one.

I hopped forward. I neared the edge and let the fresh water spill over my fins, my tail. I had arrived at last, to this natural body, neither man-made nor chlorinated; a sharp wet that would not burn, when I submerged but welcome me home. My tail hummed with a bolt of pleasure slithering up through my spine. While I shook my hair behind me, preparing to finally cross the threshold of human—mermaid boundary, I caught sight of a slither—there, by the water's edge, was a snake. It wiggled and came to rest in the clay mud along the bank, peaceful. It had a trail of long swirly ruby spots on its back past its head, resembling curly red hair.

A water-snake.

I closed my eyes, inhaled. I raised my arms in streamline, bent over, let my fingers brush the water. I dove in, letting my body tip forward into nothingness, trusting my body knew where to go. The cold embraced me. I submerged in a navy cocoon. Straining my ears, I could discern a faint mermaid song, a low harmony of hellos.

The underwater was dark. The sun had begun to set past the creek shoreline. The fading day was neither bold enough to penetrate the dense water nor strong enough to fight the silt and mud floating through. The bottom of the creek was invisible. There were no straight black lines like those painted on the pool floor, nor were there fluorescent overhead auditorium lights, nor were there lines of lane ropes interrupting the water.

I undulated forward, reveling in my tail's purring contentment. No need to emerge for air. I had no use for oxygen.

Behind me, I could sense Cathy treading water. She waited for my head to pop up, to spit out water from my mouth like a fountain. If I did, she'd shriek and swim away from my projectile, splashing me in the face in mock horror. I could predict her reactions. We'd flirted before, many times, in many pools. Here in the creek, the possibilities of expanding our relationship were fruitful.

I knew what she wanted from me. She wanted me to swim toward her, envelop my arms around her body, and let her come to rest with her legs wrapped around my waist, where my tail began, water making us weightless. She wanted me to sneak up behind her, tug her down by her ankle, shove her head underwater. She'd laugh, she'd choke, she'd reciprocate, and we'd fumble until our bodies were twisted around each other below, our mouths meeting above. She wanted me to kiss her again, and again, and again. In between the breathless meetings of our lips, she wanted me to promise I'd never leave.

But happy ending romances were for girls.

And I was not a girl—I was a mermaid. A mermaid destined to

swim in water not infected by chlorine. A mermaid destined to travel to her brethren under stars and moons and night skies. A mermaid destined to float suspended in the soothing cradle of water, abandoning her weighty human troubles. A mermaid destined to be mermaid.

A mermaid destined to be free.

As Ren Yu. As me.

I swam away.

# Acknowledgments

I have always loved reading the acknowledgments of debut novels: the sentimentality! The tenderness! The inside jokes! All of which leaves me feeling weepy and mushy, my favorite state of being—and writing my own feels no different, even when the following weepy, mushy thank-yous have been composed under the burden of knowing they'll never adequately capture the immensity of my gratitude:

To DongWon Song, my dream badass agent—thank you for believing in me.

To my brilliant editor, David Pomerico, for acquiring so many of my favorite books, and for making my own better.

To Mireya Chiriboga, Yeon Kim, Rachelle Mandik, Kelly Shi, Shelby Peak, Leah Carlson-Stanisic, Deanna Bailey, and the entire William Morrow/Voyager team for the time, care, and opportunity.

To Kenn Lam, for the kindness and radiant cover tail.

To Cristina Bacchilega and Marie Alohalani Brown for the magical *Penguin Book of Mermaids*.

To K-Ming Chang for inspiring young queer Asians everywhere to write, and for choosing to publish in *Waxwing* my first ever short story—a bloody, angry, yummy story that changed my life.

# Acknowledgments

To Mercer and Rice. Thank you for adopting me when I didn't know anything. To my day one and every day onward Mercer writing family: Chiyeung, JoAnna, Eda, Kimberly, and Emperatriz—I love the warmth we've built.

To my genius, bighearted, radiant, hilarious, messy, fierce, hot friends. From those I dine and dance with regularly. To those I can only see once a year because of distance. To those I was only able to know for a temporary time. I am in love with all of you, for what we give and gave each other. Especially to Angel, my 大屁股的知己; Sel, for making *Chlorine*'s first furry fanart; Gabriella, for truly seeing me in those early sentences; Zack, for holding my hand as we sewed flaps of skin; Derek, for reading my terrible first drafts with kindness but not niceness; and Harish, for the jackfruit, for keeping us all together, and for always picking up the phone.

To my family, and this is where the burden is heaviest, because the thank-yous will never be enough. My mother, 程翠, for taking me to the library and the pool and everywhere else I dreamt of going. My father, 宋继忠, for his love of books and for his jet lag. Ethan, for the hope that has come and will keep coming. My 姥爷, my 亲人, in 加拿大, 北京, and 郑州: 我每天都想您们.

To the libraries and bookstores, and librarians and booksellers— thank you for letting me wander endlessly around your shelves.

To every writer and artist and translator and fictional character I've ever loved, for making me feel more alive and less alone.

And to you, dear reader, because I was a reader long before I ever contemplated being a writer, and I do not take lightly the time spent to arrive at the last page of this book. Thank you, endlessly. Thank you, thank you, thank you.

## About the Author

Jade Song is an artist, art director, and writer. Their stories and essays have appeared in *Teen Vogue*, *Electric Literature*, and various literary magazines. She resides in New York City and considers Pittsburgh and Beijing home too. *Chlorine* is their debut novel.

Twitter: jadessong
Instagram: jadessong
Website: jadessong.com